**IN THE MU~~_____ _____ ~~OF RAY BRADBURY
THERE ARE SO MANY WAYS TO DIE!**

YESTERDAY I LIVED!—Her beauty on the silver screen obsessed him. Over and over she died for him, while, silent and hating, he waited for her to spell out the name of her murderer!

THE TRUNK LADY—In a family where everyone had secrets, little Johnny had found the deadliest one of all . . . and now he would have to die for it!

HELL'S HALF HOUR—Whoever had murdered Caldwell had made sure death came slowly . . . turning mere minutes into what seemed an endless night of terror!

A CAREFUL MAN DIES—For a hemophiliac, no object is innocent, and even a kiss can kill!

CORPSE CARNIVAL—The surgeon's scalpel finally brought separation to Raoul and his twin. But one of them was now a corpse, and for the strange survivor, the future was a nightmare from which there could be no waking!

A Memory of Murder

RAY BRADBURY

A DELL BOOK

Published by
Dell Publishing Co., Inc.
1 Dag Hammarskjold Plaza
New York, New York 10017

Contents

Hammett? Chandler?
Not to Worry!

AN INTRODUCTION BY RAY BRADBURY

When my first detective mystery stories began to appear in *Dime Detective*, *Dime Mystery Magazine*, *Detective Tales*, and *Black Mask* in the early '40s, there was no immediate trepidation over in the Hammett-Chandler-Cain camp. The fact is, it didn't develop later either. I was never a threat. I couldn't, in the immortal words of Brando, have been a contender.

I was a survivor, however, and one of my heroes was Leigh Brackett, who met me every Sunday noon at Muscle Beach in Santa Monica, California, there to read my drear imitations of her Stark on Mars stories or my carbon copies of her first-rate detective tales, which were beginning to appear in all the above mentioned magazines. I would lie on the beach and weep with envy at how easily her characters slid forth, adventured, died, or lived to grieve a death. How she managed to plow through my early agonized contrivances I cannot say. The word friendship arises here to oil the machinery.

Leigh Brackett knew that heart, soul, and guts, I wanted to be a writer. I still had not found my proper voice, though I was beginning to find some of my truths in the weird tale, and an occasional science fiction yarn that wasn't too embarrassing. Leigh was my loving teacher, and I had yet to work free from her influence, both creative and constricting.

Most of the stories in this collection were written to please Leigh, to get an occasional "Well done!" or, once in a while, "This is your best yet!"

Starting back in the year when I left Los Angeles High School, I put myself on a regimen of writing one story a week for the rest of my life. I knew that without quantity there could never be any quality. I sensed that my stories at that time were so bad that only practice could clean the junk out of my head and let the good stuff flow. In the meantime, I tried to cram as much literary experience as I could—good, bad, indifferent, or excellent—into my eyeballs so that eventually it would jump out of my fingertips.

So every Monday I wrote a first draft of any story that leaped into my head. On Tuesday I wrote a second draft. On Wednesday, Thursday, and Friday, third, fourth, and fifth versions followed. On Saturday the final draft went into the mail. On Sunday I collapsed for a day on the beach with Leigh, and on Monday I was back starting a new story. So it has gone for some forty-four years. I am still writing a story a week, or its equivalent. These days I do seven or eight poems a week, or a one-act play, or three chapters of a new novel, or an essay. But the same number of pages come out now as came years ago: somewhere between eighteen and thirty-two pages a week.

I hasten to add that all this was not mechanical. I didn't hold myself to account. I didn't have to. I loved what I was doing, even as a mother loves her homely or ugly babies. You may or may not like my children, but at the time I wrote them, I was plowing my typewriter and reaping the paragraphs. God protects young writers so they do not know, at the time, how badly off center they are performing. That's what quantity production is all about. The good stories you write later are an umbrella over the bad stuff you discover you left behind you in the years. It all equals out. And, if you love writing, it is all a lark.

It follows that detective fiction, as well as the fantasy, science, and weird genres, was a lark of mine. My talent developed faster in the latter fields because it was intuitive. My weird, my fantastic, my science fiction concepts came as lightning bolts and knocked me head first into my machine. The detective tales, because they required hard thinking, prevented my flow, damaged my ability to use my intuition to the full. They were, as a result, quite often walking wounded. Today, many years later, with a greater knowledge of the field and having learned lessons from Ross Macdonald meanwhile, I feel I might be able to do better. I feel it enough, I might add, that I recently finished—and Knopf will soon publish—my first mystery suspense novel, *Death Is a Lonely Business*.

Now, as to the stories in this collection. First, the titles. I would like to have changed some of them from their pulp versions, simply because I did not like the titles the editors of those magazines hung on my stories without asking permission. After all, "Hell's Half Hour" and "Corpse Carnival" are not exactly sterling examples of title-making. I was astonished when the editors let "The Trunk Lady" and "The Long Night," *my* titles, slip through.

What you have here in this collection, then, is a record of the way I wrote and tried to survive through the early '40s, with Leigh Brackett trying to help around the edges. I floundered, I thrashed, sometimes I lost, sometimes I won. But I was trying. Perhaps this collection is only of historical interest to those with an immense curiosity about my work in a field unfamiliar to many, but I can name my favorites, "The Long Night" and "The Trunk Lady," and add that "The Small Assassin" seems to me to be one of the best stories in any field that I have ever written. It was so successful, in fact, that it appears to have influenced a dozen novels and films written and produced in the last ten years.

As for the other stories, *you* must read and judge. But I hope you will judge kindly, and let me off easy. I was, after all, in my early twenties and still had a long way to go, with Hammett and Chandler and Cain way over there on the horizon, standing tall, and me on the beach, sweating it out and taking advice from Leigh Brackett. I hope that her dear ghost will not mind that this book and its stories are dedicated to her with love.

RAY BRADBURY

The Small Assassin

Just when the idea occurred to her that she was being murdered she could not tell. There had been little subtle signs, little suspicions for the past month; things as deep as sea tides in her, like looking at a perfectly calm stretch of tropic water, wanting to bathe in it and finding, just as the tide takes your body, that monsters dwell just under the surface, things unseen, bloated, many-armed, sharp-finned, malignant and inescapable.

A room floated around her in an effluvium of hysteria. Sharp instruments hovered and there were voices, and people in sterile white masks.

My name, she thought, what is it?

Alice Leiber. It came to her. David Leiber's wife. But it gave her no comfort. She was alone with these silent, whispering white people and there was great pain and nausea and death-fear in her.

I am being murdered before their eyes. These doctors, these nurses, don't realize what hidden thing has happened to me. David doesn't know. Nobody knows except me and—the killer, the little murderer, the small assassin.

I am dying and I can't tell them now. They'd laugh and call me one in delirium. They'll see the murderer and hold him and never think him responsible for my death. But here I am, in front of God and man, dying, no one to believe my story, everyone to doubt me, comfort me with lies, bury me in ignorance, mourn me, and salvage my destroyer.

Where is David? she wondered. In the waiting room, smoking one cigarette after another, listening to the long tickings of the very slow clock?

Sweat exploded from all of her body at once, and with it an agonized cry. Now. Now! Try and kill me, she screamed. Try, try, but I won't die! I won't!

There was a hollowness. A vacuum. Suddenly the pain fell away. Exhaustion, and dusk came around. It was over. Oh, God! She plummeted down and struck a black nothingness which gave way to nothingness and nothingness and another and still another. . . .

Footsteps. Gentle, approaching footsteps.

Far away, a voice said, "She's asleep. Don't disturb her."

An odor of tweeds, a pipe, a certain shaving lotion. David was standing over her. And beyond him the immaculate smell of Dr. Jeffers.

She did not open her eyes. "I'm awake," she said quietly. It was a surprise, a relief, to be able to speak, not to be dead.

"Alice," someone said, and it was David beyond her closed eyes, holding her tired hands.

Would you like to meet the murderer, David? she thought. I hear your voice asking to see him, so there's nothing but for me to point him out to you.

David stood over her. She opened her eyes. The room came into focus. Moving a weak hand, she pulled aside a coverlet.

The murderer looked up at David Leiber with a small, red-faced, blue-eyed calm. Its eyes were deep and sparkling.

"Why!" cried David Leiber, smiling. "He's a *fine* baby!"

Dr. Jeffers was waiting for David Leiber the day he came to take his wife and new child home. He motioned Leiber to a chair in his office, gave him a cigar, lit one for himself, sat on the edge of his desk, puffing solemnly for a long moment. Then he cleared his throat, looked David Leiber straight on, and said, "Your wife doesn't like her child, Dave."

"What!"

"It's been a hard thing for her. She'll need a lot of love this next year. I didn't say much at the time, but she was hysterical in the delivery room. The strange things she said—I won't repeat them. All I'll say is that she feels alien to the child. Now, this may simply be a thing we can clear up with one or two questions." He sucked on his cigar another moment, then said, "Is this child a 'wanted' child, Dave?"

"Why do you ask?"

"It's vital."

"Yes. Yes, it is a 'wanted' child. We planned it together. Alice was so happy, a year ago, when—"

"Mmmm—that makes it more difficult. Because if the child was unplanned, it would be a simple case of a woman hating the idea of motherhood. That doesn't fit Alice." Dr. Jeffers took his cigar from his lips, rubbed his hand across his jaw. "It must be something else, then. Perhaps something buried in her childhood that's coming out now. Or it might be the simple temporary doubt and distrust of any mother who's gone through the unusual pain and near death that Alice has. If so, then a little time should heal that. I thought I'd tell you, though, Dave. It'll help you be easy and tolerant with her if she says anything about—well—about wishing the child had been born dead. And if things don't go well, the three of you drop in on me. I'm always glad to see old friends, eh? Here, take another cigar along for—ah—for the baby."

It was a bright spring afternoon. Their car hummed along wide, treelined boulevards. Blue sky, flowers, a warm wind. Dave talked a lot, lit his cigar, talked some more. Alice answered directly, softly, relaxing a bit more as the trip progressed. But she held the baby not tightly or warmly or motherly enough to satisfy the queer ache in Dave's mind. She seemed to be merely carrying a porcelain figurine.

"Well," he said at last, smiling. "What'll we name him?"

Alice Leiber watched green trees slide by. "Let's not decide yet. I'd rather wait until we get an exceptional name for him. Don't blow smoke in his face." Her sentences ran together with no change of tone. The last statement held no motherly reproof, no interest, no irritation. She just mouthed it and it was said.

The husband, disquieted, dropped the cigar from the window. "Sorry," he said.

The baby rested in the crook of his mother's arm, shadows of sun and trees changing his face. His blue eyes opened like fresh blue spring flowers. Moist noises came from the tiny pink, elastic mouth.

Alice gave her baby a quick glance. Her husband felt her shiver against him.

"Cold?" he asked.

"A chill. Better raise the window, David."

It was more than a chill. He rolled the window slowly up.

Suppertime.

Dave had brought the child from the nursery, propped him at a tiny, bewildered angle, supported by many pillows, in a newly purchased high chair.

Alice watched her knife and fork move. "He's not high-chair size," she said.

"Fun having him here, anyway," said Dave, feeling fine. "Everything's fun. At the office too. Orders up to my nose. If I don't watch myself I'll make another fifteen thousand this year. Hey, look at Junior, will you? Drooling all down his chin!" He reached over to wipe the baby's mouth with his napkin. From the corner of his eye he realized that Alice wasn't even watching. He finished the job.

"I guess it wasn't very interesting," he said, back again at his food. "But one would think a mother'd take some interest in her own child!"

Alice jerked her chin up. "Don't speak that way! Not in front of him! Later, if you must."

"Later?" he cried. "In front of, in back of, what's the difference?" He quieted suddenly, swallowed, was sorry. "All right. Okay. I know how it is."

After dinner she let him carry the baby upstairs. She didn't tell him to; she *let* him.

Coming down, he found her standing by the radio, listening to music she didn't hear. Her eyes were closed, her whole attitude one of wondering, self-questioning. She started when he appeared.

Suddenly she was at him, against him, soft, quick; the same. Her lips found him, kept him. He was stunned. Now that the baby was gone, upstairs, out of the room, she began to breathe again, live again. She was free. She was whispering, rapidly, endlessly.

"Thank you, thank you, darling. For being yourself, always. Dependable, so very dependable!"

He had to laugh. "My father told me, 'Son, provide for your family!' "

Wearily, she rested her dark, shining hair against his neck. "You've overdone it. Sometimes I wish we were just the way we were when we were first married. No responsibilities, nothing but ourselves. No—no babies."

She crushed his hand in hers, a supernatural whiteness in her face.

"Oh, Dave, once it was just you and me. We protected each other, and now we protect the baby, but get no protection from it. Do you understand? Lying in the hospital I had time to think a lot of things. The world is evil—"

"Is it?"

"Yes. It is. But laws protect us from it. And when there aren't laws, then love does the protecting. You're protected from my hurting you, by my love. You're vulnerable to me, of all people, but love shields you. I feel no fear of you, because love cushions all your irritations, unnatural instincts, hatreds, and immaturities. But—what about the baby? It's too young to know love, or a law of love, or anything, until we teach it. And in the meantime we're vulnerable to it."

"Vulnerable to a baby?" He held her away and laughed gently.

"Does a baby know the difference between right and wrong?" she asked.

"No. But it'll learn."

"But a baby is so new, so amoral, so conscience-free." She stopped. Her arms dropped from him and she turned swiftly. "That noise? What was it?"

Leiber looked around the room. "I didn't hear—"

She stared at the library door. "In there," she said slowly.

Leiber crossed the room, opened the door, and switched the library lights on and off. "Not a thing." He came back to her. "You're worn out. To bed with you—right now."

Turning out the lights together they walked slowly up the soundless hall stairs, not speaking. At the top she apologized. "My wild talk, darling. Forgive me. I'm exhausted."

He understood, and said so.

She paused, undecided, by the nursery door. Then she fingered the brass knob sharply, walked in. He watched her approach the crib much too carefully, look down, and stiffen as if she'd been struck in the face. "David!"

Leiber stepped forward, reached the crib.

The baby's face was bright red and very moist; his small pink mouth opened and shut, opened and shut; his eyes were a fiery blue. His hands leapt about on the air.

"Oh," said Dave, "he's just been crying."

"Has he?" Alice Leiber seized the crib railing to balance herself. "I didn't hear him."

"The door was closed."

"Is that why he breathes so hard, why his face is red?"

"Sure. Poor little guy. Crying all alone in the dark. He can sleep in our room tonight, just in case he cries."

"You'll spoil him," his wife said.

Leiber felt her eyes follow as he rolled the crib into their bedroom. He undressed silently, sat on the edge of the bed. Suddenly he lifted his head, swore under his breath, snapped his fingers. "Damn it! Forgot to tell you. I must fly to Chicago Friday."

"Oh, David." Her voice was lost in the room.

"I've put this trip off for two months, and now it's so critical I just *have* to go."

"I'm afraid to be alone."

"We'll have the new cook by Friday. She'll be here all the time. I'll only be gone a few days."

"I'm afraid. I don't know of what. You wouldn't believe me if I told you. I guess I'm crazy."

He was in bed now. She darkened the room; he heard her walk around the bed, throw back the cover, slide in. He smelled the warm woman-smell of her next to him. He said, "If you want me to wait a few days, perhaps I could—"

"No," she said, unconvinced. "You go. I know it's important.

It's just that I keep thinking about what I told you. Laws and love and protection. Love protects you from me. But the baby—'' She took a breath. "What protects you from him, David?''

Before he could answer, before he could tell her how silly it was, speaking of infants, she switched on the bed light abruptly.

"Look," she said, pointing.

The baby lay wide-awake in its crib, staring straight at him, with deep, sharp blue eyes.

The lights went out again. She trembled against him.

"It's not nice being afraid of the thing you birthed." Her whisper lowered, became harsh, fierce, swift. "He tried to kill me! He lies there, listens to us talking, waiting for you to go away so he can try to kill me again! I swear it!'' Sobs broke from her.

"Please," he kept saying, soothing her. "Stop it, stop it. Please.''

She cried in the dark for a long time. Very late she relaxed, shakingly, against him. Her breathing came soft, warm, regular, her body twitched its worn reflexes, and she slept.

He drowsed.

And just before his eyes lidded wearily down, sinking him into deeper and deeper tides, he heard a strange little sound of aware-ness and awakeness in the room.

The sound of small, moist, pinkly elastic lips.

The baby.

And then—sleep.

In the morning the sun blazed. Alice smiled.

David Leiber dangled his watch over the crib. "See, baby? Something bright. Something pretty. Sure. Sure. Something bright. Something pretty.''

Alice smiled. She told him to go ahead, fly to Chicago, she'd be very brave, no need to worry. She'd take care of baby. Oh, yes, she'd take care of him, all right.

The airplane went east. There was a lot of sky, a lot of sun and clouds and Chicago running over the horizon. Dave was dropped into the rush of ordering, planning, banqueting, telephoning, arguing in conference. But he wrote letters each day and sent telegrams to Alice and the baby.

On the evening of his sixth day away from home he received the long-distance phone call. Los Angeles.

"Alice?"

"No, Dave. This is Jeffers speaking."

"Doctor!"

. "Hold on to yourself, son. Alice is sick. You'd better get the next plane home. It's pneumonia. I'll do everything I can, boy. If only it wasn't so soon after the baby. She needs strength."

Leiber dropped the phone into its cradle. He got up, with no feet under him, and no hands and no body. The hotel room blurred and fell apart.

"Alice," he said, blindly starting for the door.

The propellers spun about, whirled, fluttered, stopped; time and space were put behind. Under his hand David felt the door-knob turn, under his feet the floor assumed reality, around him flowed the walls of a bedroom, and in the late afternoon sunlight Dr. Jeffers stood, turning from a window, as Alice lay waiting in her bed, something carved from a fall of winter snow. Then Dr. Jeffers was talking, talking continuously, gently, the sound rising and falling through the lamplight, a soft flutter, a white murmur of voice.

"You wife's too good a mother, Dave. She worried more about the baby than herself. . . ."

Somewhere in the paleness of Alice's face there was a sudden constriction that smoothed itself out before it was realized. Then, slowly, half smiling, she began to talk, and she talked as a mother should about this, that, and the other thing, the telling detail, the minute-by-minute and hour-by-hour report of a mother concerned with a dollhouse world and the miniature life of that world. But she could not stop; the spring was wound tight, and her voice rushed on to anger, fear, and the faintest touch of revulsion, which did not change Dr. Jeffers's expression, but caused Dave's heart to match the rhythm of this talk that quickened and could not stop:

"The baby wouldn't sleep. I thought he was sick. He just lay, staring, in his crib, and late at night he'd cry. So loud, he'd cry, and he'd cry all night and all night. I couldn't quiet him, and I couldn't rest."

Dr. Jeffers's head nodded slowly, slowly. "Tired herself right into pneumonia. But she's full of sulfa now and on the safe side of the whole damn thing."

David felt ill. "The baby, what about the baby?"

"Fit as a fiddle; cock of the walk!"

"Thanks, Doctor."

The doctor walked off away and down the stairs, opened the front door faintly, and was gone.

"David!"

He turned to her frightened whisper.

"It was the baby again." She clutched his hand. "I try to lie to myself and say that I'm a fool, but the baby knew I was weak from the hospital, so he cried all night every night, and when he wasn't crying he'd be much too quiet. I knew if I switched on the light he'd be there, staring up at me."

David felt his body close in on itself like a fist. He remembered seeing the baby, feeling the baby, awake in the dark, awake very late at night when babies should be asleep. Awake and lying there, silent as thought, not crying, but watching from its crib. He thrust the thought aside. It was insane.

Alice went on. "I was going to kill the baby. Yes, I was. When you'd been gone only a day on your trip I went to his room and put my hands about his neck; and I stood there, for a long time, thinking, afraid. Then I put the covers up over his face and turned him over on his face and pressed him down and left him that way and ran out of the room."

He tried to stop her.

"No, let me finish," she said hoarsely, looking at the wall. "When I left his room I thought, It's simple. Babies smother every day. No one'll ever know. But when I came back to see him dead, David, he was alive! Yes, alive, turned over on his back, alive and smiling and breathing. And I couldn't touch him again after that. I left him there and I didn't come back, not to feed him or look at him or do anything. Perhaps the cook tended to him. I don't know. All I know is that his crying kept me awake, and I thought all through the night, and walked around the rooms, and now I'm sick." She was almost finished now. "The baby lies there and thinks of ways to kill me. Simple ways. Because he knows I know so much about him. I have no love for him; there is no protection between us; there never will be."

She was through. She collapsed inward on herself and finally slept. David Leiber stood for a long time over her, not able to move. His blood was frozen in his body; not a cell stirred anywhere, anywhere at all.

The next morning there was only one thing to do. He did it.

He walked into Dr. Jeffers' office and told him the whole thing, and listened to Jeffers' tolerant replies:

"Let's take this thing slowly, son. It's quite natural for mothers to hate their children, sometimes. We have a label for it—ambivalence. The ability to hate while loving. Lovers hate each other, frequently. Children detest their mothers—"

Leiber interrupted. "I never hated my mother."

"You won't admit it, naturally. People don't enjoy admitting hatred for their loved ones."

"So Alice hates her baby."

"Better say she has an obsession. She's gone a step further than plain, ordinary ambivalence. A cesarean operation brought the child into the world and almost took Alice out of it. She blames the child for her near death and her pneumonia. She's projecting her troubles, blaming them on the handiest object she can use as a source of blame. We *all* do it. We stumble into a chair and curse the furniture, not our own clumsiness. We miss a golf stroke and damn the turf or our club, or the make of ball. If our business fails we blame the gods, the weather, our luck. All I can tell you is what I told you before. Love her. Finest medicine in the world. Find little ways of showing your affection, give her security. Find ways of showing her how harmless and innocent the child is. Make her feel that the baby was worth the risk. After a while, she'll settle down, forget about death, and begin to love the child. If she doesn't come around in the next month or so, ask me. I'll recommend a good psychiatrist. Go on along now, and take that look off your face."

When summer came, things seemed to settle, become easier. Dave worked, immersed himself in office detail, but found much time for his wife. She in turn took long walks, gained strength, played an occasional light game of badminton. She rarely burst out anymore. She seemed to have rid herself of her fears.

Except on one certain midnight when a sudden summer wind swept around the house, warm and swift, shaking the trees like so many shining tambourines. Alice wakened, trembling, and slid over into her husband's arms, and let him console her and ask her what was wrong.

She said, "Something's here in the room, watching us."

He switched on the light. "Dreaming again," he said. "You're better, though. Haven't been troubled for a long time."

She sighed as he clicked off the light again, and suddenly she slept. He held her, considering what a sweet, weird creature she was, for about half an hour.

He heard the bedroom door sway open a few inches.

There was nobody at the door. No reason for it to come open. The wind had died.

He waited. It seemed like an hour he lay silently in the dark.

Then, far away, wailing like some small meteor dying in the vast inky gulf of space, the baby began to cry in his nursery.

It was a small, lonely sound in the middle of the stars and the dark and the breathing of this woman in his arms and the wind beginning to sweep through the trees again.

Leiber counted to one hundred slowly. The crying continued.

Carefully disengaging Alice's arm he slipped from bed, put on his slippers, robe, and moved quietly from the room.

He'd go downstairs, he thought, fix some warm milk, bring it up, and—

The blackness dropped out from under him. His foot slipped and plunged. Slipped on something soft. Plunged into nothingness.

He thrust his hands out, caught frantically at the railing. His body stopped falling. He held. He cursed.

The "something soft" that had caused his feet to slip rustled and thumped down a few steps. His head rang. His heart hammered at the base of his throat, thick and shot with pain.

Why do careless people leave things strewn about a house? He groped carefully with his fingers for the object that had almost spilled him headlong down the stairs.

His hand froze, startled. His breath went in. His heart held one or two beats.

The thing he held in his hand was a toy. A large, cumbersome patchwork doll he had bought as a joke, for—

For the baby.

Alice drove him to work the next day.

She slowed the car halfway downtown, pulled to the curb, and stopped it. Then she turned on the seat and looked at her husband.

"I want to go away on a vacation. I don't know if you can make it now, darling, but if not, please let me go alone. We can get someone to take care of the baby, I'm sure. But I just have to get away. I thought I was growing out of this—this *feeling*. But I haven't. I can't stand being in the room with him. He looks up at me as if he hates me too. I can't put my finger on it; all I know is I want to get away before something happens."

He got out on his side of the car, came around, motioned to her to move over, got in. "The only thing you're going to do is see a good psychiatrist. And if he suggests a vacation, well, okay. But this can't go on; my stomach's in knots all the time.'' He started the car. "I'll drive the rest of the way.''

Her head was down; she was trying to keep back tears. She looked up when they reached his office building. "All right. Make the appointment. I'll go talk to anyone you want, David.''

He kissed her. "Now you're talking sense, lady. Think you can drive home okay?''

"Of course, silly.''

"See you at supper, then. Drive carefully.''

"Don't I always? Bye.''

He stood on the curb, watching her drive off, the wind taking hold of her long, dark, shining hair. Upstairs, a minute later, he phoned Jeffers and arranged an appointment with a reliable neuro-psychiatrist.

The day's work went uneasily. Things fogged over; and in the fog he kept seeing Alice lost and calling his name. So much of her fear had come over to him. She actually had him convinced that the child was in some ways not quite natural.

He dictated long, uninspired letters. He checked some shipments downstairs. Assistants had to be questioned and kept going. At the end of the day he was exhausted, his head throbbed, and he was very glad to go home.

On the way down in the elevator he wondered, What if I told Alice about the toy—that patchwork doll—I slipped on on the stairs last night? Lord, wouldn't *that* back her off? No, I won't ever tell her. Accidents are, after all, accidents.

Daylight lingered in the sky as he drove home in a taxi. In front of the house he paid the driver and walked slowly up the concrete walk, enjoying the light that was still in the sky and the trees. The white colonial front of the house looked unnaturally silent and uninhabited, and then he remembered this was Thursday and the hired help they were able to obtain from time to time were all gone for the day.

He took a deep breath of air. A bird sang behind the house. Traffic moved on the boulevard a block away. He twisted the key in the door. The knob turned under his fingers, oiled, silent.

The door opened. He stepped in, put his hat on the chair with his briefcase, started to shrug out of his coat, when he looked up.

Late sunlight streamed down the stairwell from the window near the top of the hall. Where the sunlight touched it took on the bright color of the patchwork doll sprawled at the bottom of the stairs.

But he paid no attention to the toy.

He could only look, and not move, and look again at Alice.

Alice lay in a broken, grotesque, pallid gesturing and angling of her thin body at the bottom of the stairs, like a crumpled doll that doesn't want to play anymore, ever.

Alice was dead.

The house remained quiet, except for the sound of his heart.

She was dead.

He held her head in his hands, he felt her fingers. He held her body. But she wouldn't live. She wouldn't even try to live. He said her name, out loud, many times, and he tried, once again, by holding her to him, to give her back some of the warmth she had lost, but that didn't help.

He stood up. He must have made a phone call. He didn't remember. He found himself suddenly upstairs. He opened the nursery door and walked inside and stared blankly at the crib. His stomach was sick. He couldn't see very well.

The baby's eyes were closed, but his face was red, moist with perspiration, as if he'd been crying long and hard.

"She's dead," said Leiber to the baby. "She's dead."

Then he started laughing low and soft and continuously for a long time until Dr. Jeffers walked in out of the night and slapped him again and again across his face.

"Snap out of it! Pull yourself together!"

"She fell down the stairs, Doctor. She tripped on a patchwork doll and fell. I almost slipped on it the other night myself. And now—"

The doctor shook him.

"Doc, Doc, Doc," said Dave hazily. "Funny thing. Funny. I—I finally thought of a name for the baby."

The doctor said nothing.

Leiber put his head back in his trembling hands and spoke the words. "I'm going to have him christened next Sunday. Know what name I'm giving him? I'm going to call him Lucifer."

It was eleven at night. A lot of strange people had come and gone through the house, taking the essential flame with them—Alice.

David Leiber sat across from the doctor in the library.

"Alice wasn't crazy," he said slowly. "She had good reason to fear the baby."

Jeffers exhaled. "Don't follow after her! She blamed the child for her sickness, now you blame it for her death. She stumbled on a toy, remember that. You can't blame the child."

"You mean Lucifer?"

"Stop calling him that!"

Leiber shook his head. "Alice heard things at night, moving in the halls. You want to know what made those noises, Doctor? They were made by the baby. Four months old, moving in the dark, listening to us talk. Listening to every word!" He held to the sides of the chair. "And if I turned the lights on, a baby is so small. It can hide behind furniture, a door, against a wall—below eye level."

"I want you to stop this!" said Jeffers.

"Let me say what I think or I'll go crazy. When I went to Chicago, who was it kept Alice awake, tiring her into pneumonia? The baby! And when Alice didn't die, then he tried killing me. It was simple; leave a toy on the stairs, cry in the night until your father goes downstairs to fetch your milk and stumbles. A crude trick, but effective. It didn't get me. But it killed Alice dead."

David Leiber stopped long enough to light a cigarette. "I should have caught on. I'd turn on the lights in the middle of the night, many nights, and the baby'd be lying there, eyes wide. Most babies sleep all the time. Not this one. He stayed awake, thinking."

"Babies don't think."

"He stayed awake doing whatever he *could* do with his brain, then. What in hell do we know about a baby's mind? He had every reason to hate Alice; she suspected him for what he was—certainly not a normal child. Something—different. What do you know of babies, Doctor? The general run, yes. You know, of course, how babies kill their mothers at birth. Why? Could it be resentment at being forced into a lousy world like this one?"

Leiber leaned toward the doctor tiredly. "It all ties up. Suppose that a few babies out of all the millions born are instantaneously able to move, see, hear, think, like many animals and insects can. Insects are born self-sufficient. In a few weeks most mammals and birds adjust. But children take years to speak and to learn to stumble around on their weak legs.

"But suppose one child in a billion is—strange? Born perfectly aware, able to think, instinctively. Wouldn't it be a perfect setup, a perfect blind for anything the baby might want to do? He could pretend to be ordinary, weak, crying, ignorant. With just a *little* expenditure of energy he could crawl about a darkened house, listening. And how easy to place obstacles at the top of stairs. How easy to cry all night and tire a mother into pneumonia. How easy, right at birth, to be so close to the mother that *a few deft maneuvers might cause peritonitis*!''

"For God's sake!" Jeffers was on his feet. "That's a repulsive thing to say!''

"It's a repulsive thing I'm speaking of. How many mothers have died at the birth of their children? How many have suckled strange little improbabilities who cause death one way or another? Strange, red little creatures with brains that work in a bloody darkness we can't even guess at. Elemental little brains, warm with racial memory, hatred, and raw cruelty, with no more thought than self-preservation. And self-preservation in this case consisted of eliminating a mother who realized what a horror she had birthed. I ask you, Doctor, what is there in the world more selfish than a baby? Nothing!''

Jeffers scowled and shook his head helplessly.

Leiber dropped his cigarette down. "I'm not claiming any great strength for the child. Just enough to crawl around a little, a few months ahead of schedule. Just enough to listen all the time. Just enough to cry late at night. That's enough, more than enough.''

Jeffers tried ridicule. "Call it murder, then. But murder must be motivated. What motive had the child?''

Leiber was ready with the answer. "What is more at peace, more dreamfully content, at ease, at rest, fed, comforted, unbothered, than an unborn child? Nothing. It floats in a sleepy, timeless wonder of nourishment and silence. Then suddenly it is asked to give up its berth, is forced to vacate, rushed out into a noisy, uncaring, selfish world where it is asked to shift for itself, to hunt, to feed from the hunting, to seek after a vanishing love that once was its unquestionable right, to meet confusion instead of inner silence and conservative slumber! And the child *resents* it! Resents the cold air, the huge spaces, the sudden departure from familiar things. And in the tiny filament of brain the only thing the child knows is selfishness and hatred because the spell has been rudely shattered. Who is responsible for this disenchantment, this rude breaking of the spell? The mother. So here the new child has someone to hate with all its unreasoning mind. The mother has cast it out, rejected it. And the father is no better; kill him too! He's responsible in *his* way!''

Jeffers interrupted. "If what you say is true, then every woman in the world would have to look on her baby as something to dread, something to wonder about."

"And why not? Hasn't the child a perfect alibi? A thousand years of accepted medical belief protects him. By all natural accounts he is helpless, not responsible. The child is born hating. And things grow worse instead of better. At first the baby gets a certain amount of attention and mothering. But then as time passes, things change. When very new, a baby has the power to make parents do silly things when it cries or sneezes, jump when it makes a noise. As the years pass, the baby feels even that small power slip rapidly, forever away, never to return. Why shouldn't it grasp all the power it can have? Why shouldn't it jockey for position while it has all the advantages? In later years it would be too late to express its hatred. *Now* would be the time to strike."

Leiber's voice was very soft, very low.

"My little boy baby, lying in his crib nights, his face moist and red and out of breath. From crying? No. From climbing slowly out of his crib, from crawling long distances through darkened hallways. My little boy baby. I want to kill him."

The doctor handed him a water glass and some pills. "You're not killing anyone. You're going to sleep for twenty-four hours. Sleep'll change your mind. Take this."

Leiber drank down the pills and let himself be led upstairs to his bedroom, crying, and felt himself being put to bed. The doctor waited until he was moving deep into sleep, then left the house.

Leiber, alone, drifted down, down.

He heard a noise. "What's—what's *that*?" he demanded feebly.

Something moved in the hall.

David Leiber slept.

Very early the next morning Dr. Jeffers drove up to the house. It was a good morning, and he was here to drive Leiber to the country for a rest. Leiber would still be asleep upstairs. Jeffers had given him enough sedative to knock him out for at least fifteen hours.

He rang the doorbell. No answer. The servants were probably not up. Jeffers tried the front door, found it open, stepped in. He put his medical kit on the nearest chair.

Something white moved out of sight at the top of the stairs. Just a suggestion of a movement. Jeffers hardly noticed it.

The smell of gas was in the house.

Jeffers ran upstairs, crashed into Leiber's bedroom.

Leiber lay motionless on the bed, and the room billowed with gas, which hissed from a released jet at the base of the wall near the door. Jeffers twisted it off, then forced up all the windows and ran back to Leiber's body.

The body was cold. It had been dead quite a few hours.

Coughing violently, the doctor hurried from the room, eyes watering. Leiber hadn't turned on the gas himself. He *couldn't* have. Those sedatives had knocked him out, he wouldn't have wakened until noon. It wasn't suicide. Or was there the faintest possibility?

Jeffers stood in the hall for five minutes. Then he walked to the door of the nursery. It was shut. He opened it. He walked inside and to the crib.

The crib was empty.

He stood swaying by the crib for half a minute, then he said something to nobody in particular.

"The nursery door blew shut. You couldn't get back into your crib where it was safe. You didn't plan on the door blowing shut. A little thing like a slammed door can ruin the best of plans. I'll find you somewhere in the house, hiding, pretending to be something you are not." The doctor looked dazed. He put his hand to his head and smiled palely. "Now I'm talking like Alice and David talked. But I can't take any chances. I'm not sure of anything, but I can't take chances."

He walked downstairs, opened his medical bag on the chair, took something out of it, and held it in his hands.

Something rustled down the hall. Something very small and very quiet. Jeffers turned rapidly.

I had to operate to bring you into this world, he thought. Now I guess I can operate to take you out of it. . . .

He took half a dozen slow, sure steps forward into the hall. He raised his hand into the sunlight.

"See, baby! Something bright—something pretty!"

A scalpel.

A Careful Man Dies

You sleep only four hours a night. You go to bed at eleven and get up at three and everything is clear as crystal. You begin your day then, have your coffee, read a book for an hour, listen to the faint, far, unreal talk and music of the predawn stations, and perhaps go out for a walk, always being certain to have your special police permit with you. You have been picked up before for late and unusual hours and it got to be a nuisance, so you finally got yourself a special permit. Now you can walk and whistle where you wish, hands in your pockets, heels striking the pavement in a slow, easy tempo.

This has been going on since you were sixteen years old. You're now twenty-five, and four hours a night is still enough sleep.

You have few glass objects in your house. You shave with an electric razor because a safety razor sometimes cuts you and you cannot afford to bleed.

You are a hemophiliac. You start bleeding and you can't stop. Your father was the same way—though he served only as a frightening example. He cut his finger once, fairly deeply, and died on the way to the hospital from lack of blood. There was also hemophilia on your mother's side of the family, and that was where you got it.

In your right inside coat pocket you carry, always, a small bottle of coagulant tablets. If you cut yourself you immediately swallow them. The coagulant formula spreads through your system to supply the necessary clotting material to stop the seepage of blood.

So this is how your life goes. You need only four hours sleep and you stay away from sharp objects. Each waking day of your life is almost twice as long as the average man's, but your life expectancy is short, so it comes to an ironic balance.

It will be long hours until the morning mail. So you tap out four thousand words on a story with your typewriter. At nine o'clock when the postal box in front of your door clicks you stack the typewritten sheets, clip them together, check the carbon copy, and file them under the heading NOVEL IN PROGRESS. Then, smoking a cigarette, you go for the mail.

You take the mail from the box. A check for three hundred dollars from a national magazine, two rejections from lesser houses, and a small cardboard box tied with green string.

After shuffling over the letters you turn to the box, untie it, flip open the top, reach in, and pull out the thing that is inside it.

"Damn!"

You drop the box. A splash of quick red spreads on your fingers. Something bright has flashed in the air with a chopping movement. There was the whir of a metal spring, whining.

Blood begins to run smoothly, swiftly, from your wounded hand. You stare at it for a moment, stare at the sharp object on the floor, the little bestial contraption with the razor bedded in a springed trap that clipped shut when you pulled it out and caught you unawares!

Fumbling, trembling, you reach into your pocket, getting blood all over yourself, and pull out the bottle of tablets and gulp several down.

Then, while you are waiting for the stuff to clot, you wrap the hand in a handkerchief and, gingerly, pick up the contraption and set it on the table.

After staring at it for ten minutes you sit down and have yourself a cigarette clumsily, and your eyelids jerk and flicker and your vision melts and hardens and remelts the objects of the room, and finally you have the answer.

. . . *Someone doesn't like me . . . Someone doesn't like me at all.* . . .

The phone rings. You get it.

"Douglas speaking."

"Hello, Rob. This is Jerry."

"Oh, Jerry."

"How are you, Rob?"

"Pale and shaken."

"How come?"

"Somebody sent me a razor in a box."

"Stop kidding."

"Seriously. But you wouldn't want to hear."

"How's the novel, Rob?"

"I won't ever finish it if people keep sending me sharp objects.

I expect to get a cut-glass Swedish vase in the next mail. Or a magician's cabinet with a large collapsible mirror.''

"Your voice sounds funny," says Jerry.

"It should. As for the novel, Gerald, it is going great guns. I've just done another four thousand words. In this scene I show the great love of Anne J. Anthony for Mr. Michael M. Horn."

"You're asking for trouble, Rob."

"I have discovered that only this minute."

Jerry mutters something.

You say, "Mike wouldn't touch me directly, Jerry. Neither would Anne. After all, Anne and I were once engaged. That was before I found out about what they were doing. The parties they were giving, the needles they were giving people, full of morphine."

"They might try to stop the book, though, somehow."

"I believe you. They already have. This box that came in the mail. Well, maybe *they* didn't do it, but one of the other people, some of the others I mention in the book, they might take a notion."

"Have you talked to Anne recently?" asks Jerry.

"Yes," you say.

"And she still prefers that kind of life?"

"It's a wild one. You see a lot of pretty pictures when you take some kinds of narcotic."

"I wouldn't believe it of her; she doesn't look that sort."

"It's your Oedipus complex, Jerry. Women never seem like females to you. They seem like bathed, flowered, sexless ivory carvings on rococo pedestals. You loved your mother too completely. Luckily I'm more ambivalent. Anne had me fooled for a while. But she was having so much fun one night and I thought she was drunk, and then first thing I knew she was kissing me and pressing a little needle into my hand and saying, 'Come on, Rob, please. You'll like it.' And the needle was as full of morphine as Anne was."

"And that was that," says Jerry on the other end of the line.

"That was that," you say. "So I've talked to the police and the State Bureau of Narcotics, but there's a fumble somewhere and they're afraid to move. Either that or they're being handsomely paid. A little of both, I suspect. There's always someone somewhere in any one system who clogs the pipe. In the police department there's always one guy who'll take a little money on the side and spoil the good name of the force. It's a fact. You can't get away from it. People are human. So am I. If I can't clean the clog in the pipe one way, I'll clean it another. This novel of mine, needless to say, will be what will do it.''

"You might go down the drain with it, Rob. Do you really think your novel will shame the narcotics boys into acting?''

"That's the idea.''

"Won't you be sued?''

"I've taken care of that. I'm signing a paper with my publishers absolving them of any blame, saying that all characters in this novel are fictitious. Thus, if I've lied to the publishers they are blameless. If I'm sued, the royalties from the novel will be used in my defense. And I've got plenty of evidence. Incidentally, it's a corking good novel.''

"Seriously, Rob. Did someone send you a razor in a box?''

"Yes, and there lies my greatest danger. Rather thrilling. They wouldn't dare kill me outright. But if I died of my own natural carelessness and my inherited blood makeup, who would blame them? They wouldn't slit my throat, that'd be somewhat obvious. But a razor, or a nail, or the edge of the steering wheel of my car fixed and set with knife blades . . . it's all very melodramatic. How goes it with your novel, Jerry?''

"Slow. How's about lunch today?''

"Fair enough. The Brown Derby?''

"You sure ask for trouble. You know damn well Anne eats there every day with Mike!''

"Stimulates my appetite, Gerald, old man. See you.''

You hang up. Your hand is okay now. You whistle as you bandage it in the bathroom. Then you give the little razor contraption a going over. A primitive thing. The chances were hardly fifty-fifty it would even work.

You sit down and write three thousand more words, stimulated by the early morning events.

The handle of the door to your car has been filed, sharpened to a razor edge during the night. Dripping blood, you return to the house for more bandages. You gulp pills. The bleeding stops.

After you deposit the two new chapters of the book in your safety deposit box at the bank, you drive and meet Jerry Walters at the Brown Derby. He looks as electric and small as ever, dark-jowled, his eyes popping behind his thick-lensed glasses.

"Anne's inside.'' He grins at you. "And Mike's with her. Why do we wanna eat here, I ask?'' His grin dries and he stares at you, at your hand. "You need a drink! Right this way. There's Anne at that table over there. Nod to her."

"I'm nodding."

You watch Anne, at a corner table, in a monk's-cloth sport dress interwoven with gold and silver thread, a link of Aztec jewelry in bronze units around her tan neck. Her hair is the same bronze color. Beside her, behind a cigar and a haze of smoke, is the rather tall, spare figure of Michael Horn, who looks just like what he is: gambler, narcotics specialist, sensualist par excellence, lover of women, ruler of men, wearer of diamonds and silk undershorts. You would not want to shake hands with him. That manicure looks too sharp.

You sit down to a salad. You are eating it when Anne and Mike come by the table after their cocktail. "Hello, sharpster," you say to Mike Horn, with a little emphasis on the latter word.

Behind Horn is his bodyguard, a twenty-two-year-old kid from Chicago named Britz, with a carnation in his black coat lapel and his black hair greased, and his eyes sewed down by little muscles at the corners, so he looks sad.

"Hello, Rob, darling," says Anne. "How's the book?"

"Fine, fine. I've got a swell new chapter on you, Anne."

"Thank you, darling."

"When you going to leave this big heel-headed leprechaun?" you ask her, not looking at Mike.

"After I kill him," says Anne.

Mike laughs. "That's a good one. Now let's get going, baby. I'm tired of this jerk."

You upset some cutlery. Somehow a lot of dishes fall. You almost hit Mike. But Britz and Anne and Jerry gang you and so you sit down, the blood banging your ears, and people pick up the cutlery and hand it to you.

"So long," says Mike.

Anne goes out the door like a pendulum on a clock and you note the time. Mike and Britz follow.

You look at your salad. You reach for your fork. You pick at the stuff.

You take a forkful.

Jerry stares at you. "For God's sake, Rob, what's wrong?"

You don't speak. You take the fork away from your lips.

"What's wrong, Rob? Spit it out!"

You spit.

Jerry swears under his breath.

Blood.

You and Jerry come down out of the Taft building and you are now talking sign language. A wad of stuff is in your mouth. You smell of antiseptic.

"But I don't see how," says Jerry. You gesture with your hands. "Yeah, I know, the fight in the Derby. The fork gets knocked on the floor." You gesture again. Jerry supplies the explanation to the pantomime. "Mike, or Britz, picks it up, hands it back to you, but instead slips you a fixed, sharpened fork."

You nod your head violently, flushing.

"Or maybe it was Anne," says Jerry.

No, you shake your head. You try to explain in pantomime that if Anne knew about this she'd quit Mike cold. Jerry doesn't get it and peers at you through his thick goggles. You sweat.

A tongue is a bad place for a cut. You knew a guy once who had a cut tongue and the wound never healed, even though it stopped bleeding. And imagine with a hemophiliac!

You gesture now, forcing a smile as you climb into your car. Jerry squints, thinks, gets it. "Oh." He laughs. "You mean to say all you need now is a stab in the backside?"

You nod, shake hands, drive off.

Suddenly life is not so funny anymore. Life is real. Life is stuff that comes out of your veins at the least invitation. Unconsciously your hand goes again and again to your coat pocket where the tablets are hidden. Good old tablets.

It is about now you notice you are being followed.

You turn left at the next corner and you're thinking, fast. An accident. Yourself knocked out and bleeding. Unconscious, you'll never be able to give yourself a dose of those precious little pills you keep in your pocket.

You press the gas pedal. The car thunders ahead and you look back and the other car is still following you, gaining. A tap on the head, the least cut, and you are all done.

You turn right at Wilcox, left again when you reach Melrose, but they are still with you. There is only one thing to do.

You stop the car at the curb, take the keys, climb quietly out, and walk up and sit down on somebody's lawn.

As the trailing car passes, you smile and wave at them.

You think you hear curses as the car vanishes.

You walk the rest of the way home. On the way you call a garage and have them pick up your car for you.

Though you've always been alive, you've never been as alive as you are now—you'll live forever. You're smarter than all of them put together. You're watchful. They won't be able to do a thing that you can't see and circumvent one way or another. You have that much faith in yourself. You can't die. Other people die, but not you. You have complete faith in your ability to live. There'll never be a person clever enough to kill you.

You can eat flame, catch cannonballs, kiss women who have torches for lips, chuck gangsters under the chin. Being the way you are, with the kind of blood you have in your body, has made you—a gambler? A taker of chances? There must be some way to explain the morbid craving you have for danger or near danger. Well, explain it this way. You get a terrific ego lift out of coming through each experience safely. Admit it, you're a conceited, self-satisfied person with morbid ideas of self-destruction. Hidden ideas, naturally. No one admits outwardly he wants to die, but it's in there somewhere. Self-preservation and the will to die tugging back and forth. The urge to die getting you into messes, self-preservation yanking you out again. And you hate and laugh at these people when you see them wince and twist with discomfort when you come out whole and intact. You feel superior, godlike, immortal. They are inferior, cowardly, common. And you are a little more than irked to think that Anne prefers her narcotics to you. She finds the needle more stimulating. Damn her! And yet—you also find her stimulating—and dangerous. But you'll take a chance with her, any time, yes, any old time. . . .

It is once again four in the morning. The typewriter is going under your fingers as the doorbell rings. You get up and go to answer in the complete before-dawn quiet.

Far away on the other side of the universe her voice says, "Hello, Rob. Anne. Just get up?"

"Right. This is the first time you've come around in days, Anne." You open the door and she comes in past you, smelling good.

"I'm tired of Mike. He makes me sick. I need a good dose of Robert Douglas. I'm really tired, Rob."

"You sound it. My sympathies."

"Rob—" A pause.

"Yeah?"

A pause. "Rob—could we get away tomorrow? I mean, today—this afternoon. Up the coast somewhere, lie in the sun and just let it burn us? I need it, Rob, badly."

"Why, I guess so. Sure. Yeah. Hell, yes!"

"I like you, Rob. I only wish you weren't writing that damned novel."

"If you cleared out of that mob I might quit," you say. "But I don't like the things they've done to you. Has Mike told you what he's doing to me?"

"Is he doing something, darling?"

"He's trying to bleed me. *Really* bleed me, I mean. You know Mike underneath, don't you, Anne. White livered and scared. Britz, Britz, too, for that matter. I've seen their kind before, acting tough to cover up their lily guts. Mike doesn't want to kill me. He's afraid of killing. He thinks he can scare me out of this. But I'm going ahead because I don't think he'll have enough nerve to finish it. He'd rather take a chance on a narcotics rap than go up for murder. I know Mike."

"But do you know me, darling?"

"I think I do."

"Very well?"

"Well enough."

"I might kill you."

"You wouldn't dare. You like me."

"I like myself," she purrs, "too."

"You always were a strange one. I never knew, and still don't know, what makes you tick."

"Self-preservation."

You offer her a cigarette. She is very near you. You nod wonderingly. "I saw you pull the wings off a fly once."

"It was interesting."

"Did you dissect bottled kittens in school?"

"With relish."

"Do you know what dope does to you?"

"I relish that too."

"How about this?"

You are near enough so it takes only a move to bring your faces together. The lips are as good as they look. They are warm and moving and soft.

She holds you away a bit. "I relish this also," she says.

You hold her against you, again the lips meet you, and you shut your eyes. . . .

"Dammit," you say, breaking away.

Her fingernail has bitten into your neck.

"I'm sorry, darling. Hurt you?" she asks.

"Everybody wants to get into the act," you say. You take out your favorite bottle and tap out a couple of pills. "God, lady, what a grip. Treat me kindly from now on, I'm tender."

"I'm sorry. I forgot myself," she says.

"That's very flattering. But if *this* is what happens when I kiss you, I'd be a bloody mess if I went any further. Wait."

More bandage on your neck. Out again to kiss her.

"Easy does it, baby. We'll take in the beach and I'll give you a lecture on the evils of running with Michael Horn."

"No matter what I say, you're going ahead with the novel, Rob?"

"Mind's made up. Where were we? Oh, yeah."

Again the lips.

You park the car atop a sunblazed cliff a little after noon. Anne runs ahead, down the timber stairs, two hundred feet down the cliff. The wind lifts her bronze hair, she looks trim in her blue bathing suit. You follow, thoughtful. You are away from everywhere. Towns are gone, the highway empty. The beach below with the sea folding on it is wide, barren, with big slabs of granite toppled and washed by breakers. Wading birds squeal. You watch Anne go down ahead of you. "What a little fool," you think of her.

You saunter arm in arm and stand letting the sun get into you. You believe everything is clean now, and good, for a while. All life is clean and fresh, even Anne's life. You want to talk, but your voice sounds funny in the salt silence and anyway your tongue is still sore from that sharp fork.

You wade by the waterline and Anne picks something up.

"A barnacle," she says. "Remember how you used to go diving with your rubber-rimmed helmet and trident, Butch? In the good old days?"

"The good old days." You think of the time past, Anne and yourself and the things that used to work out for you together. Traveling up the coast. Fishing. Diving. But even then she was a weird creature. Didn't mind killing lobsters at all. Took a relish in cleaning them.

"You used to be so foolhardy, Rob. You still are, in fact. Took chances diving for abalones when these barnacles might have cut you badly. Sharp as razors."

"I know," you say.

She gives the barnacle a toss. It lands near your discarded shoes. As you come back up you skirt it, careful not to step on it.

"We could have been happy," she says.

"It's nice to think so, isn't it?"

"I wish you'd change your mind," she says.

"Too late," you say.

She sighs.

A wave comes in on the shore.

You are not afraid of being here with Anne. She can do nothing to you. You can handle her. You are confident of that. No, this will be an easy, lazy day, without event. You are alert, ready for any contingency.

You lie in the sun and it strikes through your bones and loosens you inside and you mold to the contours of the sand. Anne is beside you and the sun gilds her tippy nose and glitters across the minute pellets of perspiration on her brow. She talks gay talk and light talk and you are fascinated with her; how can she be so beautiful and like a hunk of serpentine thrown across your path and be so mean and small somewhere hidden inside where you can't find it?

You lie upon your stomach and the sand is warm. The sun is warm.

"You're going to burn," she says at last, laughing.

"I suppose I am," you say. You feel very clever, very immortal.

"Here, let me put some oil on your back," she says, unfolding the shiny patent leather Chinese jigsaw of her purse. She holds up a bottle of pure yellow oil. "This'll get between you and the sun," she says. "Okay?"

"Okay," you say. You are feeling very good, very superior.

She bastes you like a pig on a spit. The bottle is suspended over you and it comes down in a twine of liquid, yellow and glittering and cool to the small hollows of your spine. Her hand spreads it and massages it over your back. You lie, purring, eyes closed, watching the little blue and yellow bubbles dance across your shut eyelids, as she pours on more of the liquid and laughs as she massages you.

"I feel cooler already," you say.

She continues to massage you for a minute or more and then she stops and sits beside you quietly. A long time passes and you lie deep, baked in a sand oven, not wanting to move. The sun suddenly is not so hot.

"Are you ticklish?" asks Anne, behind your back.

"No," you say, your mouth turning up at the corners.

"You have a lovely back," she says. "I'd love to tickle it."

"Tickle away," you say.

"Are you ticklish here?" she asks.

You feel a distant, sleepy movement on your back.

"No," you say.

"Here?" she says.

You feel nothing. "You aren't even touching me," you say.

"I read a book once," she says. "It said that the sensory portions of the back are so poorly developed that most people couldn't tell exactly where they were being touched."

"Nuts," you say. "Touch me. Go ahead. I'll tell you."

You feel three long movements on your back.

"Well?" she asks.

"You tickled me down under one shoulder blade for a distance of five inches. Likewise under the other shoulder blade. And then right down my spine. So there."

"Smart boy. I quit. You're too good. I need a cigarette. Damn, I'm all out. Mind if I run up to the car and get some?"

"I'll go," you say.

"Never mind." She is off across the sand. You watch her run, lazily, sleepily, in patterns of rising hot atmosphere. You think it rather strange she is taking her purse and bottled liquid with her. Women. But all the same you notice she is beautiful, running. She climbs up the wooden steps, turns and waves and smiles. You smile back, move your hand in a brief, lazy salute. "Hot?" she cries.

"I'm drenched," you cry back, lazily.

You feel the sweat crawling on your body. The heat is in you now and you sink down into it, as into a bath. You feel the sweat pouring down your back in torrents, faint and far away, like ants crawling on you. Sweat it out, you think. Sweat it all out. Streaks of sweat well down your ribs and along your stomach, tickling. You laugh. God, what a sweat. You never sweated like this before in your life. The smell of that oil Anne put on you is sweet in the warm air. Drowsy, drowsy.

You start. Your head yanks upward.

On top of the cliff the car is started, put in gear, and now, as you watch Anne waving to you, the car flashes in the sun, turns, and drives away down the highway.

Just like that.

"Why, you little witch!" you cry irritatedly. You start to get up.

You can't. The sun has made you weak. Your head swims. Damn it. You've been sweating.

Sweating.

You smell something new on the hot air. Something as familiar and timeless as the salt smell of the sea. A hot, sweet, sickish odor. An odor that is all the terror in the world to you and those of your kind. You cry out and stagger up.

You are wearing a cloak, a garment of scarlet. It clings to your thighs and, as you watch, it encases your loins and spreads and grows upon your legs and ankles. It is red. The reddest red in the color chart. The purest, loveliest, most terrible red you have ever seen, spreading and growing and pulsing along your body.

You clutch at your back. You mouth meaningless words. Your hands close upon three long open wounds cut into your flesh below the shoulder blades!

Sweat! You thought you were sweating. And it was blood! You lay there thinking it was sweat coming out of you, laughing about it, enjoying it!

You can feel nothing. Your fingers scrabble clumsily, weakly. Your back feels nothing. It is insensible.

"Here, let me put some oil on your back," says Anne, far away in the shimmering nightmare of your memory. *"You're going to burn."*

A wave crashes on the shore. In memory you see the long yellow twine of liquid pouring down on your back, suspended from Anne's lovely fingers. You feel her massaging you.

Narcotic in solution. Novocaine or cocaine or something in a yellow solution that, after it clung to your back awhile, deadened every nerve. Anne knows all about narcotics, doesn't she?

Sweet, sweet, lovely Anne.

"Are you ticklish?" asks Anne in your mind, again.

You retch. And echoing in your blood-red swimming mind, you give an answer: *No. Tickle away. Tickle away. Tickle away. . . . Tickle away, Anne J. Anthony, lovely lady. Tickle away.*

With a nice sharp barnacle shell.

You were diving for abalones off shore and you scraped your back on a rock, in rough streaks, with a crop of razor-sharp barnacles. Yes, that's it. Diving. Accident. What a pretty setup.

Sweet, lovely Anne.

Or did you have your fingernails honed on a whetstone, my darling?

The sun hangs in your brain. The sand is beginning to melt under you. You try to find the buttons to unbutton, to rip away this red garment. Senselessly, blindly, gropingly, you search for buttons. There are none. The garment stays. How silly, you think foolishly. *How silly to be found in your long, red woolen underwear. How silly.*

There must be zippers somewhere. Those three long cuts can be zipped up tight and then that sliding red stuff will stop sliding out of you. You, the immortal man.

The cuts aren't too deep. If you can get to a doctor. If you can take your tablets.

Tablets!

You fall forward on your coat, and search one pocket and then another pocket, and then another, and turn it inside out, and rip the lining loose and shout and cry and four waves come pounding in on the shore behind you, like trains passing, roaring. And you go back through each empty pocket again, hoping that you have missed one. But there is nothing but lint, a box of matches, and two theater ticket stubs. You drop the coat.

"Anne, come back!" you cry. "Come back! It's thirty miles to town, to a doctor. I can't walk it. I haven't time."

At the bottom of the cliff you look up. One hundred and fourteen steps. The cliff is sheer and blazing in the sun.

There is nothing to be done but climb the steps.

Thirty miles to town, you think. *Well, what is thirty miles?* What a splendid day for a walk!

It Burns Me Up!

I am lying here in the very center of the room and I am not mad, I am not angry, I am not perturbed. In the first place, in order for a man to be perturbed, angry, mad, he must recognize some stimulus from outside which touches his nerves. The nerves flash a message to the brain. The brain kicks back quick orders to all parts of the body: be angry, be mad, be disturbed! Eyelashes, pull back from eyes, let eyes protrude, muscles work! Pupils dilate! Mouth pull back tight from teeth! Ears blush! Brow furrow! Heart beat! Blood surge! Get angry, get perturbed, get mad!

But my eyelashes will not pull back. My eyes simply stare vacantly at a colorless, dark ceiling, my heart lies cold, my mouth is limp, my fingers are laxed. I do not madden. I do not anger or perturb. And yet I have every reason to be irritated.

The detectives are swaggering about my house, swearing in the rooms, honking in the night, drinking from bottles in the alley. Reporters are flashing quick bulbs at my relaxed body. The flash eyes are glinting into electrical powder, exploding. The neighbors are peering in at the windows. My wife is lying in a chair, turned away from me, and instead of crying she is very glad.

You understand, then, I have reason to be mad. But no matter how hard I try to be incensed, fuming, swearing, I cannot. Nothing responds. There is only an encompassing cold weightlessness over and through me.

I am dead.

I lie here, sleeping, and these people are the fragments of my bloodless dreaming. They move about me, as carrion-eaters over a decaying carcass, carnivores lusting on the hot spilled blood of killing at night, taking that blood and respilling it upon the pages of tabloid papers. But somehow in the transition from body to thrashing presses, the blood has turned an ungodly black.

A little blood will ink a million print drums. A little blood is chemical enough to drive ten million presses. A little blood is adrenaline enough to pound thirty million literate, reading hearts.

Tonight I have died. Tomorrow morning I will die again in thirty million brains, caught like a fly in a web, sucked dry by the multitentacled public and flushed on through the transits of their minds to be replaced by:

HEIRESS MARRIES DUKE!
INCOME TAX INCREASE DUE!
COAL MINERS STRIKE!

So here are the vultures circling over me. Here is the coroner, casually examining my vitals, the hyena newsmen digging at the dead thoughts of my love. And here the fauns and the goats with synthetic lion hearts, peering timidly in the window, but safely removed from terror, watching the carnivores stalk about, pruning their manes.

Perhaps my wife is cleverest of them all. She resembles nothing more than a small soft, dark leopard whiskering and licking itself, pleased with its actions, crouched within the chair's patterned enclosure.

The detective immediately overhead now, like a gigantic lion moving in that world of live people, is a large-lipped man. His lips are vised about a long smoking cigar, and he talks with that vise, his teeth gleaming in amber flashes. Once in a while he drops gray ash on my coat. He is talking:

"Well, so he's dead. So we talk to *her* for an hour, two hours, three, four, and what do we get? Nothing! Hell, we can't stay here all night! My wife'll kill me! I'm never home nights anymore. More damn murders."

The coroner, so brisk, so efficient, his fingers like inquisitive calipers, measures my circumference, my diameter. Is there anything but the purest professional interest behind his slanted, sad green eyes? He lifts his head at an imperious angle and makes his speech importantly:

"Died quickly. That knife certainly did things to his throat. And then, whoever did it stabbed him three times in the chest. A very nice job. Impressively bloody."

The detective jerks his bronze-haired head at my wife, wincing. "And she ain't got a blood-speck on her! How you figger that?"

"What does *she* say?" asks the coroner.

"She *don't* say. She just plumps there crooning to herself and singing, 'I won't spill till I see my lawyer.' Honest to God!" The detective can't fathom the ways of cat women. But, lying here, *I* can.

"That's all she'll say. 'I won't spill till I see my lawyer,' over and over, like a damn-fool nursery rhyme."

There is a body scuffle at the door that directs all attentions immediately. A handsome, finely muscled reporter is wrestling to get in.

"Hey!" The detective pushes out his cliff of chest. He bites the cigar fiercely. "Whatinell goes on?"

A cop face pokes in, hot, struggling. "This gink wants in, boss!"

"Who in hell does he think *he* is?" asks the detective.

The reporter's voice from a distance . . . "Carlton of the *Tribune*. H. J. Randolph sent me."

The detective blows up. "Kelly, you fool! Let the guy in! Randolph and I went to school together! Sure!"

"Ha, *ha*!" says the coroner, deadpan.

The detective shoots him a hot glance while the officer Kelly gives way and the reporter Carlton strides sweating inside.

"I had to get in," laughs Carlton. "Or it was my job."

"Hello, Carlton." The detective laughs again. "Pull up a corpse and sit down."

That is a joke. Everybody laughs, except my wife, who is curled in a feminine S within the chair arms, contentedly licking her lips like a fed cat.

The other reporters resent Carlton's entrance. They say nothing. Carlton looks at me with his baby-blue eyes:

"Well, a self-surgery! Ear to ear! How will he talk to Saint Peter in that condition?"

The coroner is proud. "Oh, I will sew him up new as paint. I am pretty good at fixing stuff like that. Comes from long practice."

Carlton rushes on, ignoring the coroner, intrigued with scribbling hieroglyphics on papers, shooting questions. He grins while scribbling. "Hotsy-totsy. Love nest, maybe. All the trimmings. God, he looks like Christmas, don't he? Green around the gills and big red ribbons of blood tied in coagulated bows."

Even the detective cannot stomach this and coughs a little. For the first time my wife doesn't look calm and cool as cream in her chair. It is momentary. It passes. Again she adjusts the rim of her chartreuse skirt over her curvesome legs, blinking at the new reporter as if to fan his attention to flame.

But now the reporter is kneeling at the altar of my desecrated flesh. A cold marble altar, exquisitely carved by the original hands of God, and only recently recarved by—someone.

Mrs. McLeod from next door is looking through the south window from outside on fat tiptoe, her shining gray eyes hippopotamuslike in the night. Her voice is vague, and she is shivering on purpose:

"Wait until I write Susan in Springfield. Will she be jealous. My very own mysterious murder in my own front yard, almost. Who would have thought we'd have things like this in *our* neighborhood? I tell you, though, Anna, come look— See, that's the detective, that man with the fat under his chin. He don't look like a detective to me, does he to you? He looks like a bad guy, a villain. Now, take that young reporter guy, he looks just like Philo Vance, only younger. I bet he'll be the one who really solves the case. But they never get the credit, that's the way. Just look at that woman over there in the corner. I bet she was his mistress, not his wife—''

''Get away from the window, lady!''

''Well, I guess I got a right to look in!''

''Lady, move along!''

''Young man, I own this lawn right up to the window. This is my house! I rented it to Mr. Jameson myself.''

''Lady, move along.''

''Young man—''

That will do, Mrs. McLeod, that will do for a long time.

Now, back to the people in the room.

The reporter, Carlton, is now attracted as a planet is attracted to the sun by my wife. He is darting questions at her, and she is deliberately stalling him. The reporter is fast, and my wife is languid, heavy-lidded, and easy going. She will not be pushed, pell-melled into anything. She will simply have her say. She says it, purringly: ''I came home from the nightclub and there he was, lying on the floor, staring at the ceiling. That is all I know.''

The other reporters scribble too. They had not got a thing from her until handsome Carlton showed up. Carlton cracks back at her, ''You sing at the nightclub Bomba?''

''Yes. I'm a very good singer. I can hit a C above high C if you want. Once I had a chance with the Metropolitan Opera Company. But I didn't consider it; I don't like them.''

The coroner has an opinion of this chatter. He does not express it. But he has the same expression on his face that I once had. The coroner and the detective are both irked because the lime-light has swiveled from them and their stage to this little chittering divertissement between man and woman. The detective especially is annoyed because he was unable to pry anything out of my wife except her singsong pleading for a lawyer and now this young reporter—

Somebody outside hoists a small girl up to the window. She is framed in it momentarily.

''Look, baby, you may never see anything like that—''

''Oh, Mama, what's wrong with that man?''

''Move along, lady, please. I just chased a couple people away, and I'm tired. I been on my feet all evening. Move away—''

''Oh, Mama!''

I am now immortal! Caught in that child's mind I shall be dead forevermore, and on dark nights I will stride drunkenly through the shivering corridors of her body. And she will waken shrieking, ripping the bedclothes apart. Someday her husband will feel her red fingernails in his fleshy arm, and that will be me, in the middle dark, reaching out a constricting claw to clutch again at life!

"Can it, *can* it!" suggests the detective, glaring hotly at the reporter, Carlton. "I'm the one who interviews her! Not *you*, bozo!"

The lips of Carlton go down. He opens his hands and shrugs slightly. "But you want a good report for the paper, Captain, don't you? With pictures? Sure you do. And I got to get details."

He is getting the details fine. My wife has a thirty-three bust, twenty-eight waist, thirty-one hips. These details are being scribbled on a brain-pad somewhere within the reporter. Remind him, someone, to call her up after the funeral.

The coroner clears his throat. "Now, about this body—"

Yeah, for God's sake, gentlemen, let's get back to me. What am I lying here for?

Carlton snaps his voice like snapping his thin fingers. "You had a lot of men tagging after you, didn't you, madam?"

My wife lids her eyes and unlids them. "Yes, I've always been popular. Couldn't help it, I guess. He—" She shakes her head at me. "He never seemed to mind the other men tagging at my heels. It sort of upheld his judgment in marrying a— Thoroughbred."

The coroner quickly jabs my ribs in some medical joke. He busies himself over me to keep from snorting out a laugh at her choice of words.

The other reporters are now buzzing like a hive of tipped bees. My wife would not talk for *them*, but perhaps there is a provocative angle to Carlton's body, perhaps there is something about his look or his lips or the cast of his shoulders . . . anyway, the reporters are angry. "Come off it, Carlton, let us have a try!"

Carlton turns to the detective. "Who did the killing, Captain?"

"We're rounding up all her boyfriends," says the detective intelligently, nodding, thinking it over.

Carlton nods, too, and half listening, looking sidewise and gleaming at my wife, checks his notes solemnly, salutes my cold body, and marches across the room. "Thanks, thanks, thanks,

I'll be right back. Want to phone a call. Keep up the good work." To me, grinning, "Don't wait up for me, darling."

Slam. The door closes.

"Well," sighs the detective, "we've done all we can here. Fingerprints. Clues. Photographs. Grillings. I guess we can let the body—" He stops, flushing, giving way to the coroner, who, after all, has the right to make his little official announcements.

The coroner acknowledges this courtesy and says, after a due period of serious thought, "I think we can take the body away now. Yes."

One of the remaining reporters pipes, "Say, Sherlock, you think this is a suicide setup? If you ask me—"

"I'm not asking," says the detective. "How would you explain them stab wounds?"

"I see it this way," the coroner interrupts. "She comes home, finds him freshly dead on the floor, having just killed himself. That explains how she has no blood on her from a spurting jugular. Evidently she took the suicide weapon and stabbed him three times in a frenzy of—shall we say—delight? She was glad to find him dead and let herself go. There's no blood in these stab wounds, that proves he was stabbed later, after she found him lying there."

"No, no, now," roars the detective. "You're *all* wrong! You're dead wrong! That's not the way it worked at all! Not at all!" He launches himself, shaking his hair over his eyes, blundering off down blind alleys, kidding himself, chewing his cigar, pounding one fist into one palm. "No, no, you're all wrong!"

The coroner chucks me in the ribs. He looks at me. I look back with nothing in my eyes except cold shining light.

"Oh, but the coroner is right!" My wife, with the swiftness of a leopard paw darting, seizes upon this information and makes it her own. "He's exactly right!"

"Now wait a minute," complains the detective, seeing his case being torn from his hands.

"That's how it was," my wife insists, purring. She blinks big wet dark eyes. "I came in. He was lying there. And—something— came over me. I must've just seized the dagger and yelled I was glad he was dead and stabbed him some more!"

"But," wails the detective feebly, "that just can't be the way it happened." He knows it may be true, but he is slow coming back to reality. In a moment he will stomp his feet like a hurt child.

"That's how it happened," she says.

"Well now, it stands to reason," reasons the detective vaguely. He purposely drops his cigar so he'll have time to pick it up, brush it off, and put it in his mouth before he has to think. "Well, it just don't work out that way," he says tiredly.

The coroner takes over. "Young woman, you won't be prosecuted for murder, but you'll be fined for mutilating a corpse!"

"Shut up, you!" cries the detective, whirling in all directions.

"That's all right," confides my wife. "Fine me. Go ahead."

The reporters are yelling, adding to the wild pattern of voices.

"Is that true, Mrs. Jameson?"

"You may quote me. It is true."

"Oh, God!" cries the detective.

My wife is tearing the case to shreds with her enameled claws, fondling it, loving it, ripping it carefully and intentionally down the middle, while the detective gapes and tries to shut her up.

"Don't pay any attention to her, boys!"

"But it's the truth," she says with honesty in her eyes.

"See?" chortle the reporters.

"Everybody clear out!" yells the detective. "I've had enough!"

But the case is closed. The reporters, laughing, declare it so. Bulbs flare, my wife winks prettily for them. The detective sees the credit for solving the case go fleeting. He manages to calm down, "Say, say, boys, about those pictures of me for the paper, now—"

"What pictures? Ha. Period. Ha. Exclamation point. Ha!"

"Clear out, everybody!" The detective rams his cigar into an ashtray. Parts of it fall on me. Nobody brushes them off.

The coroner is grinning, and outside the window an audience is watching, breathless. One might expect applause at any moment.

It is all over. Peever, the detective, jerks his head. "Come on, Mrs. Jameson. You reporters want any more, come along to the station."

There is a movement of bodies through the air, over the carpet, through the door. "Boy, what a story! Hotsy, what photographs!"

"Quick, Alice, look through the window. They're going to take him out!"

Someone drops a cloth over my profile.

"Oh, darn it, we're too late. Now we can't see *any*thing!"

They leave the room, these reporters with their images of me, one of them even in color, carried under careless, joyful arms. Everybody is rushing for the early morning edition.

I am pleased. I died before midnight. Therefore I will make the morning paper. Mr. Jones will pick me up with his Sanka. Thoughtful of me.

The detective is making a face. My wife arises and leaves the room. One cop outside the door nods at another cop. "How about some hotcakes and syrup down at the White Log?"

I cannot even lick my lips.

Wearily the detective mops his brow. He unsheathes a fresh cigar and spits the bit end of it at my feet. He doesn't speak, but he thinks a lot. By his face, he is a man with a dominant wife. He is dreading going home to her now; he likes to idle, stay out all night. Bodies give him an excuse. I'm a pretty good one. But I'm not worth much now. He will make a routine report and go home.

The coroner is the only one left. He pats me on the shoulder. "Nobody asked you any questions, did they? Well, friend, what about it? Were you murdered by her or her friends, or did you kill yourself over—her. Huh? A fool in love is twice a fool."

Me, I won't talk.

It is late. The coroner leaves. Maybe he has a wife too. Maybe he likes bodies because they don't argue back like some people.

I'm alone now.

In a few minutes a couple of interns will come in in their whites, chewing gum. They'll glance casually at me, tilt me over onto a stretcher languidly, and trot me downtown in a slow wagon, in no hurry.

And a week from now a man who is worrying about his income tax will turn a handle and flames will burn me. I will rush up the flue of the crematory in so many gray flecks.

And with some sort of ironic justice, and the providence of a stiff March wind, a week from now, when these various people— Carlton, my wife, the detective, the coroner, the reporters, Mrs. McLeod—when all these people are crossing the street, maybe suddenly they'll get something in their damned eyes! *All* of them!

Little pieces of gray ash, maybe.

Half-Pint Homicide

It would be wrong to say that the Douser got the idea just as he was being pushed off Union Bridge by a man. Truth to tell, Douser tempted the man with, "Come on, push me," and then stepped aside, politely, allowing the man precedence.

The man screamed.

So did a train that passed below a moment later.

A few minutes later Douser was talking over a phone to a very bad fat man. The man's name was Schabold. Douser talked jovially with him. Nobody called anybody any names.

"Yeah, Schabold. My name's Douser Mulligan. And this corpse, under the Union Bridge, I mentioned, was one of your bodyguards—"

The news was not good to Schabold. Douser consoled him:

"Know just how you feel, Mr. Schabold. That's three of your boys hurt in one month. One shot himself accidentally and is still in the hospital. Another was picked up drunk on Main Street, dripping counterfeit money. That's sad."

Schabold spoke a few sad words, like a fat boy who had just lost a bag of candy: "You're the little sparrow who hangs around the Central Jail, are you not?"

"That's right. Well, see you around, huh, Schabold."

Douser hung the receiver back on its prong to sleep.

He walked up toward the jail in a cold winter wind. Things were becoming fun now. The next hour he'd dawdle speaking with Sarge Palmborg at the jail, keeping an eye peeled patiently for a large ebony limousine containing one fat man, well worried. Life was dull except on nights like this, when he had many people, assorted sizes, hating his miniature guts. Yes, sir!

Sergeant Palmborg was standing in front of the jail an hour later.

"Evening, Sergeant Palmborg!"

"So here you are again!" Palmborg looked down a million miles. "So." He lit his pipe in godlike movements. "Don't nothing discourage you?"

"Nothing," said the Douser.

A moment's silence. "They took away your badge a year ago for being so damn flippant."

"It was a frame. Look." Douser formed a frame with his hands. "With gilt edges too. Feel."

"And," Palmborg proceeded with his gray calm, "they robbed your holster like a bird's nest. And here you are, again, looking like a small puss who's digested the canary."

"A fine meal," said Douser.

The sarge nodded back one shoulder. "A body's cooling in there, just brought in from the railyards. One of Schabold's men. Naturally, you know nothing about him."

"Naturally."

"He was one of them gunmen connected with that Detroit bank killing. They never could get a thing on him."

"Except a locomotive."

The sergeant snorted. "You're in deep, lad. I don't know if you've pestered Schabold or not. Whoever did it is in for it deep. Schabold won't take it. Three of his men hurt since he arrived in town a month ago—"

Douser was about to comment when thunder boomed the winter night and a big ebony limousine roared out of nowhere. Schabold sprawled on its velvety rear cushion, fat cold pork, staring out. "Well—" Douser clocked him. "Right on time—" Douser waved.

"Douser," pleaded the sarge. "Take your fingers away from your nose." The car roared out of sight. The sarge bit his pipe. "I'd like to get something on that black-marketing bum, that soft ton of bacon—"

Douser babbled. "I got a theory. Schabold's rich, always has been. Why, then, did he go crooked? I ask you. Remember the old bromide, each of us carries the seed of our own doom? That's Schabold. Figure out his seed and you got him. Listen here, Sarge—"

They conversed in a rising wind. Waiting. Douser's heart thumped like a toy tambourine. Waiting. And when the ebony limousine came roaring by again, the sarge, on cue, whistled and walked out to intercept it, Douser at his heels.

The limousine rammed on its brakes, heaving Schabold into one window: "What's the meaning of this?"

The sarge smiled. "Got your draft cards?"

Schabold produced his with a glitter of hard rings on soft fingers. The sarge okayed them and nodded at the bodyguards up front. "You too."

"Uh—" said the bodyguards, "we—that is—we come out in such a rush we—forgot to bring them."

"Well, well," said the sarge. "We'll have to hold you until the FBI checks your draft status tomorrow morning. Climb out."

"Tomorrow!" Schabold emerged in large soft portions from his throne. He searched the sarge's face, found nothing, and shifted his wrath to his men. "You—careless louts!"

"You can go now," said Palmborg to the fat man. "We don't want you. You're okay."

Schabold flapped big red lips, changed his mind, got in the car behind the wheel, silent. Watching him, Douser got an idea of a large gray helpless barrage balloon maneuvered in life's winds by obedient servants forever running in its shadow. Now the balloon's tie lines were clipped. Let the blimp scream for orders, let the wind blow. Douser was here now, to answer.

Douser jumped in beside Schabold in the front seat, slammed the door, waved bye-bye at the sarge.

"Hey!" rumbled the blimp.

"Night, Sarge. You know who I'm with if I'm dead tomorrow. Remember." Douser turned to the fat man. "Let's go!"

It was hard to tell who was most amazed. Mouths were open. Somebody swore. The motor boomed and the car heaved off into the winter streets, roaring.

Douser settled cozily, worming his small bottom about, chuckling. "Slow down. We got all night to talk. About ways of you killing me and me killing you."

The car slowed. "All right, what's the deal?"

"No deal. This is a safe place to spend the night, with you. In the lion's mouth, I guess you'd say. Everybody saw you spirit me off into the night, fat man. That's just another part of my master plan. You don't dare touch me, tonight, or even tomorrow."

The road rushed under the car in a quick rubber whisper.

"Tell you how it is with me, Schabold. Sometimes I don't sleep nights worrying about the criminals walking free in this world. I get mad. Then I do things about it. I make sure a guy's a real honest-to-God criminal, then I start clicking. I eliminated your boyfriends first, because if something happened to me, you might try and frame it off on one of them. That's your usual trick. But I wanted you—*alone*. Just you, me, and the next twenty-four hours, darling. It's your move.''

Schabold strangled inside his lapels. His eyes were gray, blind, shining straight ahead, his jowls shaking.

Glancing at the swiftly running scenery Douser said, ''There's your house, Schabold. You want to stop and pick up a gun—''

Brakes screamed. Douser bounced off the windshield like a ball. Schabold looked pleased, and bulged from the car to pump across the street, Douser pattering after.

They found a gun in the kitchen. Douser cheerily helped look for it. ''Is it in the wastebasket? No. Refrigerator? I knew you wouldn't carry a gun by the jail. How about this jar of berry jam?''

Schabold found the gun. Munching crackers, Douser followed him back to the car. Nobody made any phone calls to warn anybody to come help somebody. The car roared again.

Schabold, with gun, settled down, over the shock of things. The bright eyes began to think inside the fat. He poked up the speed. They boomed through Beverly Hills, Douser whistling happily. When he finished whistling he asked the fat man a favor:

''Please, Mr. Schabold. Take out your gun.''

''What for?''

''For the hell of it.''

Schabold pulled the gun. ''Well . . . ?''

Douser gave directions. ''Stick it against my chest.''

The gun muzzled with ugly pleasure against ribs the size of a small birdcage.

Douser panted on his fingernails, rubbed them boredly on his kneecap with a slow, languid motion. ''Now—pull the trigger.''

The car purred down into a husky mutter. Schabold whispered: ''Oh, I'd love to pull this trigger. And keep on pulling it, over and over.'' The eyes in the fat opened, closed, opened again. ''Lord, what it would do to your pint-sized machinery. It'd be worth it—almost.''

''Almost?'' wondered the Douser. ''I gather there is some doubt?''

The gun chewed his ribs, more.

''Enjoy yourself. Play with me. You think you got me in a spot where you can laugh. Play with me. Go on.''

The car crawled slow, and the wind blew hard and cold

through the window. Schabold kept whispering slow and cold too:

"But I don't want a jail rap, I don't like trouble. Not now, anyway."

He put the gun away, with a great battle of will.

Douser's heart played hopscotch, marking lines on his stomach and jumping up and down on it, hard. He sweated.

Schabold sat thinking a long while as they drove toward the sea. Salt wind blew in from the stars, and Schabold chewed over an idea like a wad of gum and finally smiled, the wrong kind of smile, at Douser. Douser swallowed tightly.

The ocean rushed to meet them with a boom of surf and a stretch of snow-white sand. Schabold stopped the car and looked at the waves, his mind going out and in with them, deciding. When next he spoke his voice was thoughtful, soft. The anger was gone, the excitement and fury. In it was the sound of a man whose decision is made.

"Douser, it's either you or me. . . ."

Douser's heart leaped in its cage like a frantic red bird.

Schabold confessed a bit. "I came to the Coast to black-market gas. I'm a business man, you might say. You get in my way, hurt my men, bother me at all hours. Tonight I decided to supervise your demise myself. I never do a job alone, I need help. And my men are convenient hooks upon which to hang prison terms in case anything happens. That Detroit job, for example, they never proved a thing on us. I let Louie Martin take the rap for that cop killing in Fort Worth. There's always a way, Douser," he said indulgently, gently. "I have never been in jail in my life. I pride myself on my clever record. Never been in jail. You, now, tonight, thought to get me alone, to joke with me, work on me. Well now, little man," he finished dryly, "get out of the car, very slowly, please."

The gun was in Douser's side again. Douser gentled the door open, slid out. Schabold slid heavily after, eyes shining like a saint's.

"Good-bye, Douser."

"Don't be a fool!" Douser cried.

Schabold fired his gun.

He kept firing it until it was empty.

BANG. Douser jerked. BANG. He shriveled with it. BANG. It kicked his eardrums. Bullets sang hot songs. BANG. Ricocheting off sea pebbles. Stars shook like fireflies. BANG!

Silence.

The sea came in and went out, lifting its salty skirts.

And out of salt silence, Schabold's soft, genuine laughter.

Douser's fingers crawled like wary spiders, chest, stomach, legs, arms, then flying to his face.

Schabold kept laughing. "You should—have—seen—your—feet!"

Douser said simply, "I'm alive."

"Certainly." Schabold laughed again.

Douser looked almost disappointed. "You missed me on purpose!"

Laughter tears ran down the fat man's face. He was having fun, playing Douser's game right back at him. Now he climbed back into the car, flicked the keys in the ignition, chortling. "Well, I don't have to kill you, Douser," he said. "For the last hour I've worked on some way to kill you while I had the chance. It was tempting. My emotions got hold of me. Well, I'll wait. A week or a month. Until my boys are sprung from jail. Wait until my alibi is water tight, then you'll vanish and they'll never see you again. Why, you haven't got a thing on me." He was confident. "Not a thing. All I have to do is drive off, leave you here, go home to bed, forget the whole matter."

"There's only one thing wrong with your logic," said the Douser, reaching into the car and extracting the keys from the ignition with a deft move of fingers. "I haven't changed *my* mind. You can put off killing me, *you* think. But who changes *my* mind? You been big and fat and loud and rich for years. I'd do anything to pin something on you. Even if it meant killing myself."

Schabold looked at him as if he were a man from another star. "You're crazy. Crazy as a betel nut!"

"Maybe." Douser jangled the keys. "If you drive off, leaving me here, I'll climb the palisades and jump off the cliff. Maybe I'll get killed, maybe not. Either way, it involves you for a prison term."

Schabold couldn't understand that. "I'm talking to a moron. You keep talking that way, I'll have to shut you up."

"Ah ha!" cried Douser triumphantly. "See? You're trapped! No matter what you do, you're trapped. Kill me and you're caught with no one to pin the crime on but yourself! Don't kill me, and I'll kill you, or jump off a cliff—who knows?"

"You—you got a gun?"

That was funny. "No. Only my fists and my feet and a reputation for being a nuisance. I know you, Schabold. I've studied you a long time. Otherwise I wouldn't have risked coming with you. Some other Joe might've shot me. Not you. You're careful. Well, the fun's over. You ever been slapped in the face, Schabold?"

"No. . . ."

"Well, *there*, then!"

Douser slapped him.

"Hey!" Schabold crouched behind the wheel.

"I bet you never been kicked in the shins," said Douser. "I bet nothing ever happened to you, except one thing, the thing that made you turn crook. What happened, Schabold?"

Schabold blinked.

"You heard me." Douser leaned forward. "What happened."

Schabold waited and said, "Nineteen twenty-nine."

Douser nodded. "Thought so. Bathed, manicured all your life. Life didn't touch you. Nineteen twenty-nine slammed you, though. You couldn't take meeting reality. You turned crook and went on being rich the wrong way. That's what I figured. Well, fat man, shake hands. I'm life, I'm reality catching up with you again. I'm the stuff you been running away from for years. Life. Pain. Reality. That's me. Shake?"

Douser was on the running board, one foot inside the car, kicking softly into Schabold's shins. Gently at first. "I figure it this way—cops get killed every day. What if I get killed? It's no worse. I have fun. I get my man. There!"

"Stop it, stop it, stop!" cried Schabold.

"I dare you to kill me! Come on, fat man!"

Schabold fell heavily out the opposite side of the car. Douser scrambled after.

Schabold panted out and in. "You—you can't—bother—m-me! Keep away, keep away!" he cried.

"Ever been strangled, Schabold? Let's try it!"

With a bearlike roar and a sweep of one arm Schabold shook the clinging Douser loose like a cockroach. He threw his empty gun and missed. Douser kicked his shins again.

"Getting your temper up, huh? Good." Douser danced around. "You're getting mad, Schabold. That's fatal. You're getting mad and you're going to die! You're an oyster with its shell off, soft and white underneath!"

Schabold lumbered forward. Douser darted around the car. "Tag, you're it!"

The fat man clutched a heavy rock and heaved it like a girl playing basketball, with both hands. It clunked off the fender. Douser ducked and ran. Bellowing in a perfect fury, sounding the big expanses of his lungs, Schabold careened in heavy pursuit. He was off the edge, all the way. Instinctive self-preservation was overcome, swallowed by unthinking, bestial rage. He snarled.

"Douser, Douser, you little louse!"

They made a queer dreamy chase across deep sands with the sea-beat timing them and only the stars watching. Ahead, half a mile off, was a necklace of lights lying by the sea—Venice Amusement Pier—calling them on.

It was two in the morning when they reached Venice Pier, their tongues showing out of their mouths. The dark pier was deserted.

Slowing to a wary, quick-breathing walk, Schabold said, "Oh, how I hate you, you louse."

Under the plankings the sea walked on salt feet between the piles. Schabold's feet were heavy, thick, tired, old, sludging.

Like a hummingbird, one moment Douser poised under Schabold's engulfing arms, the next instant he was gone.

Douser made movements.

Somewhere a merry-go-round burst into brilliant, blatant light. The blind eyes of Schabold focused dully, bringing out of salt shadows horses frozen on brass poles. A calliope wheezed. Douser tossed a switch gaily. Horses shocked into leaping life, going around. Douser went around with them on a reeling world.

"Come and get me, fat man!"

Schabold obeyed, but the turntable threw him aside emotionlessly. He fell, and a moment later there were footsteps running, a night watchman flushing his huge belly and sweating face with a flashlight.

"Hey, in there!"

Schabold got up and hit the man a terrific blow. He wanted no outside distractions now. The night watchman tumbled, got up, and went off, yelling, for help.

"You just killed a man, Schabold!" taunted Douser, coming around, going away, coming around, going away. The calliope yelled with him.

Schabold began to cry frustratedly. He held out angry fingers as if they, and wishing hard enough, would cease the revolving world where all values shifted and all horses laughed.

The merry-go-round stopped. With a chunky bleat, jowls shaking, Schabold clambered aboard only to have the world jerk into life again. Screaming, he held to the swaying universe and could not find Douser, only a shadow running off down away through a corridor of awful music, like a little bird vanishing forever. . . .

They found Schabold at dawn, seated on the largest horse of the merry-go-round at Venice, going up and down and around, the music blaring, him going up and down in a heavy, mechanical, lethargic rhythm. Schabold liked the horses. He didn't want to get off.

He kicked the officer who tried to get him down off his mount. He also kicked another officer in the stomach and bit a third.

So they put him in jail.

Sitting on the sergeant's desk a few days later, Douser heard the story from the sarge's own gentle lips,

"Schabold went stir nuts. He was jailed for disturbing the peace, that's all. But he kicked an officer. Then he added to his crimes. He rattled bars, took swipes at people, tore off his clothes, threw away his diamond rings, screamed, and finally broke a little guy's arm, claiming the little guy's name was Douser. Yeah, Douser, mind you. Schabold finally confessed *everything*. Black-market deals, killings, robberies. It was like a load on his stomach he wanted to heave up, so he could feel better."

The Douser nodded philosophically. "Just like I said. We all carry the seeds of our own downfall. Schabold never knew reality in his life. He kept a roll of fat and bodyguards between himself and life. So what happened? He met me. I was real. I hurt. I was death, irritation, and stuff he'd never really known. He couldn't get away from me. So he reverted to full childhood, pulled a baby's tantrum. His type is soft; once life bumps them they fall down all the way and are dragged back up with a noose around their throats. I tell you, Sarge, it's sad."

Douser slid off the desk. "So there you are. More than one way to pin something on a guy. Let him do it himself. That's all I'm good for. I'm no sleuth. I just know how to bother people. Nuisance value. See you later, Sarge."

The sarge said, "Where do you think you're going?"

Douser scowled. "Well, this morning's paper says Dutch Corelli is arriving on the one fifteen train today. I thought I'd go down and throw a mudpie at him and study his reactions for future use."

"You might get hurt, Douser."

"Say, I never thought of that!" remarked the little guy.

A moment later he was running out into the sunshine, and the sarge was leaning back, shaking his head and cursing softly. . . .

Four-Way Funeral

"Pardon me," said the Douser, "but you look like a criminal."

The well-dressed gentleman looked down upon his neat gloves, his shining shoes, his seventy-dollar overcoat draped over one casual arm. Then the well-dressed gentleman stared at Douser Mulligan and sidled away somewhat.

"The intellectual criminal type, of course," added Douser, hastening not to offend the man. "The better species, I'll allow." Douser studied the man's tailoring. "Fine, fine." His manicure. "Good, good." His haircut. "Nice long gray hair, cut and combed. A clean collar. So."

"Go," said the gentleman, "away."

"I don't want to," said Douser.

"If you don't go," said the gentleman, "I shall summon the police."

"You are not the kind," observed the Douser. "Your use of the word *summon* indicates that you would call in a tidy, soft voice that no decent policeman would pay any attention to. You have to *yell* for cops. You, sir, are not the yelling kind. You hate publicity, shun notoriety, detest causing a scene. No, no."

The gentleman's narrow green eyes were amused. About fifty years worth. One gloved hand flexed upon a cane's handle; he seemed to be deliberating whether to ride Douser out of the square upon it, but he laughed a small laugh. "Go away, little man."

"Not," persisted the Douser, "until you admit you're a criminal."

"All right, if it'll satisfy you, I'm a criminal. Glad?"

Douser blinked. "Not very. It's not much fun this way. All the other people I ever met wouldn't admit it. Then I had to kick their shins or bite their ankle. I tell you it's a lot of work. But you, now. This is something new. A guy who admits he is a manicured louse. I'll hate putting you in jail."

"Are you going to do that?" wondered the white-haired man, putting a gray, neat hat upon that gray, neat hair.

Douser shrugged. "Can't see my way out of it. You're bad. Now, if you'd make up your mind to reform, we might work out a deal!"

The gentleman stood there, not much taller than Douser, who was very short. Behind him were the twilight trees of the park, the bushes, the peopled benches, the knots of arguing sidewalk politicians, the yellow cab traffic, the pedestrians. Beyond that the red and yellow theater neons and the square light fronts of stores. The gentleman tilted his head. "You're a peculiar little man. I sort of like you."

"That's funny; most people learn to loathe me."

"Will you have coffee with me," invited the gentleman. "My name is Earl Lajos, the lawyer. I'd like to see what makes you tick."

"Vice versa, and I do mean vice," said Douser. "We can talk awhile and I'll decide whether to jail you or not. Okay?"

"Fine, fine," said Lajos. They walked from the park, in step.

Shrimps lay upon the plate looking at Douser. Douser looked back at his delicious relatives. Lajos brandished cutlery delicately, slicing, forking, chewing deftly and quietly, nodding at Douser, who popped his like popcorn into a midget incinerator.

"Have you a detective badge?" asked the lawyer.

"I have only my heart beneath my vest," said Douser sadly. "The D.A. framed and hung me in the Museum of Extinct Mammalia. Sub category: Private Detective, a couple of years back."

"That makes me feel better," said Lajos. He speared another shrimp with cold precision and heartlessly vanquished it molecule by molecule. "I've heard of you, Mr.—Douser, is it not? Yes, the Douser, they call you. You—irritate people. Having no legal authority any longer you—bother criminals. I remember the case. Seems your brother, a policeman, was slain in San Francisco some years back and it kind of hurt your mind. A delightful little chap, but an unbelievable mania for wrongdoers." Lajos crossed knife and fork on his vacuumed plate, leaning forward earnestly. "Well, how would you like to catch *three* criminals? Not one. Not two. But *three*. Count them." He held up fingers in a manicured trio.

"Three," breathed the Douser. "Speak on, MacDuff!"

Lajos toyed with his water glass. "Naturally, you cannot have three unless you let me go scot-free, unleashed, unharmed, unhampered."

"I was afraid of that." Douser winced. "Three for one. A good deal. I'd rather have four, but I won't even get those three unless I play ball with you." He bit his lip. "It's a deal, but with a time limit." The man scowled; Douser hurried on. "I'd only guarantee not to molest you for three—well, make it four years." Lajos smiled agreeably. "But first," said Douser, "name the criminals. I don't want any second-rate winos or snow hounds!"

"I will guarantee," said Lajos, "that these fellows are A-1, bona fide, gilt-edge criminals of the first water. Their names are as follows: Calvin Drum, Hollywood's great actor; William Maxil, who is running for District Attorney next spring, and Joey Marsons, the horse-racing and bookie specialist."

"My God!" cried the Douser. "I can't believe it. Shake, Mr. Lajos, shake!"

They drove into Beverly Hills in Lajos's big roadster. Lajos gave a few details, showing how the three aforementioned were connected each to help the other, each to protect the other. But it seemed that—"these gentlemen are in my way. Their removal would give me room to live in. I will help you gather evidence against them, Mr. Mulligan."

"Funny thing," mused Douser. "I been thinking of them three birds a long time. Been doing some research on them, fact is."

"Really?" said Mr. Lajos, as if he hadn't known this.

Lajos's house was a big white cliff among dark trees. They parked on the brick drive and walked inside, down a hall, and into a room. It all worked very smoothly and Douser was prepared for anything.

A door slammed, the lock clicked, and Douser said to himself, "Goodie, goodie, a trap. I might have known. Gee, this exciting."

The Messrs. Drum, Maxil, and Marsons glanced up grimly from a game of blackjack and saw Douser standing there. The way they looked he was a dead pigeon already. Mr. Lajos, behind Douser, drew out a clean, neat little revolver and pressed it oh so delicately into Douser's spinal cord. Drum, the actor, shouted gaily, "*Surprise!*"

Drum crushed out a king-size cigarette that had been burnt down to a commoner. "You're late."

"That is because," said Douser, "we stopped by to see your woman on the way."

Drum's dark black brows went like that. "What?"

Lajos laughed. "Don't listen to him, Drum. We didn't."

"Quite a pretty woman too," said Douser.

Drum said, very low, "If you've bothered Elice—"

"Yes, Elice!" said Douser, now equipped with a name to use if he needed a wedge. His small, bright black button eyes took in the square, foggy room, quickly measuring distances between chairs, windows, the door, the people at the round table. Clickety-clickety, click. *Spung.* Fourteen by seventeen by six inches by three by—

Douser walked away from the gun in his back as if it fired rubber bands. He sat down in an empty chair, leaning back cozily. "Do we do it now, Lajos, or wait until we lull them into ignorance?"

Maxil was at Douser's right in a baggy business suit, with one double chin and one belly, but not much fat anywhere else. His eyeballs popped white, like little pale stomachs in his tired face. He had pouting lips and looked unwashed. To Douser's left was the nervous, flickering, horselike Marsons, who kept twitching cards out on the table. Across the table sat the collar-ad hero, Drum. "Boy," said Douser, "have we got plans for you, people." He smacked his lips. "Lajos and I are running for D.A. and City Council, aren't we, Grandma?"

Lajos walked primly up to Douser. "Please, keep quiet."

Douser ignored this minor interruption. "First, we eliminate you big frogs, then we muscle in and—well, you see, Lajos hates playing second fiddle to you guys and—"

The pretty little gun touched Douser's right ear. "Yes, sir," said Douser, shutting up.

Lajos looked down upon him, his aristocratic face a little on edge as he talked to his friends. "Don't believe a word he says. He's lying. I met him in the park, as we planned. I walked back and forth until he noticed. He fell for the bait. I promised him three criminals—and here we are. Simple."

Douser laughed a little. "Oh, you poor suckers."

Maxil chewed a cigar. "Cut it, Douser. We're wise to you.

We heard about how you cause trouble, bother people. You can't split us among ourselves. We're good pals, ain't we, boys?''

"Yes, certainly, of course, yeah, unh-hunh," said everybody with dim fervor.

"You can't break us up," said Maxil, reinforcing his convictions.

"That's right," said everybody, doing the same.

"You can't fool us," said Maxil.

"You can't," said everybody.

Douser drew his chair close, laid small hands like little springy spiders on the tabletop. The spiders walked around with his words. "My friends, do you think for one moment that I'd walk into an obvious trap like this? Think I'd believe Grandma Lajos's trumped-up yarn? Me, Douser? You know me better than that, boys. Maybe I don't give a damn about living, sure, but I wouldn't come to a thing like this on roller skates. Think it over.''

He let them think it over. Lajos swallowed some saliva down his Hart, Schaffner and Marx trachea. Drum, the actor, burnt the royal jewels off a king-size. Marsons clicked his deck of cards. Maxil felt of his stomach with curious big hands.

Douser continued. "The only reason I walked into this lion's den, kiddies, is because Uncle Lajos laid out the long green.''

The "kiddies" paid attention. Douser added, quickly, "And if he shoots me now, it'll prove he's guilty, trying to shut me up!''

Lajos's eyes narrowed into small green gems. His manicure tightened upon the gun impatiently.

Douser drew out cigarette papers and a tobacco bag. He began to make a cigarette quietly. He got half through rolling, fixing it into a rut to pour tobacco in when he said, "Some damn guy in some damn detective novel did this all the time. Every time there was lull in the conversation he did this. I can't for the hell of it figure why. Called the guy Sam Spade, I think.''

The square room held them in a smoke web, waiting.

Lajos snorted delicately, arching his cute nostrils. "Here go our plans. I warned you, Maxil, if we ever got hold of Douser it would be like battling flypaper. We never should have bothered. He's in the room two minutes and look—*look*—by the Holy Mary, he's turning one against the other, methodically. You see—*you see*?''

Maxil said, eyes lidded sleepily, "I'm lookin'.''

Marsons gritted the cards with a fingernail. "Let's get it over with. This guy messes in everyone's business for years now. We say we kill him before he starts on us, okay, let's kill him. We don't want him bolixing our election plans next spring, do we?"

Drum swore and looked so handsome doing it, too, kid. "Yes, that's what I say. We want him killed, so let's you kill him!"

"What is there about a mouse that makes the elephants scream?" wondered Douser, half aloud. He threw away the half-made smoke. "Someday I'll learn to do that, dammit." He glanced at Maxil. "You're running for D.A. As D.A. you'll assist the gambling interests, especially in the studios. Marsons is your right-hand man, all-around bookie president. Drum, better known as Drum-Tiddie-Um-Tum, will be the main contact among the actors and actresses. A nice business you got planned. And in case of trouble we have our Chanel Number Five and Shiny Fingernails Mr. Lajos." Douser rubbed hands together and leaned back. "*But—*" he cried. "Mr. Lajos had plans for himself. He would fain be D.A.! So tonight, on the way here, he gives me one thousand bucks on account, with nine more to come!"

Maxil said, sleepy-eyed, "Why're you telling us this? Why didn't you go ahead? Why you blabbing?"

"I happen to hate Mr. Lajos's guts. I don't like double-crossers. I figure he deserves to be double-crossed himself."

"But this way," said Maxil, "you get killed for your trouble."

"I take my chances. I should've died a long time ago. I figure we can work a deal where you guys can tip me off to other criminals who you don't like and let me have at them. I keep the road clear for you and you let me alone and I let you alone. I'm bargaining. All you got to do is let me have Lajos, who is a slimy knifer-in-the-back, I assure you."

Drum said, "It sounds like a good proposition. Doesn't it, Maxil?"

"Maybe," said Maxil, slow to be impressed, but waking up. "You'll do anything to get criminals, won't you, Douser?"

"Anything. Even if it means giving protection to a few so I can nab a dozen others. You got to play the game, I see that."

All during this palaver Lajos was getting taller and paler and more indignant and trying to think of words, but not having any good ones right on hand. Everybody began thinking too much.

"He's lying!" shrilled Lajos.

Douser said, "Call Rochester seven six eleven and ask for Bert. Bert will tell all."

Maxil looked lovingly at the phone. Lajos, catching this look, stalked back and forth around the table, piping. "We won't call anybody for anything! We won't call anybody!"

Maxil tapped about half an inch of rosy-gray ash off his cigar and said to Marsons, "Call Rochester seven six eleven—"

"If he touches the phone," declared Lajos, towering tall, "I quit! I'll be through, finished! We can't trust one another any longer!"

"It's just a precautionary routine call," said Maxil.

Lajos opened his jaw, snapped it shut, shook his head. "All right! Call! Phone! Go on!"

Marsons dialed alphabeticals and numerals and listened to the electric bee buzzing at the other end. Somebody killed the bee by unpronging it. Douser sat calmly small. Drum leaned forward like he did in that scene in *Love, It's Nice*. Maxil listened with his fat eyes. Marsons said nervously, "Bert?"

The receiver hung out in the silence, in Marsons's fist, so that Bert's voice could be heard, small and tiny and high in the smoke, far away. "Yeah?" said Bert.

Marsons blinked rapidly. "I'm calling about something that happened tonight, Bert," he said.

"You mean about the thousand dollars?" said Bert.

Lajos swallowed, paling out in his cheeks and in small lines around his mouth. Maxil mashed out his cigar. Marsons almost dropped the phone. Drum swore. Douser smiled.

"I'll keep it here for Douser," said Bert, "until he wants to pick it up. That sure is easy money."

Marsons cradled the phone in a long silence.

"It's not true," said Lajos, looking from Maxil to Drum to Marsons. "Douser's lying!"

Maxil said, "Take his gun away from him, Drum."

Drum got up, walked around the table.

Lajos said, "Stay away from me. This is a frame. You've got to listen to me, give me a decent break, be democratic!"

Drum kept coming. He didn't think Lajos would shoot. Lajos didn't think so either. It seemed instinctive. The gun went off with a loud sharp bark and a short finger of blue-red flame.

"Unh," said Drum. It was the best line he ever delivered. He stood there with a bullet in his stomach.

Marsons threw away his deck of cards like so many pigeons,

numbered, taking flight in a fluttering. Maxil sat fat and frozen. Douser moved a little, just to be out of harm's way.

Lajos looked at the bullet hole, not believing. "I didn't mean to do that," he said, amazed. "Here," he recoiled in horror. "Here, take it." He threw the gun and Marsons caught it. "I didn't mean to do that! I'm not guilty! It was an accident!" sobbed Lajos.

Drum stood there and Death stood below, cutting away his fibers, his roots of being. Death ran out of the way, cried, "Timber!" and Drum crashed down like a giant redwood to lie silent.

One away! thought Douser, satisfied. *Two, really, One dead, the other guilty of homicide! Oh, joy!*

Everybody trembled now. Even Maxil. Marsons looked like the flank of a nervous palamino horse, shivering. Lajos now lay upon the sofa in one corner of the room, wrinkling his tailored suit and getting his ten-dollar tie all wet, sobbing like a woman. Douser was very excited and thrilled, as at a circus.

"Shut up!" Marsons said to the crying Lajos.

Maxil said, "Snap out of it, Lajos. Hey, old man." When the sobbing did not stop, Maxil turned to Douser, whose heart leaped in a hot pink dance. "Why'd you really come here, Douser?"

"To get in with you guys and meet more criminals."

Maxil lit his cigar, as if warming over old thoughts and theories. "You'd risk your life for that?"

"I've risked it before, for less. This way I work from the inside out. I was on the outside before. This is better."

"Your story," said Maxil, balancing the idea with great slow dexterity upon the glowing tip of his cigar, "does not glue together. If Lajos planned on framing us, why did the two of you come here easy? Why didn't you run in shooting?"

Douser's heart moved in four directions. This was a good time to roll a cigarette. He produced tobacco and papers and began twitching the stuff together, thinking very fast, getting nowhere. Douser said, "We planned to come in and talk you off guard, first. That's how Lajos wanted it. He'd shoot you and Marsons and put the gun in Drum's hand and shoot Drum with your gun, then call the cops and scram. He needed my help in case he got scared. He figured I could kick people and yell and hit and jump on backs."

Maxil chewed on that. Lajos stopped sobbing long enough to say, "He's—he's lying—"

Douser laughed. "Trying to save your own skin. Drum, the great profile of Studio Films, is dead, and look who killed him. Not me. Not you, Maxil. But *him*. Boy, what a smell. Try and bury *that*, peoples."

Maxil nodded heavily. "There's one big thing wrong, though—" Maxil sat up in his chair and looked at his stomach. "Why didn't Lajos keep on shooting after he shot Drum, shoot me and Marsons?"

Douser fumbled with his cigarette and had to admit, "You have a point there. You have a point."

Maxil thought it was a good point too, and said so. "Lajos dropped the gun, immediately. He didn't mean to shoot Drum. It was accidental. I think the truth is, Douser, that he only wanted *you* dead, all along. As we planned. He brought you here to kill you, and you got to talking. We got a keg of cement downstairs and a boat at Santa Monica so we could feed you to the fishes—"

"Accident, hell!" cried Douser. "The old guy lost his nerve. All the way up he kept whispering, 'I hope I can do it, I hope I don't lose my nerve!' He's a double-crosser, and you can't prove he's not. Look, from now on, Maxil, I'm in with you. You're in a mess now, you have to admit—up to your chins. How'll you cover up Drum's murder?"

"I'll shoot you and put my gun in Drum's hand, Lajos's gun in yours," said Maxil.

"I never carry a gun," said Douser.

"You carried one tonight."

"I hate guns. The cops know that. They find me with one and they'll know something smells. They'll drag you in, work you over—first thing you know Lajos over there will sob out the whole works and then where will you be?"

Maxil looked worried. "I'm open to suggestions."

"Kill Lajos. Frame him for the murder. He's no good anymore. You can't trust him." Lajos burst out with renewed hysteria.

"That's a good idea," said Maxil. "Thanks."

"You're welcome."

"No," screamed Lajos.

Things went fast. Clickety-clickety—the old hot blood, the old wild shouting of excitement. The room burst with emotion. Maxil shifted in his chair. "No," screamed Lajos. Douser suggested that he be shot before he got too hysterical and Maxil nodded, drawing a gun and thinking along its bright blue barrel. Thinking, thinking, thinking. He pointed it at Lajos. "No," said Lajos, in a hoarse, raw voice. "Who's boss around here," said Douser, "you or him. Go ahead, Maxil, shoot him!"

Maxil shot him.

Douser arose in the spinning, sick universe and said, "Marsons, have you a gun?"

"Yeah." Marsons patted his arm holster.

"Point it at me, while I talk, Marsons. Go ahead. Take it out, point it. That's a good boy." Douser measured distances and timing and took in short, hot breaths. "Listen to me, Marsons, doesn't it look funny the way things have worked out, so many people shot?"

Maxil said, "Sit down, Douser!"

Everybody looked confused, irritated, unsure. Drum, lying at great length upon the carpet, did not believe for a minute that he was dead. Oh, no, not the great, the one and only Calvin Drum!

Neither did Lajos accept the reality of dissolution. His face was ridiculously angry and indignant, attached to the cooling thing that was his body! Both he and Drum had died incredulous and not understanding how in hell it could have happened this way. It wasn't fair!

"Marsons, take a look around," snapped the Douser eloquently. His black bright eyes darted from object to object. "Drum's dead. And why? Lajos shot him dead! Well, who told Drum to grab the gun away from Lajos? *Maxil* did! Maxil knew Lajos was edgy, nervous as a sick cat, and might shoot. But he told Drum to grab that gun anyhow. It was a death sentence! Look at Drum! Dead! Then, to even it up, Maxil shoots Lajos. My God, man, it's plain as the nose on your face! All your pals are dead! Peculiar, huh?"

"Douser!" shouted Maxil, lifting himself.

"Watch it, Marsons!" cried Douser, running, ferretlike now, measuring snap distances, shouting, ducking, skirting. "Shoot Maxil! Shoot Maxil before he rods you!"

Douser vanished behind Marsons, twisting him as Maxil fired his pistol. The bullet, planned for Douser's quick-moving body, pierced Marsons's hip.

"Oh, you dirty bum, Maxil!" groaned the confused, pained Marsons, realizing his position. He pressed the trigger in pain. Marsons's gun fired three times, quickly. Three bullets hit Maxil and rammed him back into his chair. Maxil examined his new stomach with curious, unbelieving fingers. His eyes popped and froze. My God, he must have been thinking as death came, I used to only have one navel; now, *look! I got four! Three more just added!*

Douser grunted, hooked fingers into Marsons's elbows, pulled back, kicked the knees out from under the gent, and fell, rolling to one side. He heard the gun scutter on the floor by itself and Marsons swore bitterly. Douser got to his feet first and kicked Marsons in his very strange face as Marsons rolled over and played sleeping dog. A great quiet pervaded the battlefield. Standing there, Douser realized that it was the first time in his life he had ever seen so many bewildered corpses in one room.

Whistling like some detective from some detective story, but a little off-key, Douser withdrew from the scene.

The drugstore phone took Douser's nickel as he dialed a number. "Hello, Bert? You did a swell job tonight, Bert, swell—"

"That's okay, Douser. Anytime, anytime. A janitor like me gets sick and tired of spending all night sweeping and washing by himself, alone. Did I remember my speech like you told me?"

"Exactly. And don't forget, Bert—every night from now on, the same speech."

Bert cleared his throat. "Is it about the thousand dollars? I'll keep it here until Douser calls for it."

"Fine, Bert, fine. Good night, Bert." Douser hung up, beaming. Outside the drugstore he took out cigarette papers and tobacco. He tried to make another cigarette. Finally he threw it down and stepped on it, hard. "The hell with it! I'll learn—someday!"

A man walked by who looked like a bank robber. Douser stared.

"Hey, mister!" Douser said, falling quickly in beside the stranger. "Got a cigarette?"

The Long Night

Outside the apartment house all the guys came together, Gomez, Tony, the Baron, the Sandman de Califa, and the others. Tony was hopping up and down socking my arm over and over, until I told him to stop or I'd knock the enchiladas out of him. Tony laughed with his mouth open so you could see his big, long white teeth, and he switched over to hitting the Baron on the arm. The Baron got tough and smacked Tony on the elbow, very hard. Tony yelled and pretended he was weaving fast punches at rum-soaked Sam.

It was the kind of night in October when things happen. When people get hurt and other people don't care. We were waiting around for Rudy Verdugos to show up. He was across the street where the juke music came out, sounding just like the red, green, blue, purple lights look inside the plastic juker. We were jigging around, showing off our big pants and our tight cuffs and our orange *huaraches*. I had my new black shirt on.

"Hi." Verdugos came up with a big sport coat, black, draped over his body, which isn't more than a lot of picked chicken bones, really, but Verdugos is a hot brain, and is okay, because we like him.

"Rudy, Rudy, Rudy!" we all said together. He is older than us.

He said, "Shut up," smiling. His face was thin like a rat's and he had little needle teeth. "What's doin' with you guys?"

"We been waiting for you, Rudy," we said.

"Yeah?" he said. "Well, *look*."

We looked at the brassies on his fist. "What is it?" someone wanted to know.

"Ah, you dumb," Tony said. "Why, them are brass knucks. For a good use."

"To hit them rioters with when they come around stripping clothes off us *pachuchos*," said Verdugos, very quiet, with a light in his eyes. "That's nothing. I got connections."

"Gee, Rudy," they said. I kept quiet, watching.

"Stick around me and make pin money," Verdugos told them, not laughing at all.

Just then three drunks came by, singing loud, walking on down Temple Street. Verdugos looked dark ugly after them. "Lousy gringos." he said. "Let me tell you, there's gonna be trouble here tonight."

"Yeah," we said.

I said, "The papers say the *pachuchos* at the waterfront last night pulled a knife on a sailor."

"Don't believe them papers," snapped Verdugos, giving me a hot, shiny glare. "We got rights to live, ain't we?"

"Sure, sure, Rudy," we said, uneasily. I felt alone. Suddenly, I didn't know these guys. I didn't know nothing. Tony and Gomez and Verdugos and the Baron. With their hair combed back into black duck feathers, shining.

Somebody screamed. Just like that. People began running around the three-story tenement like cockroaches, and fire leaped up from the cellar. Red fingers of it, climbing up the old bleached dry boardings. I heard *mamacita* screaming.

I yelled. I ran down the alley. "Okay, Mom, okay, Mom!"

Someone else yelled, "Call the fire house!"

I got a garden hose from somewhere. People ran around. Mama was down from the second floor screaming at me, "Freddie, Freddie, be careful! Ah, be careful!"

There was a hissing when the water smacked against hot wood.

I heard a siren way off and a moment later the big metal rumble as the engines arrived and firemen scrambled. I got out of the way and let real water pound through.

Verdugos and the other guys were standing out on the sidewalk, watching. Mama held on to me. "Ah," she cried, "there is someone caught down in the basement! A body!"

I held on to Mama. We tried to see through the smoke. The big hoses twisted in the vacant lot like a nest of big dying snakes. My guts felt the same way.

Five minutes later they brought the body up.

"Who is it!" On the first floor balcony Fannie Florianna made a lot of noise with her heavy feet.

We could not tell who it was, even when the body lay in front of us, all wet, smoked, and charred. The head was like charcoal.

The firemen emptied the pockets and read the name. It was Pesquarra, who made perfumed candles for Olvera Street.

Mama rocked on her heels beside me. "He had a wife and a child coming. And now he is dead. Oh."

I went down in the cellar. When things had cooled off and the firemen were scraping around further in the cellar, off to one side, I went down into the burnt wetness. I choked on the smoke.

I found the iron door of the water heater open, and a smell of burned flesh and hair coming from inside it. From *inside*. It plugged my nose like a fist, hitting. I reached in and pulled out a clot of human hair to hide in my pocket. The firemen were too busy yet to notice.

Up above, Pesquarra's wife had just seen him with his new face. The sound she made was like nothing ever made before.

I shivered. Someone had shoved Pesquarra head first into the water heater. And then pulled him out and laid him somewhere else and started a fire. It looked just like an accident.

I threw water and ashes on the heater. I didn't know why or what I was doing. Then I staggered up the wet steps like a crazy hound.

"What's wrong?" cried Mama, her eyes all over me at once.

"Nothing," I said. "Leave me alone."

I hadn't gone looking for anything in particular. It was just that kind of thing. I was just curious.

I faded Mama out and found myself in the hall of the tenement. It smelled of cabbage and people. Pesquarra's room was easy to get into. I wondered how I found my way there through the fog.

I swayed.

I didn't know what I was looking for.

Pesquarra had left this room and wasn't worrying about paying the rent ever again. He had been such a quiet, nice guy. Never talking to nobody. Never wanting trouble. That's why I figured I might find something to tell me—

I switched on a light. There were perfumed candles stacked up in colored rows, and—

Somebody tossed a switch; the lights went out. I felt the hairs on my legs edge up into cold pimples. I slipped around a table that was a thousand miles wide. The door opened in the dark and someone stood there, waiting. I wasn't the only one who'd come to Pesquarra's room looking.

An animal always knows what to do when it's cornered. I knew, then, too. My voice didn't belong to me, hissing out:

"I got a knife. Don't come in. Get out!"

For just a moment that person there in the door waited. Then the door slammed. I heard footsteps run down the hall. I also thought I heard little bells tinkling.

I was in no hurry to follow. I leaned against the silence and let my perspiration out to dry.

The lights went back on. Another noise pulled me out of my searching before even five minutes had passed. On the street there was yelling. I got out of Pesquarra's room fast. I ran to the fire escape and looked down.

Across the street where the music jumped out of the Lucky Spot, a man lay on the sidewalk with red stuff on his head. Somebody had thrown something. A couple of other men were running silently and quickly down the street, following somebody who ducked away down an alley.

The fire engines were going away. Everybody in the tenement was out there, watching. Pietro Massinello and his dogs, with his colored shirt and the bells on it. Sam, drunk and thin and bleary eyed. Gilbert Ramirez, all muscles and brute strength. Verdugos, thin like a rat. And the other kids. I wondered by myself which one of them had killed Pesquarra. And why.

Mama called me, loud and high as a time whistle.

I climbed upstairs for supper.

There is nothing like chili simmering and bubbling red on the kitchen stove. There is nothing like the table and a pyramid of enchiladas steaming and bottles of wine open, smelling ripe, and Mama yelling for us kids to come and eat.

We straddled our chairs and dished out the chili peppers, the beans, the pork, and grabbed our spoons. Everybody else stuffed. Except me and my brother, Joe. He was standing over by the window looking down.

Mama looked at me. "Whatsa matter, Freddie?" She shoved the chili beans at me. "Put some on your plate."

The chili looked like blood.

"Naw, Mom." I pushed back from the table, feeling sick. "What happened downstairs?"

"The firemen, they all go away, *sí*," said Mama, pleased.

Papa ate rapidly, his mustache working. "Not much damage, either. Except to Mr. Pesquarra. We must send flowers. Such an accident."

"Is that all it was?" I said.

"Sure. What else?"

"Nothing, I guess. What did the cops say?"

"They blamed the water heater. Bad connection or something. Pesquarra was working on it. That's all."

I stiffened. I remembered how I'd thrown water and ashes all over the heater to cover the hair and flesh smells. I didn't even know why, except maybe to save Mrs. Pesquarra from knowing her husband was pushed into it face first.

Joe was still standing silent by the window, looking down with his face like a pale cut cameo. A sad kind of face. He sang sad songs and played a guitar slow and well. I couldn't figure him out. I liked jazz tunes. Now when Mama complained to Joe about not eating, he said, "There's going to be trouble tonight, *mamacita*. Trouble all this week. I'm glad I'm no *pachucho*!"

"All right!" I sort of flushed in my ears and held my long black hair down with my fingers. "I'm no *pachucho*! Just because I like the guys!"

Joe studied me with a tall sadness. He was a quiet stranger in a loud house. "Let me catch you dressed in a zoot coat, and I'll take it off of you myself," he said.

"Be quiet, the two of you," said Papa. He jabbed his food. Mama went to Joe and looked out of the window with him. She said, "The mob . . . They come tonight, you think?"

"I don't know." Joe studied the street. "Not many. Mostly just ordinary rioters, people who like that sort of thing. There were five hundred rioters in Bell Gardens last night. They stripped ten *pachuchos* naked and threw them in a garbage wagon. In some fights, people were hurt. It's not good for good Mexicans like us, *mamacita*."

"We'll beat their damn heads off!" I said, as red as the chili on the plates. "They got no right to pick on us because we dress different!"

"Freddie!"

I shut up, trembling. Then it came to me. Suddenly I got it. I spit it out. "Look," I said. "Look." I pulled the charred hair from my pocket and threw it on the table. "See what they did to Pesquarra!"

"What is it?" said Mama. She and Joe came together.

I told them what I had found. It was like turning out the light in the room. Mama's face whitened into bones and dark wet eyes very big and fingers clenched before her teeth. Joe swallowed and Papa could not eat.

"Those rioters," I said, loud. "You see what they do! It was murder!"

"No, I will not believe this of them," sighed Mama.

Joe took the hairs into his palm, mouth tight. I let him think about it.

"They would not do that," said Mama.

I was not sure. Funny how you say things, angry, that you don't really believe. It was something to say. It sounded almost right.

Joe said, "We must tell the police."

I got up. "No. I'd be held. It's my fault they didn't know Pesquarra was pushed into that heater head first. What good would it do to tell now? They wouldn't catch anybody."

"Excuse me," said Papa. He hurried out of the room onto the balcony to get rid of his supper.

Mama sat down heavily. "What is the world coming to? What shall we do?"

Papa came back and stood in the door, eyes running, face red. "There has been talk of Germans," he said slowly. "Trying to stir up these riots. Maybe Pesquarra had something to do with them. Maybe he knew things he should not have known. There have been no strangers around the tenement today. We must not rush our minds about it. Some of the *pachuchos* may have killed him. We'll wait until morning—"

I slammed the door. I went down the stairs, picking my way through the dark, stained odors. I tried to get mad at the rioters, but that was all gone. Papa talked right. Anybody who knew where Pesquarra's room was would not be a stranger. It would be someone from inside, like a termite. The person who had come and stood in Pesquarra's door. The guy I frightened away by yelling at him. That was the murderer.

Big feet came up the stairs toward me. A big-muscled body passed me. "Hi, Freddie." Gilbert Ramirez pounded on up. I looked after him, wondering. Him, I thought. Him, maybe?

The street was filled up to the brim with noise again. Through a hall window I saw the mob coming. About fifty guys, all about eighteen or nineteen, a few hustlers a bit older, all looking tough, a crowd of a couple hundred following them. It pulled the muscles on my stomach cold and made me mad too. I knew what they were looking for.

I wanted to yell and sling a brick. The door to Fannie Florianna's room was wide open and every inch of it was filled with her big body. Her round pink face worried. "You better come in here and don't let them see you," she whispered quickly. A little voice from such a big woman. I went in.

Her astrological charts were spread all around her room in snowdrifts. Cockroaches flipped like tiddledywinks in the sink. There was a bed made up, never slept in in years. She always slept in the big chair, sitting.

Fannie shut the door. "My vibrations tell me there'll be great trouble tonight. Aries opposes Taurus and is conjugated with Gemini. That's fatal. Better go to bed early."

"I don't need your chart to tell that."

She waddled to her massive chair. "I knew things would happen all along," she confided, eyes closed. "There are so many things happening. And all for a cause."

I said nothing. I knew that she was made of ears. Two hundred and ninety of her pounds had gone into making big ears. The rest was animal shrewdness. People went around her like planets around a sun. Everyone brought her food and flattered her, waited on her. The mice would even give her their cheese because she had something on them.

Somebody walked in the hall. I held my breath and listened. So did Fannie. Somebody stood outside the door in the long tunnel.

They rapped and Fannie said come in. The door opened with a little tinkle of copper bells. Pietro Massinello danced in with his bald head throwing light, his dogs yipping at his sandaled feet.

"Hallo, my queen!" he sang, bowing. He daintily placed a platter of salad dressing on the table. "For you, your majesty." I had to laugh. You could never tell where his acting left off and he began. He waited on Fannie, too, like everyone else did. Even me. I ran errands for her, because she caught me smoking once and would tell *mamacita* if I didn't cooperate.

The little bells on Pietro's red shirt glittered, ringing in a musical fringe. I stared. I remembered that whoever killed Pesquarra had run away from his room with a rush of bells. But Pietro was such a screwy little old man.

"I must take leave now," sang Pietro, waltzing with a dog in his arms. "I dance on Main Street with my phonograph to get money for the poor. Who are the poor? Me. I put grease on my cheeks and bells on my britches. I hope you like the salad!"

Florianna sighed at the closing door. "It's a wild world tonight." Her big bosom moved in a slow, mountainous rhythm. "All of this trouble between rioters and *pachuchos*. You know, of course, that it started in this house?''

"Huh?" I said.

She closed her eyes slyly. "You think all of this trouble just happened. Ah, no." She wagged a finger like a sausage. "Such things must be slapped to life, like slapping a new baby."

"Who's responsible?" I asked.

"I'm paid to keep my mouth shut. If you pay me a little bit, maybe I can pry it open somehow."

"Nuts," I said. "Is it Verdugos? He likes trouble."

"No. He's paid by others, perhaps. Others, bigger and more secret than he is. Paid to say what he says, do what he does."

I said, "There's a rumor about Nazis causing the riots; is that it?"

She blinked lazily, like a hippo. "Maybe. Maybe lots of things. It's great fun knowing so much and telling so little."

"Oh, you talk lies!" I cried.

That got her. She bit. Chuckling, she poked a big hand down into the pocket of her dress. "You think I lie and have no proof? Look."

She pulled out a folded paper and opened it. "Don't touch it," she warned me. "Stay where you are and look at this writing."

I looked and whistled low. "It's written in German!" I couldn't understand what it said. She hid it again, quick, inside her dress, and drew out something else. It was made of cloth. A swastika. She said: "My astrological formulas help me. They tell me where to look, guided by the stars. I found this, and the paper, in *someone's* room!"

"Someone in this house?"

"Yes. You think the big Nazis live in this part of town? No. They drive by in big cars once in a while to see how their agents are doing, yes. They pay money to their poor agents. And the troublemaker is among us, acting, talking like everybody. Someone we know. Someone we see every day. I found these in his room according to my astrological predictions."

"Whose room?" I cried, moving my hand out, quick.

Florianna clutched fat arms over the paper, blubbering. "Keep away! You can't have these! I'll scream! I'll tell the police that I found the swastika and Nazi papers in your father's room, if you touch me!"

I pulled back and watched the Nazi insignia go down into the same hiding place the paper had gone to. All the trouble in the house, the tightness and festering and worry—all hidden in the secret paper she held. I stood glaring at her.

"How can you sit there while people are fighting on the streets over stuff like that?"

"What do I care for them?" she replied. "I've my own world here, and I'm in the middle of it. I don't care for the people outside. What've they done for me?" She leaned forward, smiling. "Of course, *if* you could get some money—"

There was no use talking. I turned around and held on to the doorknob, tight. I can stop the riots now, I thought. I can tell people the truth and they'll stop hating one another. Yeah. Or will they?

The fires are burning already. Maybe I'm too late to put them out.

I jerked the door open, said, "I'll be back with some money!" and stepped out and slammed the door. I was lying. I didn't have any money. I thought I heard footsteps moving away up the steps in the hall.

For the moment the streets were quiet. I stood in the hall listening to that silence caused when the rioters moved on down toward town.

With all the darkness around me I realized I was the only one who really *knew* Pesquarra had been murdered. Mom and Papa and Joe, they knew; but *I* was the one who stuck my nose in. Florianna knew, too, maybe, but that didn't help. I shivered. I ran quick down the hall in the dark. I stumbled over something, a body, and yelled. I picked myself up.

It was only Sam, smelling a little bit of rum, passed out on the floor, lying all dirty and old and wrinkled in his sleep.

I ran outside to stand by the streetlight. The house was suddenly too big and too dark. There were so many people in the house. And one of them knew all about the riots and made the *pachuchos* start them. Florianna knew who it was.

Was it Pietro who sang and danced with his barking dogs? Maybe Pesquarra had found out that Pietro was a Nazi and threatened to tell the police and Pietro had shoved him into the burner. Or Verdugos? He was smart and quick and liked money. Or maybe Sam, who loved his drink too much? How about Gilbert Ramirez? So big and hulking and dumb, but maybe smart underneath it. . . .

The stone hit my shoulder.

I almost fell. The other stone missed me, whistling.

I ran.

Five rioters came after me. "There's one of those lousy *pachuchos* who hit Pete!" they shouted.

I raced down the alley, ducked around a fence, ran across a yard, jumped another fence, and lost the sound of them swearing and panting. I held myself behind a bush, waiting. My heart beat hot. I hung over in a crouch, swaying.

They hunted around like dark animals, but they couldn't smell me for all my garlic and all my chili, and they didn't hear my heart drumming, even though it filled my world up with noise.

They got tired of hunting after a while and went away.

I picked my way back later, over fences and through alleys. I stopped and listened. Far off I heard feet running, people shouting. The riots were beginning to build up again. A couple blocks away.

I crept through the alley by the house.

Something made me stop by the steps going down into the burnt-up cellar. I thought I saw something lying at the bottom.

It was Joe.

It was so easy to find him. It was so easy to know he wouldn't argue with me again. Joe lay there, crumpled up, a gash across his skull with blood clotting it.

I fell down on my knees and grabbed him.

"Joe! Joe!" I said. Oh, God, the world went crazy. I was in the middle of things and I didn't have a side to be on. It all hit me like an earthquake shaking me. Joe had come down to the cellar to see if what I'd said about Pesquarra was true. And the murderer had seen him prowling and killed him, afraid that Joe would call the cops.

It would look like the rioters had done it. Just another accident. Just one of those things. Just like Pesquarra. Burned because he knew too much about riots. And Joe—killed—because I had poked my nose in the wrong hole. Nobody would be held for his death.

And how about me?

Someone who ran through the house on quiet feet, someone who was waiting around now to get me and finish me. It would make good headlines for tomorrow's morning papers. It would add gasoline to the fire, make people all the madder.

I had found a side to be on at last. Joe told me without a word, lying there. He told me which side was the right side. Not

Verdugos and his gang of guys following him just because he said so. They didn't think. They had air in their heads, nothing else. They didn't know what they were doing, helping Nazis.

I touched Joe's hand. "I'm with you, Joe. Honest, I am. I'm sorry we ever argued. Oh, God, honest I am, Joe. I wish I'd never told you—"

I got up. I climbed the back steps angrily and I didn't know where I was going except that I found my hand twisting the door to Fannie Florianna's room. She knew everything. In a cold anger, gritting my teeth hard, making fists, I would force her to tell me who was responsible for Joe. I'd get it out of her if I had to kill her—

I opened the door to her room and I turned colder.

This was easier. Easier than finding Joe.

Florianna lay upon her back in the middle of the floor, her face chalked white and blue. A doctor would say that she died of heart failure.

I didn't much bother to see if the Nazi insignia and the Nazi paper were gone. They were.

Standing over her, I figured it out. I looked at her bed. She hadn't slept in it for years. She couldn't lie down; she was so fat she couldn't breathe lying down.

Someone had come in, pushed her over on the floor, and held her in a prone position.

That's all they had to do. No fighting, no strangling, no clubs, no bullets. Just hold Fannie Florianna down until her fat strangled her and her pink moon face turned blue.

Another accident. All very neat, all very well done. Three murders, and all looking like accidents.

Now there was only me left.

Upstairs, on the second floor, I heard a dial phone ticking. I opened the door very quiet and listened. I heard a voice whispering. I caught only a few words:

"Police, yes . . . Send a squad car. There's a body in the alley. Rioters, yes—"

Jumping up the steps three at a time I didn't care if I made noise.

When I reached the pay phone the receiver was swinging back and forth in a pendulum. Someone ran down the hall. I yelled after that passing shadow. There were twenty doors it could have gone in, and three flights of steps. The shadow got away.

I went back to the phone and hung it up.

At that moment I knew. I knew who had killed Pesquarra. I knew who the Nazi was, and how clever he'd been to cover himself up. First Pesquarra. Then—Joe. Then—Florianna.

And now—me.

The murderer had it all worked out nice.

They came up the stairs, the mob. They caught me before I could get away. There were about twenty of them. They looked like high-school or college kids who were out for the excitement.

"Get the damn *pachucho*!"

"Any more in this house? Drag them out!"

"Rap on all the doors! Go in and get 'em!"

"Hey, you in there, open up!"

They pulled me down stairs and out onto the street. It was all lights. Hundreds of cars lined up, lights glaring. Streetcars held up by thick traffic and a thousand people milling around like a spring flood, talking, waiting, and yelling when they saw me dragged out.

The murderer had told them there was a *pachucho* in the house and they had come to get me. The murderer was in the crowd, too, now, mingling, waiting, shifting around. I tried to see.

I fought. I kicked out and swung my fists. I screamed myself hoarse. They hit my teeth, and my lips bled and puffed out, and I tried to say, "Wait—I'm on your side now! Take my clothes, leave me alone, but let me call the police! I know who killed my brother! It's about the Nazis! You don't know. Oh, God, make them let me go!"

But there was so much noise. Horns tooting, kids crying, streetcars clanging, whistles blowing, and the crowd pressing in to see what a real live *pachucho* looked like having his guts kicked out of him. I was thrust around from person to person in a dizzy circle. I fell down and somebody kicked me in the stomach. I crouched and someone threw a stone that hit my back. I crawled back against the wall and another stone hit my leg. They jeered. *I'm on your side*, I thought. *Please, let me be on your side!*

Sometimes they won't let you change sides in a war.

The police came. A squad car roared up, sirens full, blasting the echoes from all the buildings.

The mob broke back to let them run through. In all the confusion I got myself free and headed for the alley. Someone got in my way and I hit him crazily with my numb fist and he went down. I made it, sobbing. My clothes were ripped, I tasted blood as I ran, and I saw Joe lying there, still, waiting for the morgue, and I kept running on a treadmill of nightmares. I fell over a fence and crawled behind some thick bushes, lay with my face in the dirt. . . .

It was almost midnight before the police had chased the street clean and wide and empty again. Sirens whimpered back and forth.

They came and took Joe away. I heard Mama scream. I jerked, like hooks were in my lungs, ripping. *Oh, Mama, if I could hold your head now. If only I had not told Joe, he would be alive.*

But I could not go to her yet. There was a job to be done. The night was only half through and I was not finished with it. I staggered up, and I went back through the silent areaways and I met nobody. I walked into the Lucky Spot juke joint. I stood in the door. The bartender looked up and saw me.

"Stay way from here, kid," he warned me, not liking my torn clothes. "You're underage, and the police'll be around." I could hardly hear him. I was looking at all the people in the booths.

Verdugos was there with a blond woman, beer on a table in front of them. Verdugos was laughing.

Sam was there, blowsy eyed and thin, his unshaven face covered with sweat. He was pouring himself a drink of rum, standing at the bar.

Pietro Massinello was there with his little bells and his dogs sitting on the table lapping a puddle of liquor, his bright shirt rattling. The bells jangled a merry tune that wasn't merry. The juke box was blatting *La Compañera*.

I stood there.

Gilbert Ramirez was there, big and dumb-looking, and drunk. The whole place sort of pulsed like a cut in your arm that festers and begins to ache.

I looked at Verdugos and saw what he was drinking. Beer.

I looked at Pietro Massinello. He never drank. He just sang and danced and acted nuts.

Sam was drinking rum, like always. A special kind of rum nobody else ever drank.

The music stopped and I hung there like a fly in a web. Sweat trickled down my cheeks and I blinked my eyes to clear things up.

Sam turned around and shambled over and put a nickel in the jukebox slide. He didn't push it in. Blearily he looked at the twenty-four numbers to pick a tune. I waited. Then I walked up to about six feet behind him and I said, "Sam."

He turned around.

"You drink rum, Sam," I said.

"Sure, I drink rum," he said.

"You're the only one I know around here who drinks rum."

His eyelids twitched. I felt everybody in the room looking at me, holding me with their liquor eyes. "Sure," said Sam, "I drink rum. So what?"

I swallowed and bit my lips. "So, before that last riot you called the police."

Sam looked from side to side.

I told him. "You were pretty clever. Everybody thought you were just a stumblebum, a wino, a lousy old ginker of liquor. A good setup. Nobody would suspect an old wino. Now, a guy like Verdugos, he *looks* dishonest. But a guy like you, no. No!"

"You kidding?" But he was uneasy.

"Shut up. Let me finish," I said. "You called the police and told them there was a body—Joe—my brother. You phoned the cops, to be sure the rioters were blamed. Then you got downstairs again by the back way, and the mob was coming back again so you sicced them upstairs to where they could find another damn *pachucho*! Me! You're a murderer, Sam!"

"You can't prove that, you can't blame me, you can't, by hell!"

I could hardly speak. "When you talked, Sam, you left little pieces of spit inside the receiver. Everybody does that when they talk. They make the mouthpiece wet. But you made it smell of rum, Sam! The only person in the house who drinks rum!"

Sam's face was ugly. "That don't prove nothing. Why should I kill Joe?"

"Pesquarra," I said. "He was the first one. He threatened to tell the cops about you and the Nazis—how you made trouble between races—you had plenty of reason to kill him. I was in his room when you came to see if he'd left any evidence against you. You swiped one of Pietro's shirts with bells on it, so if you were heard it would sound like Pietro prowling. Then—you had to get rid of me. You saw Joe prowling around down by the water heater. You knew I'd told him. So you killed Joe and told the police the mob had done it. . . ."

Sam moved and I jerked my fist.

"You stopped Joe and at the same time you made it look like yet more rioting. That was your job from the beginning. Kill a Mexican and make Mexicans mad. Then maybe kill a white person to make whites mad at Mexicans. Riot propaganda. Joe was dead."

The bartender started coming around the bar to break it up. I said, "Then you eliminated Florianna because you were afraid me or the cops might make her spill. So you pushed her over and she couldn't breathe, and she died. Another accident, that's all."

I took a deep breath. "So now that left only me, prowling the house. You tried to use me like you used Joe, so the Nazis could burn up the whole city with riots, white against dark. Only I got away, Sam, only I got away and you made the mistake of leaving rum-smell in the phone receiver! So now we know what you are, Sam. All those people dead just for that. Three people dead just for that, Sam. Was it worth the money? Was it—"

Sam snatched into his shirt, inside his jacket, and started pulling something out. He'd had one drink too many. I got my knife first. I swung just as Sam fired his gun. His bullet knocked the plate glass window crashing.

Sam choked, looked at the knife sticking in his thin chest, wondering what it was doing there. He didn't seem to feel any pain.

Sam bent over a little, trying to grasp the knife. He dropped his gun rattling on the floor. Everybody watched as he choked; fell back against the jukebox. His body pushed the coin slide in so it clicked. The mechanism began spinning—

Sam slid down the side of the juke to the floor, not speaking, a stream of blood pouring from his lips.

Somebody was calling the police. I stood there, shivering, beginning to cry for my mama.

Loud and hard, the jukebox blatted out.

It should have sounded gay in the silence.

It didn't.

And now I'm lying here in my bed, high in the tenement. Tomorrow is Joe's birthday. He would have been twenty-one. I lie here, listening to the water dripping from a faucet that I cannot turn off because it is only my heart beating over and over, drop by drop.

And a music comes in my room. Over and above the sound of my heart, there comes the music I cannot forget.

It is the music that came out of that jukebox ten seconds after Sam was bleeding on the floor. The music that he paid for with his German nickel that went on playing as loud as thunder, alive long after Sam was dead.

I cannot smash that record. Oh, *madre mía*, I alone cannot smash that record!

Corpse Carnival

It was unthinkable! Raoul recoiled from it, but was forced to face its reality because convulsions were surging sympathetically through his nervous system. Over him the tall circus banners in red, blue, and yellow fluttered somber and high in the night wind; the fat woman, the skeleton man, the armless, legless horrors, staring down at him with the same fierce hatred and violence they expressed in real life. Raoul heard Roger tugging at the knife in his chest.

"Roger, don't die! Hold on, Roger!" Raoul screamed.

They lay side by side on the warm grass, a sprinkle of odorous sawdust under them. Through the wide flaps of the main tent, which flipped like the leathery wings of some prehistoric monster, Raoul could see the empty apparatus at the tent top where Deirdre, like a lovely bird, soared each night. Her name flashed in his mind. He didn't want to die. He only wanted Deirdre.

"Roger, can you hear me, Roger?"

Roger managed to nod, his face clenched into a shapeless ball by pain. Raoul looked at that face: the thin, sharp lines; the pallor; the arrogant handsomeness; the dark, deep-set eyes; the cynical lip; the high forehead; the long black hair—and seeing Roger was like gazing into a mirror at one's own death.

"Who did it?" Raoul struggled, got his frantically working lips to Roger's ear. "One of the other freaks? The Cyclops? Lal?"

"I—I—" sobbed Roger. "Didn't see. Dark. Dark. Something white, quick. Dark." He sucked in a rattling breath.

"Don't die, Roger!"

"Selfish!" hissed Roger. "Selfish!"

"How can I be any other way; you know how I feel! Selfish! How would any man feel with half his body, soul, and life cast off, a leg amputated, an arm yanked away! Selfish, Roger. Oh, God!"

The calliope ceased, the steam of it went on hissing, and Tiny Mathews, who had been practicing, came running through the summer grass, around the side of the tent.

"Roger, Raoul, what happened!"

"Get the doctor, quick, get the doctor!" gibbered Raoul. "Roger's hurt badly. He's been stabbed!"

The midget darted off, mouselike, shrilling. It seemed like an hour before he returned with the doctor, who bent down and ripped Roger's sequined blue shirt from his thin, wet chest.

Raoul shut his eyes tight. "Doctor! Is he dead?"

"Almost," said the doctor. "Nothing I can do."

"There is," whispered Raoul, reaching out, seizing the doctor's coat, clenching it as if to crush away his fear. "Use your scalpel!"

"No," replied the doctor. "There are no antiseptic conditions."

"Yes, yes, I beg of you, cut us apart! Cut us apart before it's too late! I've got to be free! I want to live! Please!"

The calliope steamed and hissed and chugged; the brutal roustabouts looked down. Tears squeezed from under Raoul's lids. "Please, there's no need of both of us dying!"

The doctor reached for his black bag. The roustabouts did not turn away as he ripped cloth and bared the thin spines of Raoul and Roger. A hypodermic load of sedative was injected efficiently.

Then the doctor set to work at the thin epidermal skin structure that had joined Raoul to Roger, one to the other, ever since the day of their birth twenty-seven years before.

Lying there Roger said nothing, but Raoul screamed.

Fever flooded him to the brim for days. Drenching the bed with sweat, crying out, he looked over his shoulder to talk with Roger but—*Roger wasn't there! Roger would never be there again!*

Roger *had* been there for twenty-seven years. They'd walked together, fallen together, liked and disliked together, one the echo of the other, one the mirror, slightly distorted by the other's perverse individuality. Back to back they had fought the surrounding world. Now Raoul felt himself a turtle unshelled, a snail irretrievably dehoused from its armor. He had no wall to back against for protection. The world circled behind him now, came rushing in to strike his back!

"Deirdre!"

He cried her name in his fever, and at last saw her leaning over his bed, her dark hair drawn tight to a gleaming knot behind her ears. In memory, too, he saw her whirling one hundred times over on her hempen rope at the top of the tent in her tight costume. "I love you, Raoul. Roger's dead. The circus is going on to Seattle. When you're well, you can catch up with us. I love you, Raoul."

"Deirdre, don't you go away too!"

Weeks passed. Often he lay until dawn with the memory of Roger next to him in the old bondage. "Roger?" Silence. Long silence.

Then he would look behind himself and weep. A vacuum lived there now. He must learn never to look back. How many months he hung on the raw edge of life, he had no accounting of. Pain, fear, horror, pressured him and he was reborn again in silence, alone, one instead of two, and life had to start all over.

He tried to recall the murderer's face or figure, but could not. Twisting, he thought of the days before the murder—Roger's insults to the other freaks, his adamant refusal to get along with anyone, even his own twin. Raoul winced. The freaks hated Roger, even if Raoul gave them no irritation. They'd demanded that the circus get rid of the twins for once and all!

Well, the twins were gone now. One into the earth. The other into a bed. And Raoul lay planning, thinking of the day when he might return to the show, hunting the murderer, to live his life, to see Father Dan, the circus owner, to kiss Deirdre again, to see the freaks and search their faces to see which one had done this to him. He would let no one know that he had *not* seen the killer's face in the deep shadows that night. He would let the killer simmer in his juices, wondering if Raoul knew more than he had said!

It was a hot summer twilight. Animal odors sprang up all around him in infinite acrid varieties. Raoul walked across the tanbark uneasily, seeing the first evening star, unused to this freedom, always peering behind himself to make certain Roger wasn't lagging.

For the first time in his life Raoul realized he was being ignored! The sight of him and Roger had gathered crowds anywhere, anytime. And now the people looked only at the lurid canvases, and Raoul noticed, with a turn of his heart, that the canvas painting of himself and Roger had been taken down. There was an empty space, as if a tooth had been extracted from the midway. Raoul resented this sudden neglect, but at the same time he glowed with a new sensation of individuality.

He could run! He wouldn't have to tell Roger: "Turn here!" or "Watch it, I'm falling!" And he wouldn't have to put up with Roger's bitter comments: "Clumsy! No, no, not *that* direction. I want to go this way. Come on!"

A red face poked out of a tent. "What the hell?" cried the man. "I'll be damned! Raoul!" He plunged forward. "Raoul, you've come back! Didn't recognize you because—" He glanced behind Raoul. "That is, well, dammit, welcome home!"

"Hello, Father Dan!"

Sitting in Father Dan's tent they clinked glasses. Father Dan was a small, violently red-haired Irishman and he shouted a lot. "God, boy, it's good to see you. Sorry the show had to push on, leave you behind that way. Lord! Deirdre's been a sick cow over you, waiting. Now, now, don't fidget, you'll see her soon enough. Drink up that brandy." Father Dan smacked his lips.

Raoul drank his down, burning. "I never thought I'd come back. Legend says that if one Siamese twin dies, so does the other. I guess Doc Christy did a good job with his surgery. Did the police bother you much, Father Dan?"

"A coupla days. Didn't find a thing. They get after you?"

"I talked a whole day with them before coming west. They let me go. I didn't like talking to them anyway. This business is between Roger and me and the killer." Raoul leaned back. "And now—"

Father Dan swallowed thickly. "And now—" he muttered.

"I know what you're thinking," said Raoul.

"Me?" guffawed Father Dan too heartily, smacking Raoul's knee. "You know I never think!"

"The fact is, you know it, I know it, Papa Dan, that I'm no longer a Siamese twin," said Raoul. His hand trembled. "I'm just Raoul Charles DeCaines, unemployed, no abilities other than gin rummy, playing a poor saxophone, and telling a very few feeble quips. I can raise tents for you, Papa Dan, or sell tickets, or shovel manure, or I might leap from the highest trapeze some night without a net; you could charge five bucks a seat. You'd have to break in a new man for *that* act every night."

"Shut up!" cried Father Dan, his pink face getting pinker. "Damn you, feeling sorry for yourself! Tell you what you'll get from me, Raoul DeCaines—hard work! Damn right you'll heave elephant manure and camel dung, but—maybe later when you're strong, you can work the trapezes with the Condiellas."

"The Condiellas!" Raoul stared, not believing.

"Maybe, I said. Just maybe!" retorted F.D., snorting. "And I hope you break your scrawny neck, damn you! Here, drink up, boy, drink up!"

The canvas flap rattled, opened, a man with staring blind eyes set in a dark Hindu face felt his way inside. "Father Dan?"

"I'm here," said Father Dan. "Come in, Lal."

Lal hesitated, his thin nostrils drawing small. "Someone else here?" His body stiffened. "Ah." Blind eyes shone wetly. "They are back. I smell the double sweat of them."

"It's just me," said Raoul, feeling cold, his heart pumping.

"No," insisted Lal gently. "I smell the two of you." Lal groped forward in his own darkness, his delicate limbs moving in his old silks, the knife he used in his act gleaming at his waist.

"Let's forget the past, Lal."

"After Roger's insults?" cried Lal softly. "Ah, no. After the two of you stole the show from us, treated us like filth, so we went on strike against you? Forget?"

Lal's blind eyes narrowed to slits. "Raoul, you had better go away. If you remain you will not be happy. I will tell the police about the split canvas, and then you will not be happy."

"The split canvas?"

"The sideshow canvas painting of you and Roger in yellow and red and pink which hung on the runway with the printed words SIAMESE TWINS! on it. One night four weeks ago I heard a ripping sound in the dark. I ran forward and stumbled over the canvas. I showed it to the others. They told me it was the painting of you and Roger, ripped down the middle, separating you. If I tell the police of that, you will not be happy. I have kept the split canvas in my tent—"

"What has that to do with me?" demanded Raoul angrily.

"Only you can answer that," replied Lal quietly. "Perhaps I'm blackmailing you. If you go away, I will not tell who it was who ripped the canvas in half that night. If you stay I may be forced to explain to the police why you yourself sometimes wished Roger dead and gone from you."

"Get out!" roared Father Dan. "Get out of here! It's time for the show!"

The tent flaps rustled; Lal was gone.

The riot began just as they were finishing off the bottle, starting with the lions roaring and jolting their cages until the bars rattled like loose iron teeth. Elephants trumpeted, camels humped skyward in clouds of dust, the electric light system blacked out, attendants ran shouting, horses burst from their roped stalls and rattled around the menagerie, spreading tumult; the lions roared louder, splitting the night down the seams; Father Dan, cursing, smashed his bottle to the ground and flung himself outside, swearing, swinging his arms, catching attendants, roaring directions into their startled ears. Someone screamed, but the scream was lost in the incredible dinning, the confusion, the chaotic hoofing of animals. A swell and tide of terror sounded from the throats of the crowd waiting by the boxes to buy tickets; people scattered, children squealed!

Raoul grabbed a tent pole and hung on as a cluster of horses thundered past him.

A moment later the lights came on again; the attendants gathered the horses together in five minutes. The damage was estimated as minor by a sweating, pink-faced, foul-tongued Papa Dan, and everything quieted down. Everybody was okay, except Lal, the Hindu. Lal was dead.

"Come see what the elephants did to him, Father Dan," someone said.

The elephants had walked on Lal as if he were a small dark carpet of woven grasses; his sharp face was crushed far down into the sawdust, very silent and crimson wet.

Raoul got sick to his stomach and had to turn away, gritting his teeth. In the confusion, he suddenly found himself standing outside the geeks' tent, the place where he and Roger had lived ten years of their odd nightmarish life. He hesitated, then poked through the flaps and walked in.

The tent smelled the same, full of memories. The canvas sagged like a melancholy gray belly from the blue poles. Beneath the stomaching canvas, in a rectangle, the flake-painted platforms, bearing their freak burdens of fat, thin, armless, legless, eyeless misery, stood ancient and stark under the naked electric light bulbs. The bulbs buzzed in the air, large fat Mazda beetles, shedding light on all the numbed, sullen faces of the queer humans.

The freaks focused their vague uneasy eyes on Raoul, then their eyes darted swiftly behind him, seeking Roger, not finding him. Raoul felt the scar, the empty livid stitchings on his back take fire. Out of memory Roger came. Roger's remembered voice called the freaks by the acrid names Roger had thought up for them: "Hi, Blimp!" for the Fat Lady. "Hello, Popeye!" This for the Cyclops Man. "And you, Encyclopaedia Britannica!" That could only mean the Tattooed Man. "And you, Venus de Milo!" Raoul nodded at the armless blond woman. Even six feet of earth could not muffle Roger's insolent voice. "Shorty!" There sat the legless man on his crimson velvet pillow. "Hi, Shorty!" Raoul clapped his hand over his mouth. Had he said it *aloud*? Or was it just Roger's cynical voice in his brain?

Tattoo, with many heads painted on his body, seemed like a vast crowd milling forward. "Raoul!" he shouted happily. He flexed muscles proudly, making the tattoos cavort like a three-ring act. He held his shaved head high because the Eiffel Tower, indelible on his spine, must never sag. On each shoulder blade hung puffy blue clouds. Pushing shoulder blades together, laughing, he'd shout, "See! Storm clouds over the Eiffel! Ha!"

But the sly eyes of the other freaks were like so many sharp needles weaving a fabric of hate around him.

Raoul shook his head. "I can't understand you people! You hated both of us once for a reason; we outshone, outbilled, outsalaried you. But now—how can you still hate *me*?"

Tattoo made the eye around his navel almost wink. "I'll tell you," he said. "They hated you when you were more abnormal than they were." He chuckled. "Now they hate you even more because you're released from freakdom." Tattoo shrugged. "Me, I'm not jealous. I'm no freak." He shot a casual glance at them. "They never liked being what they are. They didn't plan their act; their glands did. Me, my mind did all this to me, these pink chest gunboats, my abdominal island ladies, my flower fingers! It's different—mine's ego. Theirs was a lousy accident of nature. Congratulations, Raoul, on escaping."

A sigh rose from the dozen platforms, angry, high, as if for the first time the freaks realized that Raoul would be the only one of their number ever to be free of the taint of geekdom and staring people.

"We'll strike!" complained the Cyclops. "You and Roger

always caused trouble. Now Lal's dead. We'll strike and make Father Dan throw you out!''

Raoul heard his own voice burst out. "I came back because one of you killed Roger! Besides that, the circus was and *is* my life, and Deirdre is here. None of you can stop me from staying and finding my brother's murderer in my own time, in my own way.''

"We were all in bed that night," whined Fat Lady.

"Yes, yes, we were, we were," they all said in unison.

"It's too late," said Skyscraper. "You'll never find anything!"

The armless lady kicked her legs, mocking. "I didn't kill him. I can't hold a knife except by lying on my back, using my feet!''

"I'm half blind!" said Cyclops.

"I'm too fat to move!" whined Fat Lady.

"Stop it, stop it!" Raoul couldn't stand it. Raging, he bolted from the tent, ran through darkness some ten feet. Then suddenly he saw her, standing in the shadows, waiting for him.

"Deirdre!"

She was the white thing of the upper spaces, a creature winging a canvas void each night, whirling propeller-wise one hundred times around to the enumeration of the strident ringmaster: "—eighty-eight!" A whirl. "Eighty-nine!" A curling. "Ninety!" Her strong right arm bedded with hard muscles, the fingers bony, grasping the hemp loop; the wrists, the elbow, the biceps drawing her torso, her tiny bird-wing feet on up, over, and down; on up, over, and down; with a boom of the brass kettle as she finished each roll.

Now, against the stars, her strong curved right arm raised to a guy wire, she poised forward, looking at Raoul in the half-light, her fingers clenching, relaxing, clenching.

"They've been at you, haven't they?" she asked, whispering, looking past him, inward to those tawdry platforms and their warped cargo, her eyes blazing. "Well, I've got power too. I'm a big act. I've got pull with Papa Dan. I'll have my say, darling.''

At the word "darling" she relaxed. Her tight hand fell. She stood, hands down, eyes half-closed, waiting for Raoul to come and put his arms about her. "What a homecoming we've given you," she sighed. "I'm so sorry, Raoul." She was warmly alive against him. "Oh, darling, these eight weeks have been ten years.''

Warm, close, good, his arms bound her closer. And for the

first time in all his life, Roger was not muttering at Raoul's back: "Oh, for God's sake, get it over with!"

They stood in the runway at nine o'clock. The fanfare. Deirdre kissed his cheek. "Be back in a few minutes." The ringmaster called her name. "Raoul, you must get up, away from the freaks. Tomorrow you rehearse with the Condiellas."

"Won't the freaks detest me for leaving them on the ground? They killed Roger; now, if I outshine them again, they'll get me!"

"To hell with the freaks, to hell with everything but you and me," she declared, her iron fingers working, testing a practice hemp floured with resin. She heard her entrance music. Her eyes clouded. "Darling, did you ever see a Tibetan monk's prayer wheel? Each time the wheel revolves it's one prayer to heaven— *oom mani padme hum.*" Raoul gazed at the high rope where she'd swing in a moment. "Every night, Raoul, every time I go around one revolution, it'll mean I love you, I love you, I love you, like that—over and over."

The music towered. "One other thing," she added quickly. "Promise you'll forget the past. Lal's dead, he committed suicide. Father Dan's told the police another story that doesn't implicate you, so let's forget the whole sorry mess. As far as the police know Lal was blind and in the confusion of the lights going off, when the animals got free, he was killed."

"Lal didn't commit suicide, Deirdre. And it wasn't an accident." Raoul could hardly say it, look at her. "When I returned, the real killer got panicky and wanted a cover-up. Lal suspected the killer, too, so there was a double motive. Lal was pushed under those elephants to make me think my search was over and done. It's not. It's just beginning. Lal wasn't the kind to commit suicide."

"But he hated Roger."

"So did *all* the geeks. And then there's the matter of Roger's picture and mine torn in two pieces."

Deirdre stood there. They called her name. "Raoul, if you're right, then they'll kill you. If the killer was trying to throw you off-trail, and you go on and on—" She had to run then, off into the music, the applause, the noise. She swung up, up, high, higher.

A large-petaled flower floated on the darkness and came to rest on Raoul's shoulder. "Oh, it's you, Tattoo."

The Eiffel Tower was sagging. Twin flowers were twitching at Tattoo's sides as in a high storm. "The geeks," he muttered sullenly. "They've gone on hands and knees to Father Dan!"

"What!"

"Yeah. The armless lady is gesturin' around with her damn big feet, yellin'. The legless man waves his arms, the midget walks the table top, the tall man thumps the canvas ceiling! Oh, God, they're wild mad. Fat Lady'll bust like a rotten melon, I swear! Thin Man'll fall like a broken xylophone!

"They say you killed Lal and they're going to tell the police. The police just got done talking with Father Dan and he convinced them Lal's death was pure accident. Now, the geeks say either Father Dan kicks you out or they go on strike and tell the cops to boot. So Father Dan says for you to hop on over to his tent, *tout de suite*. Good luck, kid."

Father Dan sloshed his whiskey into a glass and glared at it, then at Raoul. "It's not what you did or didn't do that counts, it's what the geeks *believe*. They're boiling. They say you killed Lal because he knew the truth about you and your brother—"

"The truth!" cried Raoul. "What *is* the truth?"

Father Dan couldn't face him, he had to look away. "That you were fed up, sick of being tied to Roger like a horse to a tree, that you—that you killed your brother to be free—that's what they say!" Father Dan sprang to his feet and paced the sawdust. "I'm not believing it—yet."

"But," cried Raoul. "*But*, maybe it would've been worth risking, isn't that what you mean?"

"Look here, Raoul, it stands to reason, if one of the geeks killed Roger, why in hell are you alive? Why didn't he kill you? Would he chance having you catch up with him? Not on your busted tintype. Hell. None of the geeks killed Roger."

"Maybe he got scared. Maybe he wanted me to live and suffer. That would be real irony, don't you see?" pleaded Raoul, bewildered.

Father Dan closed his eyes. "I see that I've got my head way out *here*." He shoved out his hand. "And this business of the torn painting of you and Roger that Lal found. It points to the fact that someone wanted Roger dead and you alive, so maybe you paid one of the other geeks to do the job, maybe you didn't have the nerve yourself—" Father Dan paced swiftly. "And after the job was done, your murderer friend tore the picture triumphantly in two pieces!" Father Dan stopped for breath, looked at

Raoul's numbed, beaten face. "All right," he shouted, "maybe I'm drunk. Maybe I'm crazy. So maybe you *didn't* kill him. You'll still have to pull out. I can't take a chance on you, Raoul, much as I like you. I can't lose my whole sideshow over you."

Raoul rose unsteadily. The tent tilted around him. His ears hammered crazily. He heard his own strange voice saying, "Give me two more days, Father Dan. That's all I ask. When I find the killer, things will quiet down, I promise. If I don't find him, I'll go away, I promise that too."

Father Dan stared morosely at his boot tip in the sawdust. Then he roused himself uneasily. "Two days, then. But that's all. Two days, and no more. You're a hard man to down, aren't you, number two twin?"

They rode on horseback down past the slumbering town, tethered up by a creek, and talked earnestly and kissed quietly. He told her about Father Dan, the split canvas, Lal, and the danger to his job. She held his face in her hands, looking up.

"Darling, let's go away. I don't want you hurt."

"Only two more days. If I find the murderer, we can stay."

"But there are other circuses, other places." Her gray eyes were tormented. "I'd give up my job to keep us safe." She seized his shoulders. "Is Roger that important to you?" Before he knew what she intended, she had whirled him in the dark, locked her elbows in his, and pressured her slender back to his scarred spine. Whispering softly, she said, "I have you now, for the first time, alone, don't go away from me." She released him slowly, and he turned and held her again. She said, so softly, "Don't go away from me, Raoul, I don't want anything to interfere again. . . ."

Instantly time flew backward. In Raoul's mind he heard Deirdre on another day, asking Roger why he and Raoul had never submitted themselves to the surgeon's scalpel. And Roger's cynic's face rose like driftwood from the tide pool of Raoul's memory, laughing curtly at Deirdre and retorting, "No, my dear Deirdre, no. It takes two to agree to an operation. I refuse."

Raoul kissed Deirdre, trying to forget Roger's bitter comment. He recalled his first kiss from Deirdre and Roger's abrupt voice: "Kiss her this way, Raoul! Here, let *me* show you! May I cut in? No, no, Raoul, you're unromantic! That's better. Mind if I fan myself?" Another chortle. "It's a bit warm."

"Shut up, shut up, shut up!" screamed Raoul. He shook

violently, jolting himself back into the present—into Deirdre's arms—

He woke in the morning with an uncontrollable desire to run, get Deirdre, pack, catch a train, and get out now, get away from things forever. He paced his hotel room. To go away, he thought, to leave and never know any more about the half of himself that was buried in a cemetery hundreds of miles away— But he *had* to know.

Noon bugle. The carnies, geeks, finkers, and palefaces, the shills and the shanties, lined the timber tables as Raoul picked vaguely at his plated meat. There *was* a way to find the murderer. A *sure* way.

"Tonight I'm turning the murderer over to the police," said Raoul, murmuring.

Tattoo almost dropped his fork. "You mean it?"

"Pass the white top tent," someone interrupted. Cake was handed past Raoul's grim face as he said:

"I've been waiting—biding my time since I got back—watching the killer. I saw his face the night he got Roger. I didn't tell the police that. I didn't tell anybody that. I been waiting—just waiting—for the right time and place to even up the score. I didn't want the police doing my work for me. I wanted to fix him in my own way."

"It wasn't Lal, then?"

"No."

"You let Lal be killed?"

"I didn't think he would be. He should have kept quiet. I'm sorry about Lal. But the score'll be evened tonight. I'll turn the killer's body over to the police personally. And it'll be in self-defense. They won't hold me, I'll tell you that, painted man."

"What if he gets you first?"

"I'm half dead now. I'm ready." Raoul leaned forward earnestly, holding Tattoo's blue wrist. "You won't tell anyone about this, of course?"

"Who? Me? Ha, ha, not *me*, Raoul."

The choice news passed from Tattoo to Blimp to Skeleton to Armless to Cyclops to Shorty and on around. Raoul could almost see it go. And he knew that now the matter would be settled; either he'd get the killer or the killer'd get him. Simple. Corner a rat and have it out. But what if nothing happened?

He frequented all the dark places when the sun set. He strolled under tall crimson wagons where buckets might drop off and crush his head. None dropped. He idled behind cat cages where a sprung door could release fangs on his scarred spine. No cats leaped. He sprawled under an ornate blue wagon wheel waiting for it to revolve, killing him. The wheel did not revolve, nor did elephants trample him, nor tent poles collapse across him, nor guns shoot him. Only the rhythmed music of the band blared out into the starry sky, and he grew more unhappy and solemn in his death-walking.

He began walking faster, whistling loudly against the thoughts in his mind. Roger had been killed for a purpose. Raoul was *purposely* left alive.

A wave of applause echoed from the big top. A lion snarled. Raoul put his hands to his head and closed his eyes. The geeks were innocent. He knew that now. If Lal or Tattoo or Fat Lady or Armless or Legless was guilty, they'd have killed both Roger and Raoul. There was only one solution. It was clear as a blast of a new trumpet.

He began walking toward the runway entrance, shuffling his feet. There'd be no fight, no blood spilled, no accusations or angers.

"I will live for a long time," he said to himself, wearily. "But what will there be to live for, after tonight?"

What good to stick with the show now, what good if the freaks did settle down to accepting him? What good to know the killer's name. No good—no damned good at all. In his frantic search for one thing he'd lost another. He was alive. His heart pounded hot and heavy in him, sweat poured from his armpits, down his back, on his brow, in his hands. Alive. And the very fact of his aliveness, his living, his heart pulsing, his feet moving, was proof of the killer's identity. It is not often, he thought grimly, that a killer is found through a live man being alive, usually it is through a dead man's being dead. I wish I were dead. I wish I were dead.

This was the last performance in the circus in his life. He found himself shuffling down the runway, heard the whirling din of music, the applause, the laughter as clowns tumbled and wrestled in the red rings.

Deirdre stood in the runway, looking like a miracle of stars and whiteness, pure and clean and birdlike. She turned as he came up, her face pale, small blue petals under each eye from sleepless nights; but beautiful. She watched the way Raoul walked with his head down.

The music held them. He raised his head and didn't look at her.

"Raoul," she said, "what's wrong?"

He said, "I've found the killer."

A cymbal crashed. Deirdre looked at him for a long time.

"Who is it?"

He didn't answer, but talked to himself, low, like a prayer, staring straight out at the rings and the people: "You get caught. No matter what you do, you're helpless. With Roger I was unhappy; without him I'm worse. When I had Roger I wanted you; now, with Roger gone, I can never have you. If I'd given up the hunt, I'd never have been happy. Now that the hunt is over, I'm even more miserable with what I've found."

"You're—you're going to turn the killer in, then?" she asked, finally, after a long time.

He just stood there, saying nothing, not able to think or see or talk. He felt the music rise, high. He heard, far off, the announcer giving Deirdre's name, he felt her hard fingers hold him for a moment, tightly, and her warm lips kiss him hard.

"Good-bye, darling."

Running lightly, the sequins all flashing and flittering like huge reflecting wings, Deirdre went over the tanbark, into the storm of applause, her face upward, staring at her ropes and her heaven, the music beating down on her like rain. The rope pulled her up, up, and up. The music cut. The trap drum pattered smoothly, monotonously. She began her loops.

A man walked out of the shadows when Raoul motioned to him, smoking a cigar, chewing it thoughtfully. He stopped beside Raoul and they were wordless for a time, staring upward.

There was Deirdre, caught high in the tent by a white beam of steady light. Grasping the slender rope strand, her legs swung up over her curved body in a great circle, over, up and down.

The ringmaster bawled out the revolutions one by one: "One—two—three—four—!"

Over and over went Deirdre, like a white moth spinning a cocoon. *Remember, Raoul, when I go around; the monk's prayer wheel.* Raoul's face fell apart. *Oom mani padme hum. I love, I love you, I love you.*

"She's pretty, ain't she?" said the detective at Raoul's side.

"Yes, and she's the one you want," said Raoul slowly, not

believing the words he had to speak. "I'm alive tonight. That proves it. She killed Roger and ripped our canvas painting in half. She killed Lal." He passed a trembling hand over his eyes. "She'll be down in about five minutes, you can arrest her then."

They both stared upward together, as if they didn't quite believe she was there.

"Forty-one, forty-two, forty-three, forty-four, forty-five," counted the detective. "Hey, what're you crying about? Forty-six, forty-seven, forty- . . . ''

Hell's Half Hour

The room was in a terrible state. The pictures were flung violently from the walls, the furniture was tumbled, overturned, there were deep gashes in the woodwork and wallpaper where Mr. Caldwell, the blind man, had dug, clutched, searched with his fingernails. The amount of damage was phenomenal.

Chris Priory, lieutenant of homicide for the town of Green Bay, California, stood beside me for a long while, just looking.

Caldwell, his dark glasses ground into powder, lay against the farthest wall, at its center, one hand struck up as if to claw through its frustrating thickness, the back of his skull caved in. He was a young, fine-looking, sensitively featured man, with dark, curly hair and a smooth complexion. Death had done things to his handsomeness.

"Lord, what a mess," I said.

Downstairs on the first floor we could hear the landlady weeping.

Priory looked at me and said, wonderingly, "Caldwell was blind."

"Yes," I said. "The landlady said he arrived here on October seventeenth, with his sight rapidly failing. Two weeks later he was stone blind, and he's been that way ever since. That was six weeks ago."

"Strange," muttered Priory. "It stands to reason that if someone came to murder Caldwell last night, he could have killed him right off, without all this muss. It must have taken a good twenty minutes to have done all this to the room. No need for it. A blind

man's at the mercy of any killer. One good blow on his unde-
fended and unsuspecting head—'' Priory broke off, walking
across to bend beside the corpse. "He was trying to get away,
escape, trying to find the door in a wild, hysterical frenzy, when
he died."

I glanced at the slashed furniture, the scarred walls. "Or else
the place was wrecked to make it look like a fight?"

Priory shook his head. "Caldwell did most of it. Look. Under
his fingernails: crescents of wallpaper, plaster, a sliver from the
door, a thread of material from the couch. And here—his pants,
at the knee, scuffed with violent rubbing. The tips of his shoes
bruised with kicking at the locked door."

"Brutal," I said.

"Brutal, yes," admitted Priory. "And his forehead, too, you
see. Those bruises came from colliding headlong with the wall,
in flight. That cut on his cheek derives from shattering a picture
and being cut by the falling glass. The death blows were delivered from the rear as he tried to scoop a hole through the wall
with cut and bleeding raw fingernails. . . ."

I swallowed uneasily. "Granted all that's true, what's the
motive? Perhaps the killer searched afterward for money, letters,
other valuables."

Priory bent and pointed to the outer material of a chair. He
showed me how it had been slashed by fingernails, but none of
the stuffing pulled out or disturbed. The same way with the
davenport. The desk was gashed, but the drawers were all closed
and the pens, pencils, and writing paper neat inside them. Nowhere,
either around or behind the pictures, were the scratches more
than superficial. A man looking for something would have pounded
gaping holes in plaster and ripped the cotton guts from the
furniture. I had to admit this was true. Everywhere the marks
were simply those of a man who'd raked fingers swiftly over
surfaces in violent moves. The picture backs were not pried in
any manner, nor were tacks lifted from the carpet at any spot.

I stood up. "That fixes that. Perhaps Caldwell carried something on his person?"

"Then the killer would have knocked him down and taken it,
wouldn't he? But no, the killer was very methodical, cold-
blooded, took his time. Or maybe he *had* to take his time.
Maybe—"

"Maybe what?"

Priory shrugged. "Let's go talk to the landlady."

*   *   *

The landlady lay in bed, her small, thin face so white it almost blended with the wrinkled pillow. She lifted a weak hand and began to talk.

"Mr. Caldwell came two months ago, exactly to the day. Almost hysterical he was. I was very sympathetic to him. He was going blind and two weeks after he took the room he was totally in the dark. I often heard him sobbing upstairs. I'd knock on his door—that was before I took ill in bed—and he'd quiet down and come open the door with his cheeks all wet and when I'd try comforting him, he'd say, 'I've done a horrible thing. I've done a horrible thing. I know what it is now. Oh, my God, it's dark.' "

"Was Caldwell his real name?"

"I don't know. He seemed awfully jumpy, as if he were running from someone. When anyone came near he'd cry, 'Who's there!' and I'd say, 'No one but Miss Tarvey, sir,' or 'It's only the butcher's boy, bringing poultry.' An ordinary blind man would have asked politely. Not Mr. Caldwell. His face always paled out and his hands trembled and he cringed at people's footsteps."

The landlady paused to get her breath.

"I'm all alone here, and Mr. Caldwell was one of two roomers. My other roomer, Miss Tarvey, works nights, so she was gone. This man who came to visit Mr. Caldwell called earlier yesterday. Miss Tarvey answered the phone. The man asked where the blind man lived. He didn't ask by name, he just asked where the blind man lived. I thought that queer. And Miss Tarvey told him upstairs on the second floor and the voice on the phone asked which room, on which side of the hall, and Miss Tarvey said the first door on the right. Then the phone suddenly clicked, without so much as a thank-you. And an hour later, at nine o'clock, when Miss Tarvey had gone, this man came into the front hall."

"He didn't rap on the front door?" Priory asked.

"No. Just walked right in. I remember calling to see who it was. There was no answer, but I didn't worry much about it. He went upstairs and knocked on Mr. Caldwell's door. Then I heard the door open, Mr. Caldwell cry out, and the door slammed and locked."

"And then the noises began?"

The landlady sighed, closing her eyes, her voice weak, pale, far away. Her fingers twisted the bed quilt as she continued.

"The little noises began. And me lying here in bed, not able to do a thing. First of all, a man walking across the floor. It wasn't Mr. Caldwell, I could tell by his shoes. Then I heard a sharp thump. Mr. Caldwell cried out. I pushed myself up in bed. I called, 'Mr. Caldwell, you all right?' but he didn't hear me, I guess. Then I heard Mr. Caldwell, walking now, toward the door.''

"Walking? At a regular, even pace?''

"Yes. Like you might stroll through the park. And then this other man began walking, too, and for three or four minutes they did nothing but walk around upstairs. I tensed myself, listening.''

"They just walked around?''

The landlady lay listening to the memory of it; it was vivid and real to her still. "Yes. It sounded so—queer. Walking around—and talking. I couldn't figure out a word. Mr. Caldwell would say something and then this other man would say something,'' she remembered. "They began to walk a little faster. It kept speeding up, faster and faster. Mr. Caldwell would make a little run across the floor, then the man would make a little run after him. Then Mr. Caldwell would run some more, bump something, fall, get up, run on, and the man coming right after him, striding like.''

I looked at the ceiling. The landlady flicked her tongue over her withered lips, stretched her eyes wider, staring, made wild, remembering movements, with white eyeballs and focused pupils, dark, turned upward, at that room.

"Back and forth, back and forth, faster and faster, faster and faster. And they began to shout things I can't remember, things I didn't understand. Walking, walking, walking, the two of them. Running now, quickly, like waltzing mice. Queer, odd. I kept lifting myself, calling, 'Mr. Caldwell, stop that, I can't sleep!' But they shouted louder and finally thumps and scratchings sounded, like mice, rats in the walls. Pictures fell crashing. Furniture tipped back like tons of hard lumber, shaking the lights! I heard glass tinkle. I heard a table fall like a young tree cut. I heard a knob rattle, quick, quick; Mr. Caldwell started screaming. Then—then there was more scurrying—'' She breathed it out, gasping, eyes fixed, immovable. "More shouting, blundering back and forth, back and forth, like a gigantic pendulum in that room; more rats in the wall. Mr. Caldwell collapsed down. I heard him fighting, scratching, digging right up there, *there*, you *see!* Digging like a dog at a gopher hole, sobbing wild! And then—''

The landlady stopped, stiffened her entire thin body.

"Then I heard the last sounds. The sounds of something striking Mr. Caldwell over and over again. Again and again!''

The landlady relaxed, sinking back on the bed, resting, perspiration on her brow, sighing to a finish.

"Right after that, the man came downstairs, silent, and went out the door. I tried screaming, but it was six hours before Miss Tarvey arrived to call the police.''

I had sat down. Priory was scowling and nervous himself. "Of all the damnable things,'' he murmured. "You heard Mr. Caldwell's voice right up to the last?'' The landlady nodded. "That proves it all occurred with Caldwell alive and moving, anyway. There was little time for the killer to search.''

"No, sir. He came down immediately and went away.''

I lighted a cigarette and looked at the match flame awhile. "That killer must have enjoyed himself immensely. Immensely.''

"Half an hour it was,'' said the landlady. "Thirty minutes they walked and ran around up there like nightmares on a treadmill.''

"Thirty minutes to toy with his victim,'' I said.

Priory grunted. "It doesn't hold water.'' He turned to the door. "If you'll pardon me, I've some phone calls to make. Then I'm going out into the town for a few hours and see if I can't find myself a waltzing mouse. You stay here and watch the other homicide boys go over the room with a comb, eh? Good boy.''

"Are you serious?'' I asked, but Priory walked off.

Priory returned late in the afternoon, beaming. He talked excitedly and paced back and forth. "Douglas, suppose you were a killer. It wouldn't be hard tracing a blind man. A blind man can't run far with much secrecy. Or fast. And people remember him. So if you were the killer, how would you approach your victim if he lived in the next town, say?''

"I'd drive to where he was, kill him, and leave town.''

"Why?''

"If I took the train or bus or cab, people would remember me. A cabbie might describe me from memory.''

"And if you had a scar on your face?''

"All the more reason for me to drive my own car and then get back home quickly as possible, preferably at night, so even my own neighbors wouldn't know I had gone away at all.''

"And you wouldn't take half an hour to commit that murder?''

"No,'' I cried. "I'd get it over with.''

"Ah, and that is exactly where our killer gave himself away. Remember it took him half an hour. Because of that, I know what he looks like! I've gone up and down the street asking people if they've seen the murderer, checked every yellow-cab driver, every bus depot. No soap. The killer *must* have come by his own car.''

"How could you describe the killer on such flimsy evidence!''

Priory looked at me sadly, as at a faithful but very ignorant puppy. "Simply on the basis of the half hour it took for the murder. Like to bet on it, Douglas, boy?''

"You're damn right I do. You can't tell me that's enough of a clue to catch a criminal on!'' We shook hands.

Priory now drew a list from his pocket. "Here are three people, the only suspects in town, who might have, but didn't, kill Caldwell.''

"What kind of people?''

"People who'd take half an hour to commit murder,'' he said maddeningly. "But their alibis were all good. So what have I done but turned up my main suspect over in Orange City. A young, fairly well-to-do gentleman by the name of John Melton who was attacked on the morning of October sixteenth—''

"And Caldwell arrived here on October seventeenth, the next day.''

"Right. Caldwell was fleeing after what he'd done. This Orange City suspect fits in every way my mental picture of the killer. The police file is all too clear on that point. And I've discovered a very concise and horrible motive for this murder. This man Melton, after the attack, refused to name his assailant; therefore there's no mention of Caldwell, but the very nature of the attack leaves little doubt that it was he who attacked Melton. Shall we drive over and arrest Melton as our murderer?''

"You're that certain, are you?''

"Positively. I haven't one other clue to my name. Not a damn one. No one saw the killer. No positive corpse identity. Just the waltzing mice. If—I emphasize the 'if'—if the murder had occurred instantly I might never have guessed the solution. It was simply the fact that the murderer took half an hour. Think it over,

Douglas, while you drive me over to Orange City to arrest our man.''

We drove to Orange City. Myself very irritated. Priory very quiet and certain about the whole affair.

In Orange City, an elderly, kind-faced but tired-looking, plump woman, Mrs. Melton, the mother of our suspect, answered the door when we rang. She listened to Priory explain that it was just a routine call, cautioned us to be quiet, because John was very tired, and then let us in, adding the fact that the last two months had been a severe shock to John. Priory said that he understood perfectly and, as we entered the hall of the medium-wealthy family, nodded me to a chair and went on ahead into a side room where I could hear Melton and him conversing. Mrs. Melton went away into another part of the house.

I had begun to fidget when finally, through the door, I heard him say, ''Frankly, Mr. Melton, I'm investigating a friend of yours named Caldwell.''

Melton's voice was very young, clear, and self-assured. ''I don't know anyone by that name, Lieutenant.''

Priory cleared his throat. ''He was about your age, on the verge of blindness last October, when he suddenly moved from this town over to Green Bay. Does that help recall him?''

A long silence. ''Oh, you mean Bill Calder.''

''Calder—Caldwell, it's pretty nearly the same. He was going blind, was he not?''

''He was.''

''And on the morning of October sixteenth, in a discussion concerned with his blindness, didn't this Calder—or Caldwell— attack you?''

After a much longer silence, Melton replied. ''He did.'' And his voice was older, suddenly. ''How could I ever forget that?''

''He was a friend?''

''We were never friends. We loved the same woman, if that means anything.''

''It does. After attacking you, Calder-Caldwell moved to Green Bay in a highly emotional state, seeming to expect someone to follow and hurt him. Could you tell me more about your fight with him on that October morning? How did it begin?''

''It was all over Doris. She's a very beautiful woman. Calder was supposed to marry her at that time, but then his old eye ailment recurred. He discovered he was going progressively blind. It almost drove him crazy, I imagine.''

''And then—''

''Doris broke off with him. She didn't want marriage to a blind man. She realized that in a matter of weeks he'd be totally helpless, with no hope for a cure.'' A pause. ''Doris and I became engaged almost immediately.''

Priory observed, ''She doesn't sound like a very kindly person.''

Melton laughed bitterly. ''She isn't.''

''You didn't marry her?''

Again, bitterness. ''No. *It* happened.''

''What do you mean by—*it*?''

Melton took a deep breath. I leaned forward on my chair in the hall. Melton explained.

''I was happy, triumphant, swell-headed. One morning, October sixteenth, I visited Calder, or Caldwell, as you know him. We'd always hated each other's guts, so I guess I talked too much. I said something I shouldn't have said. It crushed him down. I could see him wither under it. I shouldn't have said it. Christ, if I'd kept my mouth shut I'd be happy with Doris today—''

Melton seemed to have difficulty continuing. Priory asked him, ''What did you say to Calder that made him attack you?''

''I looked at him, laughed, and declared, 'Doris and I are getting married. She doesn't want to be married to a blind man!' ''

''Good Lord,'' exclaimed Priory.

''Yes,'' said Melton dully, ''that's what I said. I was a fool. Calder screamed, 'I can still see enough to fix you!' and he leaped toward me!''

Silence.

''Next day, Calder left town. The police interviewed me, but I wouldn't prefer charges, or tell them who it was attacked me.''

''And then Doris didn't marry you?''

''No. She went off with someone else.''

Priory said, ''Well, Calder's finally turned up again. He was murdered in Green Bay last night. Mr. Melton. You didn't happen to be in Green Bay last night, did you—after a tedious six weeks' search located Caldwell?''

''No. My mother will tell you I was here, resting.''

''Your mother loves you; she'd say anything. She'd pay good

money to your chauffeur who *had* to drive you there too,'' retorted Priory. ''Sorry; you're under arrest.''

''Where's your proof?''

''Proof? First, your motive. A strong, terrible motive. But above all else was the condition in which we found Caldwell's room and the *length of time it took to kill Caldwell*. There were other clues which would probably have tripped you up much later, but the one clue of the time length pointed right at you. I was able to locate you immediately.''

''I don't understand!''

''The two of you, scrambling, falling, slashing walls, furniture, doors, rugs, smashing pictures, darting from wall to wall faster and faster, for thirty minutes until you finally got to him and crushed in his head with your cane!''

I rose from my chair, shaking.

I heard Melton's voice break and tremble and husk.

''All right, all right. I don't care! It was luck I got home! I intended giving myself up, anyway. There's not a damn thing worth living for. All I wanted was to find and kill him! Two blind men groping about a room, one dodging to escape, behind tables, chairs, sofas, the other going on and on and on trying to find and kill him! It took me quite half an hour's search until I got him, Mr. Priory.''

''Douglas,'' Priory called to me through the door. ''Come in.''

I opened the hall door, stepped in. The case was over.

There sat Mr. Melton, looking at but not seeing me, a red-and-white striped cane with a heavy lead tip leaned across his knee, his eyes scarred and blinded from that October morning when he had joked at Caldwell's eye failure, and when Caldwell in a wild, screaming rage had attacked, thrown Melton down, and destroyed his eyes with merciless fingernails!

The Long Way Home

Charlie Guidney's heart was shaking inside him as he made the top of the stairs. He wore a hunted look as he leaned against the bannister and thought, Well, another day's over. The office is behind me; the comptometers are behind me. I have a nice evening to look forward to. He winced. Inside, his heart sounded like a broken comptometer, off rhythm, totaling up a colossal No Sale. What had his doctor said?

"That heart of yours needs a rest. Take it on a vacation."

Small and pale, Charlie Guidney moved slowly along the fourth-floor hall. He dreaded telling his wife about his health, his heart—

He blinked sweat from his tired eyes. Through the long hot day the comptometers had sung like a million metal crickets in all the long, echoing office rooms. Mr. Sternwell had yelled at him. He'd like to kill Sternwell. Couldn't he understand that Charlie was a sick man?

Charlie stopped at his own apartment door. Inside waited the red-haired, half-alive woman he had once loved. Would she approve of his going away for a rest? No. Her mouth would bang shut like a trap when he spoke of his illness. Her eyes would hold sharp amusement while her lips said he was all right, he just needed more sleep nights.

He put his shaking hand on the knob. Either he got away on a long vacation or someday, in a righteous fury, he'd push Mr. Sternwell out the tenth-story window.

Oh, the monotony of coming-going on streetcars, work, the endlessly dull conversations with Lydia over half-fried foods! He feared for his sanity. Sometimes he even entertained ideas of killing Lydia. The way she stared fixedly, feverishly, at all the younger men in the apartment house—as if they were toys to be played with.

The door opened from the inside. A young man appeared, bobbing his blond head at Charlie Guidney in surprised welcome. "Oh, hi, Mr. Guidney. Just been fixing your radio."

Charlie watched Travis go down the hall, then entered. His wife sat spread out on a gray sofa with a brilliant magazine for a head. Behind the slowly fluttered pages Lydia's voice said coolly, "You're late!"

She had him off balance, as always. "It's only five after six," he said.

"And tomorrow night'll be ten after, the next night twenty after," she said sharply behind her reading. "And later and later and *later*!"

He fidgeted around so he could see her large white nose, her wide jaw, her eyes as shiny as two bits of blue glass. "My heart, the doctor—" he began.

"Your heart," she scoffed. "Your damned heart again is it? I don't see you dead, much the worse for me, God save me," she muttered.

"Oh," he cried helplessly, "you're trying to cover up, confuse me. That young radio man, Travis, has been up here visiting again." She simpered and scanned her magazine, not reading it. This so infuriated him. He looked wildly about the drab room as if seeking some means of getting back at her.

"Look," he cried. "A mouse!"

"Ah, where!" she shrieked. She seized her huge feet from the floor, paling under her blazing wig of red hair, eyes searching, frightened.

There was no mouse. He had used the old trick again. Her eyes glittered straight at him. "Just for that," she pronounced slowly, "I'll take an extra ten dollars from your paycheck this week. Ten dollars or you fix your own suppers for a week, like you did last month!"

He stood wordlessly gesturing toward her, wanting to speak simply and say, "We've let marriage make us mean and small. Let's get out of Los Angeles, Lydia. Maybe if we got away we'd start living again. Maybe you'd be like you used to—"

He knew it was useless, Lydia was the kind of woman who viciously creamed your coffee if you loved it black, played the radio at a thunder if your head ached. How could he confess his illness and spiritual want to her? She'd say they couldn't afford travel for his health. She'd sit watching him die. His head swam. Sternwell. Office. Doctor. Lydia. Murder. He hesitated. *Murder.* Hold on! He lifted his head, laughing inwardly.

"Close the door, and hang up that dirty hat of yours," she snapped.

He said dully, "No, that won't do any good," frantically searching for something to say, "I just killed a man!"

Lydia didn't seem to understand. "*Really?* What's his name?"

Charlie flushed. "I said I *killed* a man!" he cried. "K-i-l-l-e-d! Killed. Murdered!"

"Killed!" she screamed, on her feet now. Charlie leaned his head against the door, shut his eyes. He was in for it now. He had to go through with it. There was no backing out. Make it good, he told himself frantically, make it good. Tell her. *Go on.* "I shot him right through his heart," he said in awed wonder. "Very pretty."

"Oh, Charlie—"

"I couldn't help it," said Charlie. "I didn't like his face. He was one of those people with no chin. . . ."

"Oh, now, Charlie!"

"Yes." He laughed gently, slowly. "Oh, now, Charlie. That won't help. I blew his heart back through his spinal cord. He looked surprised."

It was almost as if he *had* killed someone. He imagined the explosion, the blood, the excitement. His heart pounded. His voice was high, shrill as the ring of alarm clocks in dreams.

He liked what it was doing to Lydia. She had forgotten her Mr. Travis and her radio and her scornful cruelty. She watched him as if he were a mechanical man for whom she'd lost the key. He sat down. His feet tracked mud across the green carpet.

She wanted to complain about the mud. It was easier to understand a dirty floor than a Charlie Guidney who had killed a human being.

He looked at the mud and then at her in strange triumph. "Everything's shot to hell," he said. "He folded over my gun like a marionette. God, it was exciting!" Lydia stared at him like a blind woman, her hands twisting, the blood gone from her face. Heaven help him *now* if he slipped!

"I got the idea today in the office. Mr. Sternwell yelled at me, and I thought to myself, He shouldn't yell so loud, I don't like it. And then I thought, He's no good to the world, he's getting old and somebody should stop him from shouting—" He leaned forward. "Somebody. Who? All of a sudden I —"

He pointed at himself then, smiling. "Me. Mr. Charles Guidney, white-collar worker, tidy, meek, and pale, Charles C. Guidney. Blood all over the place." Lydia shivered, so he very carefully repeated, "Blood all over the place!"

Lydia's face was as it hadn't been in ten years. Everything bad was gone out of it in this moment. She was worrying. It was suddenly the greatest thing in the world to lie.

"I left work early," he said. "On Main Street you can't buy a gun without a permit, so I stole one. When the dealer went into the back room for a moment I got one. Then I went back to the office and I followed Mr. Sternwell downstairs and in the alley I killed him!"

Lydia sat down unsteadily.

"So now I'm a fugitive," said Charlie simply. "We'll have to leave town, take a trip—"

"We can't afford—" Lydia caught herself. Perhaps the vision of the five thousand dollars at the bank, under her name, stopped her. Perhaps, too, she'd often wanted to get away, but never admitted it. She was not one to come out and agree to other people's plans.

This might be the turning point. They could go off, start again together, if she stuck by him now. But if she really hated him, she'd turn him over to the police now, instantly. This was a test of her love for him, thought Charlie, astounded at the implications he had not considered when starting his lie. The embarrassment if she *did* turn him over to the cops. He'd have to tell the truth in front of her and she'd glower and simper, hate him even more.

Lydia was very calm. "What do you want me to do?" she asked.

"You mean you'll help me? You love me enough to go with me?"

She examined him quietly. Maybe she knew he lied. Maybe she saw new possibilities in him because he showed enough imagination to frame a story such as this. Perhaps her pride prevented her accepting the plan on just its vacation merits. Perhaps she liked playing this game, too. She was a gunmoll now. He almost laughed.

She repeated, "What do you want me to do?"

"I'll pack suitcases. You reserve tickets on tonight's San Diego bus!" He hurried around the room. "We'll forget the whole thing in Mexico for six months. Oh, it'll be good with you, Lydia!"

Her expression was thoughtful as she put on her hat and coat. "And hurry," he said, giving her the bus-ticket money. She walked out the door, shut it. Laughing, singing, Charlie stuffed clothes into suitcases. "She loves me!" he whispered, amazed. "There *is* something to live for, then. She's actually helping *me*, going with *me*. She doesn't care about anyone but *me*!"

While shaving, he deliberately left the top off the cream tube. He did not dry the brush nor rinse the bowl nor hang the towel straight.

Lydia stood stiff and calm in the bathroom door. "Here are the tickets, Charlie," she announced.

"You're late," he said.

"I'm sorry," she said.

"Don't do it again," he said. "There's no excuse."

"There was a crowd," she explained, looking straight at him in the mirror, taking off her hat. "I was lucky to get these. The bus leaves at nine sharp."

"Lydia," he said. He hesitated. He looked down at the bowl, at his wet hands, then at her level eyes. "Lydia, you don't know what this means to me. To have you backing me up—"

"Yes, Charlie, yes," she said, without tone.

A siren sounded below in the darkening street. For a moment Charlie did not comprehend it. Then he jerked his hands up and let out a mock cry of despair, hurled himself from the bathroom. "They'll surround the house!" He thrashed into his coat, crammed his hat on, seized the two suitcases, put them down, took the tickets from Lydia, stuck them dangling in his lapel pocket and whispered swiftly. "Quick. Down the back way into the alley!"

Lydia stood very straight, her eyes to one side, her head tilted. "The police car went on by, Charles," she told him.

"Well, we'd better go down the front way then, huh? I guess it'd look funny for us running down the alley. Go on ahead, Lydia!"

She marched out. He walked around the room, laughing at the walls and the ceiling. He wiped his shoes on the sofa they'd bought on an installment plan. He smashed two gaudy pictures on the wall. Nodding to the shattered frames, he was ready for the world. He went out and slammed the door hard.

A fat man waited below the steps outside as Charlie closed the front door cautiously and glanced around. Lydia gripped Charlie's elbow and croaked, "Mr. Kelly!"

Officer Kelly, mistaking this for a salutation, saluted them. "Ah, and hello to the two of you, Mr. and Mrs. Guidney!" he said cheerily.

Lydia, stumbled and weaved and blinked many times, jerking

her head first toward Charlie, then the policeman. "Oh, Mr. Kelly please, Charlie didn't mean to kill that man!"

Charlie dumbfounded, balanced on the top step, caught his wife and propelled her back. "No, no, no," he hissed frantically. "Control yourself!"

Lydia, over Charlie's shoulder, pleaded with the cop. "He didn't know what he was doing. Don't shoot him, oh, please."

Kelly said from a great distance, "He didn't know he was doing what to who?"

"Nothing, nothing." Charlie smiled at the officer. "You don't understand."

Lydia cringed against Charlie. "He'll shoot us!" she screamed.

Charlie's heart began to kick up; it got the familiar pains.

"Hold on, hold on." Officer Kelly came up the steps with long slow movements of big heavy feet. Charlie groaned to his wife, "Go inside, go inside, Lydia. Nothing's wrong, Lydia. Oh God!"

"What," Mr. Kelly wanted to know, "are you two talking about?"

"It's Mr. Sternwell, he was old and mean and somebody should have shot him and Charlie did!" sobbed Mrs. Guidney in a wild torrent. Charlie managed to pump her through the door, slam it, and stand against it facing Officer Kelly.

"Well?" asked Kelly, scowling darkly.

"My wife's nervous. She—she thinks I—I shot a man. I didn't. No, sir, I didn't. All a joke. Just a joke."

"All a joke," said Kelly. "Ha ha." He thumped the suitcases with one foot. "And of course you're taking them clothes on over to the laundry to be rough-dried?"

Charlie made a surprised face. "Clothes?" Charlie discovered the baggage at his feet and his shoulders sagged.

"And," said Kelly as he very delicately plucked a paper from Charlie's lapel. "And this little piece of green tissue," he said politely. "This wouldn't be a bus ticket for San Diego?"

"I tell you my wife has the whole thing messed up."

"Suppose *you* tell me," said Kelly earnestly.

Charlie got indignant. "Call precinct headquarters! Ask them if any old men've been killed in the past three hours!"

"I am not that dense," said Kelly. "Maybe you hid the remains."

"Aw, now, Kelly, do I look like a fiend? Come here." And he led Kelly down a couple of steps and whispered the whole

setup into one of Kelly's hairy ears. "You see?" He finished off.
"And if she finds out it's a frame-up, I'll never lift my head
again! She'll peel the hide off me."

Kelly's eyes flashed a squinting, understanding blue glance at
him. Kelly put his hand on Charlie's shoulder, patting him.
"That's different, now. I won't let the cat out. I know just how
you feel. Sometimes *my* wife—but that's a long story better
saved. I hope you will not mind if I make a phone call anyways,
Mr. Guidney?"

Charlie laughed. "Sure, sure." He slapped Kelly's broad back.
They went across the street.

Kelly talked into the round metal mouthpiece of the phone,
feeling good. "This is Kelly. Yeah." Kelly listened. Charlie
whistled and rocked on his heels. Mexico. Peace. Easy living. A
dream coming true. "Yeah?" said Kelly. "Well, this is what I'm
inquiring about. Listen—" and he told them. And he smiled.
Charlie watched him. Kelly's smile faded, like smoke in a cold
wind. "Yeah?"

Charlie shifted his feet. "What's up, Kelly?"

Kelly listened again and said, "Oh, he *did*, did he?"

Charlie swallowed hard. He hung onto Kelly's elbow. "There
isn't anything wrong—is there?"

Kelly listened. "Oh, it did, did it? I will."

"Will what, Kelly?" asked Charlie.

Kelly looked at him, talked in the phone. "He's standing right
here beside me." Mr. Kelly hung up.

Charlie said, "No. No. Don't look at me that way. No!"
Kelly replied, "Oh, yes, Mr. Guidney, it *can* be. Mr. Guidney, I
hereby arrest you for the murder of one John Pastor, found bleeding to death from a gun wound half an hour ago. Shot dead with
a twenty-two caliber pistol, he was, in an alley behind some trash
bins, over on Temple Street. That's just eight blocks from here,
close enough to make me think—"

Charlie kicked Mr. Kelly's shins just as Mr. Kelly was taking
out his handcuffs. Kelly grunted. Charlie hit him with his fist.
Kelly fell down and lay motionless on the sidewalk. His head had
struck the pole on the way down.

Lydia lay against the wall inside the door as Charlie yanked it
open. She was like ice. "Charlie, we can't escape—we can't
escape. We were fools to try."

His jaw hung down. "But this is different. Something's
happened. Wait for me, Lydia! I'll come back!"

"But what about the bus tickets?"

"We can't use them now!" he cried. "Good-bye, Lydia!"

"Charlie, come back! Where are you going?"

"I don't know!" The door slammed. His footsteps died out down the alley.

It was dark. Charlie grieved to himself, walking along in the shadows. How had he gotten into this? A lifetime of sturdy mediocrity and now—boom-crash-bang—Jack the Ripper! He shivered. Talk about the chill hand of Fate—

He looked around. This was the drab shopping district where he and Lydia often walked to pick up some Chinese chop suey, or some Russian rye bread, or kosher corned beef. Liquor stores, gun stores, little cafés. Empty lots and dark alleys. Drunken men roaming, drunken men in the lots and in the alleys.

Thousands of people in Los Angeles. Any one of them could be a murderer brushing by him as he walked, watching for prowl cars. How could you tell which one: the man with the limping foot over there; the woman with the shopping bag?

You fool, he told himself. The cops will never believe your story now. How can you explain the bus ticket, the packed bags, the running away—except as fleeing from a crime you just committed?

You're looking for an old man you never saw before and someone who killed him. You've got to find the real murderer. Out of a population of a million and a half that should be simple!

In the darkness most shops were shuttered and padlocked. A few hardware and credit shops were still lighted, their proprietors living in the doorways to catch a breeze from the warm summer night.

Charlie paused in one door. "I hear there was some excitement around here?" The man to whom Charlie spoke folded his arms. "Yeah. In the alley down there."

"An old man, wasn't it? Who was he? Who killed him?"

"I don't know. An old wino, that's all. Am *I* worried?"

"Did you see anything?"

"Nothing. I saw blue serge and badges, and sirens I heard."

Charlie thanked him and walked away and the night came in to get him. He felt like stopping people and looking into their faces and saying, "You didn't happen to kill someone an hour ago, did you? No? Thanks, anyhow." On a few steps. Stop again. "Mister, are you a killer?" He haunted every open shop. Nobody had seen from nothing. It was a real hot night, wasn't it? Rain tomorrow, maybe? Would you like to buy a real piece of goods, mister? Step in, have a look!

The popcorn vendor stood at the corner of Temple Street and Boylston. Blue-yellow flame danced in the glass cube and popcorn was trembling within a metal-grid cage. The little dark vendor took Charlie's nickel, and they talked.

"The dead man? Johnny? He drank a lot. He prowled around the alleys here all the time; slept in them at night. Still, there was no reason for nobody to kill him. He didn't have no money." The vendor looked at Charlie with his trembling-flame eyes. "You know him?"

"I'm—very closely related to him."

A trolley car roared down the asphalt hill behind him in a mechanical cataclysm. In that riot of wheels on hard tracks, Charlie rushed with thoughts, saw himself in his drab office totaling up numbers for years, jangling up accounts, fingering reports, Sundays off, half a day Saturday, coming home on loud streetcars through the monotonous streets, meeting Lydia in their forty-a-month coffin where they argued coffee-cocoa-tea, switched radio on-off, conflicted over double features, swore about the heat, damned the cold.

So one night, while thinking about killing Mr. Sternwell, his boss, on the way home, Charlie Guidney changed his life. With the shot of a gun he propelled himself and wife out of a workaday world into change, movement, chaos.

But he hadn't killed anybody. He was disgusted with his imagination. Well, then smart guy, his mind replied, if you aren't insane and not the murderer—*who* is?

He began to walk. He wandered into gunsmiths and hardware stores and swap shops. He asked the only question he could: "Mister, did anyone buy a gun from you today?" he said. "A twenty-two?"

And the answers came back:

"You kidding?" said one. "No," said another. "Hell, no," said a third.

"Don't bother me," said the last one. "It takes a permit to buy a gun. People don't buy guns every day."

"Did anyone ask to *see* your guns? Anyone at all?" pleaded Charlie.

"One or two people. I don't remember."

"Are any of your guns missing?"

The man looked annoyed. "No."

He went back to the other dealers, one by one. He was getting tired. "Are any of your guns missing?" he asked.

"Hold on just a minute," said the proprietor of the first shop he'd started with. "I don't think so, but—" He counted the clutter of guns in his glass case. "Only eight. There should be nine. I'll count again. One, two, three—" He choked and his eyes bulged. "I'll be damned, one's gone!"

"Do you remember who was in here today to look at them?"

"Sure, sure! Only one person. They didn't have a permit. So they couldn't buy the gun. I went back into the little room there and when I came out they were gone. They needed the gun so they swiped it!"

"Can you describe the person?" asked Charlie.

The proprietor then proceeded into a wealth of detail concerning the person responsible for the disappearance of a .22-caliber pistol.

Charlie slapped his hand to his face. His knees gave out from under him. The shop dissolved around him. Finally he got the proprietor back in focus.

"A murderer could steal your gun, shoot someone a few blocks from here, and bring the gun back before you noticed it was missing, couldn't he?"

"Sure, sure, I guess so. But they didn't bring it back. It's still gone."

Charlie was trying to think, a fog in his eyes. "That way a person could get a gun, use it; the police would never trace it; the gunseller would never suspect either. The police wouldn't think to check the guns you've had here for years; they might ask if any were missing, or if you'd sold any twenty-twos, but that's all." He rose unsteadily from the chair.

"Hey, come back here—" said the shopkeeper.

Very paralyzed, not feeling anything, Charlie headed toward home.

On the way he saw a little store lighted up and there were things in the window—certain kinds of weapons for which you needed no license. He went in and laid some money on the counter and when he emerged his hand cuddled the weapon in his right coat pocket. . . .

*   *   *

It was about ten o'clock. Officer Kelly was looking up at those stars over the city, cursing to himself, when he heard footsteps behind him. He turned and almost bumped into Charlie Guidney.

"I guess you'll have your killer this evening, Kelly," Charlie said amiably.

"So there you are!" Kelly grabbed him. "It's a good thing for you, me lad, you came back under your own power!"

"Can I say good-bye to my wife first?"

Kelly hemmed and hawed. "I guess I can let you say good-bye. Go along."

They climbed the dim interior of the house. Charlie put his hand on that very familiar doorknob. "Could you wait outside, Kelly?"

Kelly could. Charlie shut the door. Lydia snapped off the radio, turned to him.

"Oh, Charlie, you're all right. I was afraid they'd shoot—"

"They almost did. They might yet."

She sank upon the couch. "We'll never escape. Charlie, why did you do it?"

"I didn't."

"What?" Her eyes widened.

"I lied. Didn't you guess I was lying from the very first Lydia?"

"Why, no, I didn't," she said.

"And didn't you have a nice setup, my dear wife?"

"I don't understand, Charlie."

"I sent you to buy tickets. All you had to do was stop in a shop that sold guns, ask for some article that would get the owner out of the room a moment, steal the gun, walk down Temple Street, find any one of the dozens of winos and stumblebums that sleep in the alleys there, in the dark, shoot the man, then go on down to the bus depot, buy the tickets, and come home.

"Then when you saw the policeman you pretended hysteria to give me away. A good frame! Except you didn't think I'd escape to check the gunsellers. You planned to return the gun probably tomorrow. Your testimony against me would be devastating. I came home, you would say, and told you I'd killed someone. Exactly what I *did* say, even though I lied. You hoped the police might even shoot me in a struggle. The bus tickets, our packed baggage, my employers not even notified, our friends unaware of our plans—all that was damning evidence against me!"

"Oh, now, Charlie!"

"Me in prison for years, or executed maybe, and you—*free!* Free with your bus tickets anytime you wanted to travel, taking along your friend, Mr. Travis—taking that five thousand dollars from the bank with which to coax him? No more boredom, Lydia?"

He shut his eyes tight. "I'm sorry it worked this way. We could've been happy, trying again. Even when you guessed I lied about the murder, you should've played along. It would have been good, exciting. Have you hated me this much all these years? Didn't you see a change was what we needed to make us over?"

"You're insane!" she cried.

"First," he said, "Lydia, take a look at *this*!"

Yanking the weapon from his pocket he pointed it, advanced on her swiftly. She stared, unbelieving, at it, fell back against the couch, screaming, clawing to escape him.

"Charlie, Charlie, Charlie!" It was like a high whistle shrieking. Something broke, exploded in her. He shoved the weapon closer. "I did it, I did it, I killed him! But take that thing away, take it away!" she sobbed.

The door burst open. Kelly ran in, gun leveled. "Okay, Mr. Guidney, I heard her! Leave her alone. I'll take care of her now. Hand over your weapon!"

Charlie turned, his eyes shut. He held out his hand and dropped the weapon into Kelly's amazed fingers.

The white rat with the shiny pink eyes scampered inside Kelly's hand.

Wake for the Living

There was any amount of banging and hammering for a number of days, along with deliveries of metal parts and oddments that Mr. Charles Braling took into his little workshop with feverish anxiety. He was a dying man, a badly dying man, and he seemed to be in a great hurry, between racking coughs and spitting, to piece together one last invention.

"What are you doing?" inquired his younger brother, Richard

Braling. He had listened with increasing difficulty and much curiosity to that banging and rattling about, and now he stuck his head through the workroom door.

"Go far, far away and let me alone," said Charles Braling, who was seventy, trembly, and wet-lipped most of the time. He trembled nails into place and trembled a hammer down with a weak blow upon a large timber and then stuck a small metal ribbon down into an intricate machine, and, all in all, was having a carnival of labor.

Richard looked on, bitter eyed, for a long moment. There was a hatred between them. It had gone on for some years and now was neither better nor worse for the fact that Charlie was dying. Richard was delighted to know of the impending death, if he thought of it at all. But this busy fervor of his brother's stimulated him.

"Pray tell," he asked, not moving from the door.

"If you must know," snarled old Charles, fitting in an odd thingamabob on the box before him, "I'll be dead in another week and I'm—I'm building my own coffin!"

"A coffin, my dear Charlie; that doesn't *look* like a coffin. A coffin isn't that complex. Come on now, what *are* you up to?"

"I tell you it is a coffin! An odd coffin, yes, but, nevertheless"—the old man moved his fingers around within the large box—"nevertheless a coffin!"

"But it would be easier to buy one."

"Not one like this! You couldn't buy one like this anyplace, ever. Oh, it will be a really fine coffin, all right."

"You're obviously lying." Richard moved forward. "Why, that coffin is a good twelve feet long. Six feet longer than normal size!"

"Oh, yes?" The old man laughed quietly.

"And that transparent top; who ever heard of a coffin lid you can see through? What good is a transparent lid to a corpse?"

"Oh, just never you mind at all," sang the old man heartily. "La!" And he went humming and hammering about the shop.

"This coffin is terribly thick," shouted the younger brother over the din. "Why, it must be five feet thick; how utterly unnecessary!"

"I only wish I might live to patent this amazing coffin," said old Charlie. "It would be a godsend to all the poor peoples of the world. Think how it would eliminate the expense of most funerals. Oh, but, of course, you don't know how it would do that, do you? How silly of me. Well, I shan't tell you. If this coffin could be mass-produced—expensive at first, naturally—but then when you finally get them made in vast quantities, ah, but the money people would save."

"To hell with it!" And the younger brother stormed out of the shop.

It had been an unpleasant life. Young Richard had always been such a bounder he had never had two coins to clink together at one time; all of his money had come from old brother Charlie, who had the indecency to remind him of it at all times. Richard spent many hours with his hobbies; he dearly loved piling up bottles with French wine labels in the garden. "I like the way they *glint*," he often said, sitting and sipping and sipping and sitting. He was the man in the county who could hold the longest gray ash on a fifty-cent cigar for the longest recorded time. And he knew how to hold his hands so his diamonds jangled in the light. But he had not bought the wine, the diamonds, the cigars—no! They were all gifts. He was never allowed to buy anything himself. It was always brought to him and given to him. He had to ask for everything, even writing paper. He considered himself quite a martyr to have put up with taking things from that rickety old brother for so long a time. Everything Charlie ever laid his hand to turned to money; everything Richard ever tried in the way of a leisurely career had failed.

And now here was this old mole of a Charlie whacking out a new invention that would probably bring Charlie additional specie long after his bones were slotted in the earth!

Well, two weeks passed.

One morning the older brother toddled upstairs and stole the insides from the electric phonograph. Another morning he raided the gardener's greenhouse. Still another time he received a delivery from a medical company. It was all young Richard could do to sit and hold his long gray cigar ash steady while these murmuring excursions took place.

"I'm finished!" cried old Charlie on the fourteenth morning, and dropped dead.

Richard finished out his cigar and, without showing his inner excitement, he laid down his cigar with its fine long whitish ash, two inches long, a real record, and arose.

He walked to the window and watched the sunlight playfully

glittering among the fat beetlelike champagne bottles in the garden.

He looked toward the top of the stairs where dear old brother Charlie lay peacefully sprawled against the banister. Then he walked to the phone and perfunctorily dialed a number.

"Hello, Green Lawn Mortuary? This is the Braling residence. Will you send around a wicker, please? Yes. For brother Charlie. Yes. Thank you. Thank you."

As the mortuary people were taking brother Charles out in their wicker, they received instructions. "Ordinary casket," said young Richard. "No funeral service. Put him in a pine coffin. He would have preferred it that way—simple. Good-bye."

"Now!" said Richard, rubbing his hands together. "We shall see about this 'coffin' built by dear Charlie. I do not suppose he will realize he is not being buried in his 'special' box. Ah."

He entered the downstairs shop.

The coffin sat before some wide-flung French windows, the lid shut, complete and neat, all put together like the fine innards of a Swiss watch. It was vast, and it rested upon a long long table with rollers beneath for easy maneuvering.

The coffin interior, as he peered through the glass lid, was six feet long. There must be a good three feet of false body at both head and foot of the coffin, then. Three feet at each end, which, covered by secret panels that he must find some way of opening, might very well reveal—exactly what?

Money, of course. It would be just like Charlie to suck his riches into his grave with himself, leaving Richard with not a cent to buy a bottle with. The old tightwad!

He raised the glass lid and felt about, but found no hidden buttons. There was a small sign studiously inked on white paper, thumbtacked to the side of the satin-lined box. It said:

THE BRALING ECONOMY CASKET
Simple to operate. Can be used again and again by mortician and families with one eye to the future.

Richard snorted thinly. Who did Charlie think he was fooling? There was more writing:

DIRECTIONS: SIMPLY PLACE BODY IN COFFIN—

What a fool thing to say. Put body in coffin! Naturally! How else would one go about it? He peered intently and finished out the directions:

SIMPLY PLACE BODY IN COFFIN—AND MUSIC WILL START.

"It can't be!" Richard gaped at the sign. "Don't tell me all this work has been for a—" He went to the open door of the shop, walked out upon the tiled terrace, and called to the gardener in his greenhouse. "Rogers!" The gardener stuck his head out. "What time is it?" asked Richard.

"Twelve o'clock, sir," replied Rogers.

"Well, at twelve fifteen, you come up here and check to see if everything is all right, Rogers."

"Yes, sir," said the gardener.

Richard turned and walked back into the shop. "We'll find out—" he said quietly.

There would be no harm in lying in the box, testing it. He noticed small ventilating holes in the sides. Even if the lid were closed down there'd be air. And Rogers would be up in a moment or two. Simply place body in coffin—and music will start. Really, how naive of old Charlie. Richard hoisted himself up.

He was like a man getting into a bathtub. He felt naked and watched over. He put one shiny shoe into the coffin, and crooked his knee and eased himself up and made some little remark to nobody in particular; then he put his other knee and foot and crouched there, as if undecided about the temperature of the bath water. Edging himself about, chuckling softly, he lay down, pretending to himself—"for it was fun pretending"—that he was dead, that people were dropping tears on him, that candles were fuming and illuminating, and that the world was stopped in mid-stride because of his passing. He put on a long pale expression, shut his eyes, holding back the laughter in himself behind pressed, quivering lips. He folded his hands and decided they felt waxen and cold.

Whirr! Spung! Something whispered inside the box wall. *Spung!* The lid slammed down on him!

From outside, if one had just come into the room, one would have imagined a wild man was kicking, pounding, blathering, and shrieking inside a closet! There was a sound of a body dancing and cavorting. There was a thudding of flesh and fists.

There was a squeaking and a kind of wind from a frightened man's lungs. There was a rustling like paper and a shrilling as of many pipes simultaneously played. Then there was a real fine scream. Then—silence.

Richard Braling lay in the coffin and relaxed. He let loose all his muscles. He began to chuckle. The smell of the box was not unpleasant. Through the little perforations he drew more than enough air to live comfortably on. He need only push gently up with his hands, with none of this kicking and screaming, and the lid would open. One must be calm. He flexed his arms.

The lid was locked.

Well, still there was no danger. Rogers would be up in a minute or two. There was nothing to fear.

The music began to play.

It seemed to come from somewhere inside the head of the coffin. It was fine music. Organ music, very slow and melancholy, typical of Gothic arches and long black tapers. It smelled of earth and whispers. It echoed high between stone walls. It was so sad that one almost cried listening to it. It was music of potted plants and crimson-and-blue stained-glass windows. It was late sun at twilight and a cold wind blowing. It was a dawn with only fog and a faraway foghorn moaning.

"Charlie, Charlie, Charlie, you old fool, you! So this is your odd coffin!" Tears of laughter welled into Richard's eyes. "Nothing more than a coffin which plays its own dirge. Oh, my sainted grandma!"

He lay and listened critically, for it was beautiful music and there was nothing he could do until Rogers came up and let him out. His eyes roved aimlessly; his fingers tapped soft little rhythms on the satin cushions. He crossed his legs idly. Through the glass lid he saw sunlight shooting through the French windows, dust particles dancing on it. It was a lovely blue day with wisps of clouds overhead.

The sermon began.

The organ music quieted and a gentle voice said: "We are gathered together, those who loved and those who knew the deceased, to give him our homage and our due—"

"Charlie, bless you, that's *your* voice!" Richard was delighted. A mechanical, transcribed funeral, by God! Organ music and lecture, on records! And Charlie giving his own oration for himself!

The soft voice said, "We who knew and loved him are grieved at the passing of—"

"What was *that*?" Richard raised himself, startled. He didn't quite believe what he had heard. He repeated it to himself just the way he had heard it.

"We who knew and loved him are grieved at the passing of Richard Braling."

That's what the voice had said.

"Richard Braling," said the man in the coffin. "Why, *I'm* Richard Braling."

A slip of the tongue, naturally. Merely a slip. Charlie had meant to say *Charles* Braling. Certainly. Yes. Of course. Yes. Certainly. Yes. Naturally. Yes.

"Richard was a fine man," said the voice, talking on. "We shall see no finer in our time."

"My name, *again*!"

Richard began to move about uneasily in the coffin.

Why didn't Rogers come?

It was hardly a mistake, using that name twice. Richard Braling. Richard Braling. We are gathered here. We shall miss . . . We are grieved. No finer man. No finer in our time. We are gathered here. The deceased. Richard Braling. *Richard* Braling.

Whirrrr! Spunng!

Flowers! Six dozen bright blue, red, yellow, sun-brilliant flowers leaped up from behind the coffin on concealed springs!

The sweet odor of fresh-cut flowers filled the coffin. The flowers swayed gently before his amazed vision, tapping silently on the glass lid. Others sprang up, and up, until the coffin was banked with petals and color and sweet odors. Gardenias and dahlias and petunias and daffodils, trembling and shining.

"Rogers!"

The sermon continued.

". . . Richard Braling, in his life, was a connoisseur of great and good things. . . ."

The music sighed, rose, and fell, distantly.

". . . Richard Braling savored of life as one savors of a rare wine, holding it upon the lips. . . ."

A small panel in the side of the box flipped open. A swift bright metal arm snatched out. A needle stabbed Richard in the thorax, not very deeply. He screamed. The needle shot him full of a colored liquid before he could seize it. Then it popped back into a receptacle and the panel snapped shut.

"Rogers!"

A growing numbness. Suddenly he could not move his fingers or his arms or turn his head. His legs were cold and limp.

"Richard Braling loved beautiful things. Music. Flowers," said the voice.

Rogers!

This time he did not scream it. He could only think it. His tongue was motionless in his anesthetized mouth.

Another panel opened. Metal forceps issued forth on steel arms. His left wrist was pierced by a huge sucking needle.

His blood was being drained from his body.

He heard a little pump working somewhere.

". . . Richard Braling will be missed among us. . . ."

The organ sobbed and murmured.

The flowers looked down upon him, nodding their bright-petaled heads. Six candles, black and slender, rose up out of hidden receptacles and stood behind the flowers, flickering and glowing.

Another pump started to work. While his blood drained out one side of his body, his right wrist was punctured, held, a needle shoved into it, and the second pump began to force formaldehyde into him.

Pump, pause, *pump*, pause, *pump*, pause, *pump*, pause.

The coffin moved.

A small motor popped and chugged. The room drifted by on either side of him. Little wheels revolved. No pallbearers were necessary. The flowers swayed as the casket moved gently out upon the terrace under a blue clear sky.

Pump, pause. *Pump*, pause.

"Richard Braling will be missed by all his . . ."

Sweet soft music.

Pump, pause.

"Ah, sweet mystery of life, at last. . . ." Singing.

"Braling, the gourmet . . ."

"Ah, I know at last the secret of it all. . . ."

Staring, staring, his eyes egg-blind, at the little card out of the corners of his eyes:

THE BRALING ECONOMY CASKET
DIRECTIONS: SIMPLY PLACE BODY IN COFFIN—
AND MUSIC WILL START.

A tree swung by overhead. The coffin rolled gently through the garden, behind some bushes, carrying the voice and the music with it.

"Now it is the time when we must consign this part of this man to the earth. . . ."

Little shining spades leaped out of the sides of the casket.

They began to dig.

He saw the spades toss up dirt. The coffin settled. Bumped, settled, dug, bumped, and settled, dug, bumped, and settled again.

Pump, pause, *pump*, pause, *pump*, pause, *pump*, pause.

"Ashes to ashes, dust to dust. . . ."

The flowers glistened and waved. The box was deep. The music played.

The last thing Richard Braling saw was the spading arms of the Braling Economy Casket reaching up and pulling the hole in after it.

"Richard Braling, Richard Braling, Richard Braling, Richard Braling, Richard Braling. . . ."

The record was stuck.

Nobody minded. Nobody was listening.

"I'm Not So Dumb!"

Oh, I'm not so dumb. No, sir. When those men at Spaulding's Corner said there was a dead man hereabouts, you think I ran quick to the Sheriff's office to give in the news?

You got another think coming. I turned around and walked off from them men, looking over my shoulder every second or so to see if they was smiling after me, their eyes shining with a prank, and I went to stare at the body first. It was Mr. Simmons's body in that empty-echoed farmhouse of his where the green weeds grew thick for years and there was a larkspur, bluebird sprouts, and morning-fires fringing the path. I tromped up to the door, knocked, and when nobody said they was home, I squeaked the door open and looked in.

Only then did I get going for the Sheriff.

On the way some kids threw rocks at me and laughed.

I met the Sheriff coming. When I told him he said yes, yes, he knew all about it, get outa the way! and I shied off, letting him and Mr. Crockwell smelling of farm dirt and Mr. Willis smelling of hardware hinges and Jamie MacHugh smelling of soap and scent and Mr. Duffy smelling of bar beer past.

When I got back to the lonely gray house they were inside bending around like a labor crew working a ditch. Can I come in, I wondered, and they grumbled no, no, go away, you would only be underfoot, Peter.

That's the way it is. People always shake me to one side, chortling at me. Those folks who told me about the body, you know what they expected? Expected me to call the Sheriff without stopping to see if they was lying or not. Not me, not anymore. I realized what went on last spring when they sent me jogging for a skyhook and shore line for the twenty-seventh time in as many years; and when I sweated all the way down the shore curve to Wembley's Pier to fetch a pentagonal monkey wrench which I never found in all my tries from the age of seventeen on up to now.

So I fooled them this time by checking first and then running for help.

The Sheriff slouched out of the house half an hour later, shaking his dusty head. "Poor Mr. Simmons, his head is all rucked in like the skin of a rusted potbelly stove."

"Oh?" I asked.

The Sheriff flickered a mean yellow glance at me, switching his mustache around on his thin upper lip, balancing it. "You damn right it is."

"A murder mystery, hunh?" I asked.

"I won't say it's a mystery," said the Sheriff.

"You know who done it?" I asked.

"Not exactly, and shut up," snapped the Sheriff, thumb-rolling a cigarette; and sucked it into half ash with his first flame. "I'm thinking."

"Can I help?" I asked.

"You," snorted the Sheriff, looking up at me on top of my mountain of bones and body, "help? Ha!"

Everybody laughed, holding rib bones like bundles of breathing sticks and blowing out cheeks and glittering their sharp shiny eyes. Me help, that was sure something to tickle.

Mr. Crockwell, he was the farmer man, he laughed, and Mr.

Willis, he was the hardware-store man and tough as a rail spike, he laughed like tapping a sledge on a beam iron, and Mr. Duffy's Irish bartender laugh made his tongue jig around pink in his mouth; and Jamie MacHugh, who would run away if you yelled boo, he laughed too.

"I been reading Sherlock Holmes," I said.

The Sheriff raked me over. "Since when you reading?"

"I can read, never mind," I said.

"Think you can solve mysteries, eh?" cried the Sheriff. "Get the hell away afore I boot the big rump off you!"

"Leave him be, Sheriff," laughed Jamie MacHugh, waving one hand. He clicked his tongue at me. "You're a first-rate sleuth, ain't you, Peter?"

I blinked at him six times.

"Sleuth, detective, Sherlock Holmes, I mean," said Jamie MacHugh.

"Oh," I said.

"Why, why-high," laughed Jamie MacHugh, "I'd bet my money on big Peter here any day, *ann-eee* day! Strong, strapping lad, Sheriff. He could solve this case with one shuffle of his big left shoe, couldn't he, men?"

Mr. Crockwell winked at Mr. Willis and Mr. Willis tonked a laugh out like cleaning your pipe on a flat stone, and everybody shot little sly glances at the Sheriff, nudging one another's ribs and chuckling.

"Sure, I'd bet good money any autumn on Peter there. Here's fifty cents says Peter can solve the case afore the Sheriff!" said Jamie.

"Now, look here!" bellowed the Sheriff, standing stiff.

"Here's seventy cents says the same," drawled Mr. Willis.

And here came round money silver shining, and green money like little wings flapping on their hairy hands.

The Sheriff kicked a boot angrily. "Odd dammit. No feeble-minded giant can solve any murder case with me around!"

Jamie MacHugh tilted back and forth on his heels. "Scared?"

"Hell's gate, no! But you're all riding my goat!"

"We mean it. Here's our money, Sheriff; you meeting it?"

The Sheriff crackled he sure as hell would, and did. Everybody boomed out laughter like on bass drums and with brass trumpets. Somebody slapped me on the back but I didn't feel it. Someone yelled for me to go in there and show him. Peter, show him, but it was all underwater, far away. Blood pounded around on big red boots in my ears, kicking my brain back and forth like a wrinkled football.

The Sheriff looked at me. I looked at him with my heavy hands hanging. He laughed right out.

"God, I'll solve this case before Peter has time to open his mouth for spit!"

The Sheriff wouldn't let me be in the room with the corpse unless I stood on one leg and put both hands out in the air. I had to do it. The others said it was fair. I did it. I must have stood there during most the time we talked, on one leg, hands out to balance, and them snickering when I toppled.

"Well," I said, over the corpse, "he's dead."

"Brilliant!" Jamie MacHugh had a bone of laughter caught in his throat, choking him.

"And he's been head-bashed," I said, "with a heavy thing."

"Colossal! Wonderful!" spluttered Jamie.

"And no woman done it," I said. "Because a woman couldn't have done it so heavy and hard."

Jamie laughed less. "True enough." He glanced at the others, eyebrows up a tremor. "That's true; we didn't think of that."

"That counts out all females," I said.

Mr. Crockwell teased the Sheriff. "You didn't say *that*, Sheriff."

The Sheriff's cigarette hissed sparks in a Fourth of July pinwheel. "I was *going* to say it! Damn, anyone can see a woman didn't do it! Peter, you go stand in the corner and do your talking!"

I stood in the corner on one foot.

"And—" I said.

"Shut up," said the Sheriff. "You've had your say, let me have mine." He hitched up his trousers on his rump. Silence. The Sheriff scowled. "Well, like he says, the man's dead, head stove in, and a woman didn't do it and—"

"Ha-ha," said Mr. Crockwell.

The Sheriff shot him a blazing look. Mr. Crockwell covered his mouth with his hand.

"And the body's been dead twenty-four hours," I said, sniffing.

"Any dimwit knows that!" yelled the Sheriff.

"You didn't say that before," said James MacHugh.

"Do I have to say, can't I think a few?"

I looked around the empty room. Mr. Simmons was a strange man, living alone with no furniture in the house and only carpets here and there, and one cot upstairs. Didn't want to spend money on stuff. Saved it.

I said, "There wasn't much fuss or fight; nothing's upset. Must've been killed by someone he trusted."

The Sheriff started to swear but Jamie MacHugh said for him to let me talk, this was damn interesting. The others said so too. I smiled. I closed my eyes, grinning soft, and opened them again and everyone looked at me for the first time in my life as if I was good enough to stand beside them. I stepped from the corner, slowly.

I crouched beside Mr. Simmons, looking. He was blood ripe. The Sheriff quick followed, imitating me, on his knees. I peered close. The Sheriff peered close. I fussed with the rug. Sheriff fussed with the rug. I smoothed Mr. Simmons's right sleeve. Guess who smoothed Mr. Simmons's left sleeve? I made a humming sound like a comb and tissue in my throat. The Sheriff ground his teeth together. Everybody stood high and sweating sour in the summer-heated quiet.

"What was that about him being murdered by a friend?" Mr. Crockwell wanted to know.

"Sure," I said. "Someone he trusted, no commotion."

"That's right," said Mr. Willis, who didn't speak much.

Everybody said it was right, all right.

"Now," I said, "what people didn't like the cold man here?"

The Sheriff's voice was high and stringy with irritation. "Simmons wasn't liked by many. Always fightin' with folks, tetchy-like."

I looked at the men, wondering which one I could detect to be the murderer. My eyes kept snapping in rubber-band moves to Jamie MacHugh. Jamie always was flighty. You lost your match-box and stared at Jamie, he'd whine, guilty, "I didn't take it." If you dropped a nickel and it went away Jamie'd say, "I didn't do it!"

Funny. Something scared him as a kid, all the time he felt guilty, whether or not he was. So I couldn't help but see him now, and go up and down him with my eyes, him so nervous and losing his head over things. Just opposite of Hardware Willis, who would stand rock stiff while lightning bounced around him.

"I heard Jamie say Mr. Simmons should be killed," I said.

Jamie opened his eyes. "I never said that. And if I did, you know how you say things you never mean."

"I heard you say it, anyways."

"Now, now, now," said Jamie three times. "You, you, you are not Sheriff for this city, city. You just shut your trap."

The Sheriff fox-grinned. "What's the matter with you, Jamie? Second ago you was egging Peter on, all het up for his side."

"I don't want anybody accusing me, that's all, you big slob," said Jamie to me. "Go stand on one foot in the corner!"

I didn't blink my eyes. "I heard you say Mr. Simmons should be dead."

"You look sort of nervous, Jamie?" remarked the Sheriff.

"I remember," said Mr. Willis. "You did say that, Jamie. Say, Peter, you got a good memory." He nodded at me smartly.

"I bet fingerprints of Jamie are around here," I said.

"Sure," cried Jamie, pale. "Sure, they're here. I was here early yesterday afternoon to try and get back my thirty dollars from that damn scoundrel lying limp on the floor, you elephant!"

"You see," I said. "He was here. His fingerprints all around like ants at a picnic." And I added, "I bet if we looked in his pocket we'd find Mr. Simmons's wallet full of money, I bet we would."

"Nobody looks through my pockets!"

"I'll do it," I said.

"No," said Jamie.

"Sheriff," I said.

The Sheriff looked at me, looked at Jamie. "Jamie," he said.

"Sheriff," said Jamie.

"Who was it picked me to solve this case?" I said. "Jamie did, Sheriff."

The Sheriff's cigarette hung cold on his lip, twitching. "That's right."

"Why'd he want me solving it, Sheriff?" I asked, and answered, "Because he thought I'd only kick up mud in the creek, rile you so you wouldn't get nothing done."

"Well odd damn, imagine that," murmured the others, moving back.

The Sheriff squinted tight.

"Peter, I got to admit, you got something. Jamie was sure hot to bring you up to mess around. He started them goddamn bets. Irritated me with you until I can't see beans from breakfast!"

"Yes," I said.

"Well now, I didn't kill nobody, I didn't sic Peter on you for that purpose, Sheriff, oh, no, I didn't," said Jamie MacHugh, sweat gobbering out his head like water from them fancy park sprinkling systems in the concrete skulls of them pretty naked women statues.

The Sheriff said, "Let Peter search you."

Jamie said no, as I grabbed his wrists with one big hand and held them while I put my other hand in his rear pants pocket and pulled out the dead man's wallet.

"No," whispered Jamie like a ghost.

I let him go. He swung around next thing, gibbering, and slammed out the door, crying, before anybody could stop him.

"Go get him, Peter!" everybody yelled.

"You really want me to?" I asked. "You're not kidding like with the skyhook and shore line?"

"No, no," they cried. "Get him!"

I thundered out the door and ran after Jamie in the hot sun over a green hill, through a little woods. What if Jamie gets away, I thought. No, he can't do that. I'll run fast.

Just near the edge of town I caught up with Jamie.

He never should have tried to fight me.

Crunch.

So now people sit around the Sheriff's office on summer evenings dangling their shoes in a little laced pattern and speaking with smoke blowing from their easy mouths about how the Sheriff let me solve the case. And the Sheriff says he don't care, he's just as pleased that I caught the criminal as if he'd done it himself; but the Sheriff winces when he says this.

Kids on the street don't kick my shins no more or throw rocks at me. They come ask to hold my hands as we walk downtown. They ask me to tell how I did it. Even ladies in pretty blue or green dresses look over back fences and ask. And I shine up the battered silver star the Sheriff had left over from twenty years ago, catch it on my chest where it sparkles, and I tell everybody again how I solved the Simmons case and caught the murderer Jamie MacHugh, who broke his neck trying to get out of my hands.

Nobody ever tells me to run get a skyhook or shore line or a left-handed screwdriver no more. They think my silences are thinking ones. Men nod at me from cars and say hello Peter and they don't laugh so much, they sort of admire me, and just this morning asked if I intended solving any more cases.

I'm very happy. Happier than in all my days. I'm certainly

glad now that Mr. Simmons died and I had a chance to catch
Jamie MacHugh that way. No telling how much longer these
people might have pestered me.

And if you'll promise, cross your heart, hope to die, spit over
your left shoulder, not to tell nobody, I'll let you in on a little
secret.

I killed Mr. Simmons myself.

You understand why, don't you?

As I said at the beginning—I'm not so dumb.

The Trunk Lady

Johnny Menlo kicked his shoes and sat down hard on the bottom
of the attic stairs. His teacher, his special private tutor, was *not*
coming after all. So he *wouldn't* have someone in the house all to
himself.

Downstairs the party was running full blast. The sounds of it
came up mockingly—the laughter, the cocktail shakers clinking,
the music. Johnny thought he had got away from its sounds,
sitting way up here, so lonely. His teacher was supposed to have
come today. She hadn't.

Mom and Dad, so busy drinking with people, gave Johnny the
kind of look you give your shadow.

Johnny retreated farther up the stairs into the complete musty
asylum of the abandoned attic. Even up here the dust and warm
afternoon quiet was rustled by the party noises from below.

Johnny glanced around. There were four trunks sitting under
veils of webs in the dim corners. A sunbeam fell through a small
dirty window, lighted things for Johnny's curious blue eyes.

The trunk in the north corner, for instance. It was always
locked, the key hidden somewhere. The hasps were down now,
but the brass tongue in the middle was flipped up, unlocked.

Johnny walked to the trunk and pried the hasps open. He
pulled the lid up. Suddenly the attic was very cold.

She was inside.

Curled up, her body was, young, pretty. Her slender face was
like chalk etched against the blackboard of her hair. Johnny

gasped, but not too loudly. He held onto the trunk rim. Only her perfume was still alive. She looked as lonely and abandoned as he felt. He sympathized. Attics are places for things neglected and forgotten.

Death had apparently come through suffocation. Someone had slammed the heavy airtight lid down upon her curled loveliness. Her hand was like a white fragment of it against her filmy pink cocktail dress.

A moment later he found the balled wad of paper on the floor. It was only part of a note, with *her* writing on it.

> —you've got to make it up to me, the way I've been treated. It shouldn't be difficult. I could be Johnny's teacher. That would explain my presence in the house to everyone. ELLIE.

He looked at her quiet beauty. It seemed as if she might have fallen asleep during the cocktail party and had been carried here and the lid slammed down upon her while in slumber!

The attic dimness moved in about Johnny, shaking him, then drawing out, leaving him numbed and saying, "Are you my teacher? Are you the one I was going to have for myself alone? But they—they killed you? Why should anyone kill my teacher?"

Another thought rushed the first away. He, Johnny Menlo, of the society Menlos, had found a body, hadn't he? *Sure.* His eyes widened. Mom and Dad'd *have* to notice him now, more often.

Why, even Grandma would quit playing chess all day with Uncle Flinny, choke on her brandy, stare at him through thick glasses, and cry, "My God, child, your snooping finally came to a profit, did it?"

Sure! Sure! Johnny blinked rapidly, his heart pounding.

Cousin William might even *faint* at the news!

He, Johnny Menlo, had found the body. Pictures in the papers of *himself* instead of Mother beaming out of the society columns!

Hiding the note in his pocket, Johnny took one last long look at the pretty lashes and the pink lips and the dark black hair of the Trunk Lady. He closed the lid on her sleeping.

He'd scream. Yes, at the top of the grand stairs. Scream till the sky fell down, and the party with it! Scream!

His screaming wasn't bad at all.

Down the stairs, across the hall, making a path with his

screaming through the startled ranks of people, Johnny reached Mother's glittering cocktail gown and held onto it very tightly.

"Johnny, Johnny, why are you downstairs? What's the matter? I told you—" Mother's girl-face looked down over the glitter. He grabbed another fistful of spangles. He yelled it:

"Mom, there's a body in the attic!"

Like faces in a football stadium, the faces watching them. Mother stiffened, then relaxed. "Let go my dress, darling, you'll get it dirty. Look at your hands, cobwebs and all. Now run up to your room like a good boy." She patted his head.

"But Mom!" he wailed. "There's a body—"

"Good Lord," someone murmured. "Just like his father."

Johnny spun angrily. "You shut up! There is *so* a body!"

Mother didn't see him. She looked at her guests, and all Johnny could see was her lovely swanlike throat, the firm chin with the pulse beating under it, her fingers fixing the chestnut shine of hair swept up from her ears.

"Please forgive Johnny," she was saying. "Children are so imaginative, aren't they?"

Her chin came down. There was no light in her blue eyes. "You'd better go upstairs, Johnny."

"Oh, but, Mom—"

His world was crashing. The spangles slipped from between his fingers. He suddenly hated everyone at the party looking at him.

"You heard what your mother said, General."

That was Dad's resonant voice and it meant the fight was lost. Johnny jerked around, shot one last glare at the people, and ran upstairs, tears coming into his eyes.

He twisted the brass knob of Grandma's door. She sat playing chess with Uncle Flinny before the great glaring window. Sunlight glinted off her glasses. She hardly looked up.

"Pardon me, Granny, but—"

She shifted her cane against her thin knee. "Well?"

"There's a body in the attic and nobody'll believe me—"

"Go away, Johnny!"

"But," he cried, "there's a body!"

"We know it, we know it! Now run get Cousin William a bottle of cognac! Scat! Go!"

Johnny went and got the cognac from the wine pantry, rapped on Cousin William's door, and thought he heard indrawn breath behind the paneling. Then Cousin William whispered quickly.

"Who's there?"

"Cognac."

"Oh, fine, fine!" Cousin William's weak-chinned, rabbity face poked out, his soft hands darting after the offered liquor. "Thank God. Now go away and let me get drunk!"

The door slammed, but before it did Johnny got a brief glimpse of the cluttered, disorderly interior of Cousin William's Designing Room—the mannequins standing stiff around with brilliant silks draped, cut, fixed to them, watercolor sketches of capes, hats, suits, thumbtacked to the plaster walls. Bright heaps of woolens, threaded spools, and all. The door cut it off, locked it in, and Cousin William was nervously attending his cognac behind the shining knob.

Johnny eyed the hall phone, his anger simmering. He thought of Mom and Dad dancing, Uncle Flinny and Grandma playing their eternal chess, Cousin William drinking—and himself a stranger in this great old echoing house. He snatched up the phone.

"Uh—I want—that is—give me the police station."

Another deep voice cut in on the operator's.

"Hang up the phone, Johnny. Hang up and go to bed." Dad's very resonant and cultured voice.

Johnny hung up slowly. So this was his reward for finding a body? He sat and cried with frustration. He felt like the lady in the trunk, the lid slammed in his face by five people! *Slammed!*

He was twisting in bed when Uncle Flinny softly opened the door and poked his curly, soft-haired, big head into the room. His eyes were round, black, gentle, peaceful-looking. He came in with slow, soft movements, sat on the edge of the chair beside the bed like a very quiet little bird. He folded his birdlike fingers.

"Since you're retiring early," he said, "I thought I'd better come tell your bedtime story early too. Yes?"

Johnny felt himself too old for stories. Being raised in such an adult house with few contacts with children, and having an advanced education with such mature talk and mature people around, he felt himself far above bedtime stories. But he resigned himself, sighed, and said, "Okay, Uncle Flinny. Go ahead. Shoot."

Uncle Flinny held onto his neatly pressed black trousers at the knees as if they'd explode and slowly pieced out his tale.

"Well, once there was a young woman who was very beautiful—"

Oh-oh! Johnny'd heard this story a thousand times before. He fidgeted. *A body in the attic and he had to listen to this.*

"And," continued Uncle Flinny, "this beautiful young girl fell in love with and married a young knight. They lived happily for years. Until one day a Dark One kidnapped the beautiful woman and ran away with her." Uncle Flinny looked sad and old.

"And then the husband came home," prompted Johnny.

Uncle Flinny didn't hear him at all. He just kept talking in a funny soft monotone. "The husband chased the Dark One into a Dark Land. But no matter how hard he pleaded, or tried to catch up with the Dark One, he never could. His wife was gone forever. Forever."

Uncle Flinny's breathing was uneven, harsh. His eyes glowed dark, round. His lips trembled. He wasn't himself. He was someone else off a million miles in that Dark Land. He seized his knees tighter and bent over them.

"But the husband searched and searched, vowing that someday he would find and kill the Dark One, and, wonder of wonders, he did! He struck the Dark One down, but oh God above, after striking the Dark One he found that somehow the Dark One looked like his beautiful wife! And he found to his horror that he himself was growing—darker and darker. . . ."

The end. Johnny hoped there'd be no more. Uncle Flinny sat sighing in the atmosphere he'd built from the story. He'd forgotten Johnny was a part of the room. His hands were shaking and he was out of breath. He just sat there.

Johnny shivered for no reason he knew. "Thanks. Thanks very much, Uncle Flinny," he said. "Thanks for the swell story."

Uncle Flinny turned blind eyes. "Unh?" He relaxed, recognizing Johnny. "Oh, yes. Anytime. Anytime at all."

"You sure get steamed up, Uncle Flinny."

Uncle Flinny quietly opened the door. "Good night, Johnny."

"Oh, Uncle!"

"Yes?"

Johnny stopped himself. "Never mind."

Uncle Flinny shuffled out. The door closed gently.

Johnny bounced furiously on the springs. "The things I've had to do the last few days, to keep this family happy! Listen to Uncle Flinny—wait on Grandma—get out of the way of Mother—obey Father. And keep Cousin William drunk. Guh!"

He was tired of them all. For a change why not some attention for *himself*? He could hear the party continuing downstairs. Slipping from bed, he listened against the door.

In the next hour he heard all varieties of feet upon the stairs, like heartbeats in the house. The crisp, snapping moves of Grandma and her pert cane feeling the layers of altitude. The shuffle of Uncle Flinny. The even long and easy stride of Dad. The glide of Mother. The nervous, uneasy tripping of Cousin William.

And there were voices talking, some arguing, some urging, others hysterical, mixed—Dad calm, Mother criticizing, Grandma stern, Cousin William whimpering, Uncle Flinny quiet. Once or twice the attic door creaked.

No one even came near Johnny's room. The party still existed downstairs, unaware of all this badinage. Night was coming swiftly on with an autumn chill.

Finally it was quiet again. Johnny hurried up the dark, dusty stairs into the attic, heart beating quickly. He'd show *them*!

The trunk was not heavy, strangely enough. One could easily tip it toward the stairs, and the stairs led down to the landing. One more push from the landing and down, down, down into the living room. Yes. They'd have to believe him now!

Johnny tipped the trunk.

People were talking. Music was playing on the radio-phonograph. Mom and Dad mingled with the bright swarm, flames about which social moths beat their sophisticated wings.

It was in the very midst of these things that Johnny's small voice made some sort of declaration from atop the hall staircase. He yelled loudly.

"Mom! Dad!"

Everybody turned and looked, as at a reception.

The woman came down the stairs.

Somebody had to scream. It sounded almost like Cousin William. But everybody watched, falling back, as the woman came down the stairs in her filmy cocktail dress. Well, she didn't exactly *come* down. She *rolled*.

Over and over, arms limp, legs limp, head bobbing, hair flailing in a dark whip, around and down, softly nudging the steps, jointless, boneless, and lifeless. When she reached the bottom Johnny was right after her.

"I told you, Mother! Dad, I found her again! I found her!"

He'd always and forever remember Mother's face in that moment and the way she said his name. "Johnny . . . !" And the way she struck him across the face.

Someone said, "Call the police!"

Someone else had the phone, ticking it. Dad's face was like a wet gray calm, suddenly old and tired. Johnny fell back from Mother's blow, holding to the banister. He thought She's never hit me before. Never before. Always kind and good, thoughtless at times, maybe, but she never went and hit me before today.

Then it happened. Everybody began laughing. Somebody pointed at the body, their faces got red, and they laughed. Dad laughed, too, with everything but his eyes.

"I'll be damned," someone said. "So that's the body the child found upstairs?"

"A mannequin!" someone declared.

"Of course. A store-window dummy. Easy to see how a child might think it a body." Again, laughter. Lots of it.

"A mannequin." The laughter grew and grew upon itself.

Johnny, trembling, crept and bent and touched the outflung hand, pulled away, touched it again, felt tremblingly the hard cold plastic.

"That's not the body," he said, looking up, bewildered. He shook his head, moving back. "That's not the body at all," he said. "The other body was different. Warmish and soft. It was a real woman!"

"Johnny!"

Dad had stopped smiling. Mother clenched a fist with white knuckles.

Johnny said, "Just the same, it's not the one!" He began to cry. Tears came as on the windshield of a car in a storm, erasing the world in wet portions. "Just the same, she was dead and she wasn't made of plaster!"

The house was full of sounds late that night. People talking in locked rooms. Arguments. Once he thought he heard Cousin William sobbing. Feet climbed stairs, lights clicked on and off. Finally everyone was in bed, and Johnny sat up, throwing back the covers. That clicking was Cousin William double-locking his door. Why? . . . Because someone or something was walking around in the house?

Johnny started. His doorknob was turning. The door pushed open a few inches. Someone was standing there in the darkness, looking in. A heart is an erratic thing. Like mercury. It scurries all over a person's insides. Johnny's heart was like mercury.

The door remained open. The shadow remained standing in the doorway, staring, looking in. Johnny said nothing. Then, very matter-of-factly, the shadow withdrew, and the door closed.

Rapping the lock home hard, Johnny threw his breath out and lay trembling on the door. Pressure from outside a moment later, from that withdrawn shadow, could not force the bolt. Johnny listened. The shadow went away.

Very weakly Johnny returned to bed, trembling. "Mom! Mom," he said to himself, "are you mad at me for making a scene before all of society? Would *you* kill me, Mom? Was there something about the Trunk Lady and Dad, something you didn't like, and did *you* kill her because of it? Now, when I come around, in the way, what will you do to me? Oh, Mom, it *can't* be you!"

"Dad," he said, the same way, "*you* made me hang up the phone. Are *you* afraid it will get out too? Afraid of your business, your money, your reputation at the club, huh, Dad? Was that you standing in the door, silent and dark and thinking? You've been my favorite in the family. But now, today, you're so quiet and *you* don't even look at me."

Cousin William. He could have changed the bodies, tried to fool Johnny. He could have put one of the mannequins in the trunk instead. Was she Cousin William's girlfriend? Was she causing trouble somehow? Or was Cousin William just afraid for his reputation? Him and his mannequins and his famous, expensive dresses for expensive women. Was it him, twisting the doorknob a moment ago?

Maybe it was Uncle Flinny, with his bedtime stories and his quiet ways. He loved Mother so much—his sister. He'd do anything for her or Dad or Grandma or Cousin William. Would he kill for her or Dad or the others to keep this house whole, intact and untouched?

Grandma. Played her cold game of chess day by day and drank her brandy neat. Her whole life was keeping the house moving together. Her whole life was society and position and taste. What if someone came into the house and tried to do all the ordering instead of her? What would she do to her?

All of them! All of them!

Johnny sank shivering back on the springs. A woman walked

into a big mothballed old mansion like this and suddenly everyone was afraid. Just *one* woman.

On the table beside his bed Johnny groped and found the note
he'd discovered in the attic dust. He felt of it, and read it again in
his mind:

> —you've got to make it up to me, the way I've been
> treated. It shouldn't be difficult. I could be Johnny's teacher.
> That would explain my presence in the house to everyone.
> ELLIE.

Johnny turned over.

"Ellie, my teacher, where are you now?" he asked the darkness.
"Lonely and resting in Cousin William's studio with all the other
stiffened mannequins? Playing chess with Grandma, only not
moving? In the cold, dark basement like the wine casks put away
for all the years? Somewhere in this big house tonight. But
maybe not tomorrow. Unless I find you before then. . . ."

There was a huge back yard with many acres to it, fruit trees, a
flower garden, the swimming pool, the bathhouse, servants'
quarters immediately behind the big house. Sunlight caught between a row of sycamore trees and a high green fence that
shielded all this from the street. There was an oak tree to dangle
from in the afternoon, and a policeman who walked his beat just
under that tree on the sidewalk beyond the fence. Johnny climbed
up and waited.

The policeman walked below. Johnny rattled leaves.

"Hi, son." The policeman looked up. "Better watch out.
You'll fall."

"I don't care," said Johnny. "We got a dead lady in our
house and everybody keeps it secret."

The policeman made a smile. "You have, have you?"

Johnny shifted himself. "I found her in a trunk. Somebody
killed her. I tried to call the police last night, but Dad wouldn't
let me. I tipped the trunk over, and she fell downstairs but she
turned out to be a wax doll. It wasn't the lady after all."

"So." The policeman chuckled, enjoying it.

"But the other lady was real," insisted Johnny.

"What other lady?"

"The first one I found. Cousin William's a dress designer. He
changed bodies. You should have seen everyone at breakfast this

morning. Trying to be happy. Like in the movies. But they can't fool me. They're not happy. Mother looks tired, and she's real touchy. I wonder how long they can go around like this without yelling?''

The policeman scowled. ''Honest to God, you sound just like my kid. Him and his Buck Rogers disintegrators and his comic books. Honest to God, it's a crime what they give the younger generation to read. Ruin their minds with it. Killing. Corpses. Ah!''

''But it's true!''

''See you later,'' said the policeman, and walked on.

Johnny clung there, and the tree trembled in the wind. Then he dropped down across the fence and gave chase. ''You got to come look. They'll take her away if you don't—then nobody'll ever find her.''

The policeman was patient. ''Look, little boy, I can't go nowhere without no warrant. How do I know you're not lying?'' He was joking now.

''You've just *got* to believe me—that's all.''

The policeman stuck out his hand. ''Here.''

Johnny took it. The policeman walked.

''Where are we going?'' asked Johnny.

''To see your mother.''

''No!'' Johnny squirmed frantically. ''That won't help! She'll hate me for it! She'll lie about it!''

The policeman firmly escorted him around front and thumbed the bell. First a maid, and then Mother was at the door, her face pale as milk, her lips a red smear against the white. Her pompadour was a little toppled over. There were blue pouches under her suddenly dull eyes.

''Johnny!''

''Better keep him inside, ma'am.'' The policeman touched his cap. ''He'll get hurt running in the street.''

''Thank you, officer.''

The officer looked at her, then at Johnny. Johnny started to speak, but he could only sob. Two tears ran down his cheeks as the door closed, shutting the officer outside.

Mother didn't say anything to Johnny. Not a word. She just stood there, lost and white, twisting her fingers. That was all.

Hours later in the day, Johnny wrote it all down upon a nickel tablet of paper. Everything he knew about the Trunk Lady, everything he knew about Cousin William, Mom, Dad, Uncle Flinny, Grandma. Wetting his pencil, Johnny put it out in lines like this:

"The Lady in the Trunk loved Dad. Dad killed her when she came to the house." Johnny pouted over that one. "Either that or Mom killed her." Long years of viewing motion picture murders went through Johnny's mind. "Then, of course, Grandma or Uncle Flinny could have killed her because their authority and security was threatened." Yeah. Johnny scribbled quick. Let's see, now. "And Cousin William? Maybe it was his woman friend, after all." Johnny sort of hoped it was. He wasn't very partial to Cousin W. "Maybe, maybe there was something in Grandma's past? Or Uncle Flinny's?" Now, how about—

"Johnny!"

Grandma's voice. Johnny put away the pad.

Grandma came in the door and guided Johnny out through the hall and into her room, using her cane as a nervous prod. She seated him before the chessboard and nodded at the pale pieces. "Those are yours. Mine are black." She thought it over, eyes closed.

"Mine are always black."

"We can't play," Johnny announced. "Two of your black pieces are missing." He pointed.

She looked. "Uncle Flinny again. He's always taking some of my players. Always and forever. We'll play anyway. I'll use what I have. Move." She jabbed a skinny finger.

"Where's Uncle Flinny?"

"Watering the garden. Move," she ordered.

Her eyes watched his fingers in their path. She leaned forward slowly over the shining pieces. "We're all good people, Johnny. We led a good life these twenty years in this house. You've been in it only part of that twenty. We never asked for no trouble. Don't make us any, Johnny."

He sat there. A fly buzzed against the large window. Far away, below, water ran from a faucet. "I don't want no—trouble," he said.

The chess board blurred and ran away like colored water. "Dad looked so white and funny at breakfast today. Why should he feel that way over a wax doll, Grandma? And Mom, she looks like she's all twisted up like a spring inside a clock, ready to bust loose. That's no way to act over a doll, is it?"

Grandma deliberated over her bishop, withdrawn into herself

like an old hermit crab in a shell of lace. "There was no body. Just your imagination. Forget it. Forget it." She glared at the child as if he were responsible. "Walk light from now on, sonny. Keep quiet and keep out of the way and forget it. Someone's got to tell you these things. Don't know why it's always me. But just forget it!"

They played chess until twilight. Then the house got dark again too quickly, everybody hurried through supper, and it seemed that everybody went to bed early too.

Johnny listened to the hours chiming out one by one. Someone rapped on the door. Johnny said, "Who is it?"

"Uncle Flinny."

"What do you want, Uncle Flinny!"

"Time for your bedtime story, Johnny."

"Oh, well—not tonight, please, Uncle Flinny."

"Yes. Please. This is a very special story. A very extra special bedtime story."

Johnny waited. Then: "I'm tired, Uncle Flinny. Some other time, huh? Not tonight, please."

Uncle Flinny went away and after a while the clock chimed again. It was after ten. More time. After eleven. More time. Almost twelve.

Johnny opened the door.

The house was completely asleep. You could tell by the quiet, untouched gleam on the long hall stairs, clear moonlight pouring through great areas of glass, and no shadow moving.

Johnny closed the door behind him. From off somewhere in a quiet land, Grandma breathed heavily in her great four-postered bed. There was a tinkling noise, very faintly, as if bottles were being cautiously rattled behind Cousin William's door.

Johnny paused at the staircase. All he had to do would be to return to bed and forget about it, believe that it was all a mistake, and there would be no trouble. It would be forgotten and things would take up where they'd been a few days ago.

Mother would laugh at her parties. Dad would drive back and forth to the office with his thick briefcase. Grandma would sneak her brandy on the side. Cousin William would insert needles into mannequin flesh, and Uncle Flinny would go on forever telling his feverish bedtime stories that meant nothing.

Yet it was not so easy as that. Things could not go back now. Only ahead. You *can't* forget. Dad, his only friend, was a stranger now, since the—incident. Mother was worse than ever.

Her eyes looked like they cried at night. Down under the glitter she had to live too. And Grandma, she'd drink two bottles instead of one bottle of brandy a week. And Cousin William, every time he stuck a pin into a mannequin he'd think of the Trunk Lady, blanch, cringe, and start whimpering over his cognac.

And she—the lovely dark-haired stranger in the musty trunk—had looked so lonely up there where he'd found her. So apart. There was a bond between them. She was a stranger to the house—and was killed for it. Johnny was a stranger in the house now too. He wanted to find her again, because of that. They were almost brother and sister. She needed finding. She needed to be remembered, not to be forgotten.

Johnny went down each step with careful footing. He clung to the banister, sliding his fingers. She would not be in the attic now, nor would she be in any of the upstairs rooms. How could *they* sleep with her so near them? . . . Downstairs perhaps. Somewhere in the accumulated night of the house. Not in the servants' quarters.

He had just reached the stair bottom when he heard one of the upstairs doors open very slowly and close. After that there was not a sound, but quite calmly, quietly, someone came and stood at the top of the stairs, looking down.

Johnny froze. He leaned against the wall like a shadow. Sweat came out on his face and trickled in the small palms of his hands. He could not see who it was. They just stood there, watching, looking down, silent and waiting.

Things had to go on. You can't lie in bed and forget. Johnny couldn't just forget the stranger, the Trunk Lady, in her lonely attitude of death. The murderer, too, could not forget easily—nor that there was a small boy in the house who was too curious, too incautious.

Johnny breathed very slowly. He waited a moment. Then, when he saw that the person at the top of the stairs was not coming down, he moved quickly down the hall, into the kitchen, and out the back door into the moonlit veldt of the garden.

The swimming pool lay flat and shining square, with a fringe of trees beyond it, stars over it, the bathhouse near it, the low garden rows to left and right. Farther down was the greenhouse and the garden toolshed. Johnny ran.

The shadows of the toolshed offered temporary haven. Looking back, he detected no movement in the house, no light. The body would most probably be in one of these outlying houses.

His bed would feel nice now. The lock on the door would be nice. Johnny trembled like the water in the pool. Suddenly he saw someone standing in the upstairs hall window. There was just a hint of a standing figure there. Looking down, as it had looked from the top of the stairs. . . . Then—it was gone.

Now, down the gravel drive on the side of the house, footsteps sounded. Someone was coming from the front of the house, around under the sycamores. Someone moving in sycamore shadows, stealthily and unseen.

Then, very suddenly, breaking into half-light, *she* was there. She! Not Mother, nor Grandmother. But emerging half into moonlight, half in flecked shadow—was the Trunk Lady.

She looked at Johnny, far across the garden, and said nothing.
Johnny swallowed tightly and blinked. He held onto himself, his thighs, his knees, with clenched fingers. He crouched and squinted and stared in raw disbelief. A night wind set the sycamore leaves to shivering. From a way off an auto horn hooted like a lonely owl.

She was not dead after all. The whole house had tried to fool him. This was some fantastic jest he could not understand. They were all against him. His teacher was *alive*! There was no murder, no death! She was here, for him alone! In his hour of loneliness, she was here!

He darted out into the moonlight. Panting, not yelling, not laughing, he ran toward her across the grass, to the tiles of the swimming pool, across the tiles, around the pool and toward the sycamores.

She stood waiting for him, arms outstretched to take him into their soft embrace, sycamore shadows stirring over her cocktail dress, setting it into dreamy motion.

He said, "Ellie, is that you?"

He reached the rim of stirring shadow and screamed. The universe seemed to explode. The cocktail dress whirled madly, toppling in a drunken insanity. The Trunk Lady bent and there came a hoarse panting sound. She was fainting.

No! She was falling! A shadow hit him across the face, jarring his senses, once, twice, three times. He fell to his knees and before he could rise fingers were over his face, fingers that numbed him, gripping tight his sobbing mouth.

Mother!
The thought slammed him! Mother, dressed in the Trunk

Lady's cocktail dress. Decoying him out into her arms, fooling him.

Mother, don't kill me! Don't kill me! he tried to cry. *I'm sorry I tried to bring the police! Mother, you love Father—is that why you killed Ellie? Mother, let me go! Mother, you looked so much like her standing in the sycamore shadows!*

But the hands would not let him go. There was a rushing, a body against him. A series of shocks. The fingers were so strong, so much thicker than they should be. Much thicker! Johnny screamed inwardly, drawing air in an awful slobbering whistle.

The house leaned over him as if to collapse and crush him in its fall. The great old sleeping house with everyone sleeping in it, unaware that this silent struggle was happening by the flat shine of the pool.

Suddenly he realized that it was not Mother, not the Trunk Lady. The fingers were too strong. Who is stronger than Mother, sterner, more quick and hard?

Grandmother, perhaps?

The body was too hard against him. He half broke free and saw the flat of moonlight, the filmy cocktail dress lying alone, sprawled—and a mannequin hand thrown out into light. The mannequin was on the ground, dead, plastic, cold. Someone else was behind Johnny, holding, fighting.

Cousin William!

But there was no smell of cognac. The actions were the actions of a sober man. The breath was clean and clear and quick, almost sobbing.

Father!

Dad he tried to yell. *Don't, don't, please* don't!

Then a voice was talking. Something black and small clattered on the tiles beside the swirling water, and Johnny suddenly *knew*. The hands were tight, the voice tighter, whispering. "You hurt your mother!"

I didn't mean to, Johnny screamed inwardly.

"If it hadn't been for you," said the voice, whispering, "your mother would never have known about the Dark One dying!"

I didn't mean to find the Trunk Lady, cried Johnny silently, fighting.

"It'll *kill* her, the shock of it. If she dies, I won't want to live. She's all I've had ever since twenty years ago when it all happened!"

The voice husked on: "Ellie came to the party. They tried to fool me, make out she was somebody else. But I guessed. She came upstairs in her cocktail gown and I gave her a glass of brandy with sleeping powder in it, and I put her to gentle sleep in the old old trunk. Nobody would have known if *you* hadn't looked. Ellie would have just disappeared forever. Only Grandma and me would know! But you're Dark, too, you're Dark, just like Ellie!" the voice whispered. "Sometimes, when I look at you, I see *her* face! So, now—"

The Dark One. Johnny's mind spun, ached, and thrust to get free. *Uncle Flinny!*

Uncle Flinny, he thought. Why do you call Ellie the Dark One? Why? Your bedtime stories, Uncle Flinny. For so many years you've told the same story, the same strange story about the Dark One and the beautiful woman, and now the Dark One came to be my teacher, and why did you kill her! What did she do to *you*? Why do you call her the Dark One? What does the bedtime story mean? I don't know.

"Don't kill me, Uncle Flinny. The water's cold and shining tonight. I don't want to be under the cold shine of it."

Johnny grabbed onto the body behind him and fell forward. The two of them plunged screaming into the pool. There was a great plunging nausea. The fingers released him. There was a fighting in wet darkness, water stabbing his nostrils, bubbles breaking from his lips.

When Johnny broke surface there was a great sound of air rising from below, a dim surging of an old man jerking against the lazy tide. The man never came to the surface again. Just the bubbles came. . . .

Johnny was crying, screaming to himself as he dragged himself from the pool and saw her lying there so lonely and tired—the mannequin in the cocktail dress. His foot knocked something dark and small rolling on the tiles. He picked it up. One of the dark chess pieces Uncle Flinny was always stealing from the chess set in Grandma's room.

Johnny held it tight, not seeing it really, and looked at the pool with the slowing ripples on it where Uncle Flinny slept below. It was crazy, so crazy he couldn't stand it.

He looked at the house through blurred eyes, and he was shaking like a sick dog. Lights were clicking on all over it. Windows in squares of yellow and orange. Father was running downstairs, shouting, and the back door was opening, just as Johnny collapsed, sobbing, upon the cold hard tiles. . . .

*   *   *

Mother sat on one side of the bed, Dad on the other side. Johnny got his crying all out of him and lay back and looked at Dad, then Mom. "Mom?"

She said nothing, but smiled weakly and held onto his hands so tightly.

"Mom, oh, Mom," Johnny said. "I'm so tired, but I can't sleep. Why? Why, Dad?" He looked at Dad again. "Dad, what happened? I don't know."

Dad found it hard to say. He said it anyway. "Uncle Flinny was married twenty years ago. His wife died when their baby was born. Uncle Flinny loved his wife very much. She was very beautiful and good. Uncle Flinny hated the baby. He'd have nothing to do with it. He thought the baby was a murderer. You can understand how he felt, can't you? You can understand how *I'd* feel if Mother died?"

Johnny nodded weakly, not too sure at all that he understood.

"Uncle Flinny put the baby in a girl's home somewhere. He wouldn't tell us where. She grew up, bitter, hating Uncle Flinny because he treated her unfairly. After all, she didn't ask to be born. You see, son?" he said.

"Yeah, Dad."

"Well, just a month ago, Ellie, the baby, grown up now, found out where we lived somehow. She wrote a letter. We offered her a job as your teacher, which was only right and deserving. We thought to keep it secret from your uncle. When Ellie came, and went upstairs during the party, Uncle Flinny guessed who she was."

Dad couldn't speak for a moment. He closed his eyes. "Then— you found her in the attic. We tried to keep it quiet. We tried to make you forget. It was no use. We could never forget, ourselves. It was bound to come out. There was so much at stake, though, all our lives, we tried to work it out quietly. Things like money and reputations and business and what people would say made us do it, son. . . . And—really—they're not worth a damn!"

Johnny turned his head. "I kept poking my nose in—"

"You were our conscience, I guess. A rather active symbol. You kept the house stirred up. Uncle Flinny thought you were hurting your mother. Your mother—his sister—was all he had after his wife's death."

"So he tried to make it look like I was drowned in the pool—"

Mother suddenly bent and held on to Johnny closely. "I'm sorry, Johnny. Sometimes we're blind. I didn't think he'd do that."

"What about the police?"

"The truth. Flinny killed her and committed suicide."

Mother's voice seemed distant and removed and tired. Johnny heard himself talking. "Uncle Flinny used to tell me bedtime stories, Mom. I still don't understand. All about the Dark One and the beautiful wife, and—"

"Someday, when you're older, you'll understand. Poor Ellie. She was always the Dark One."

Things were fading away, away. It was all over, done. "No more bedtime stories, Mom, please. No more, huh?"

Out of the tired darkness, Mom said, "No more, Johnny."

Johnny rolled wearily over into dreams. His left hand opened and the small black object in it fell clattering to the bedroom floor. He was asleep even before the Black Knight ceased rolling.

Yesterday I Lived!

Years went by and after all the years of raining and cold and fog going and coming through Hollywood Cemetery over a stone with the name Diana Coyle on it, Cleve Morris walked into the studio projection room out of the storm and looked up at the screen.

She was there. The long, lazy body of hers, the shining red hair and bright complementary green eyes.

And Cleve thought, *Is it cold out there, Diana? Is it cold out there tonight? Is the rain to you yet? Have the years pierced the bronze walls of your resting place and are you still—beautiful?*

He watched her glide across the screen, heard her laughter, and his wet eyes shimmered her into bright quivering color streaks.

It's so warm in here tonight, Diana. You're here, all the warmth of you, and yet it's only so much illusion. They buried you three years ago, and now the autograph hunters are crazy over some new actress here at the studio.

He choked on that. No reason for this feeling, but everyone felt that way about her. Everyone loved her, hated her for being so lovely. But maybe *you* loved her more than the others.

Who in hell are you? She hardly ever saw you. Cleve Morris, a desk sergeant spending two hours a day at the front desk buzzing people through locked doors and six hours strolling around dim sound stages, checking things. She hardly knew you. It was always, "Hello, Diana," and "Hi, Sarge!" and "Good night, Diana," when her long evening gown rustled from the stages, and over her smooth shoulder one eye winking. "Night, Sarge; be a good boy!"

Three years ago. Cleve slid down in his projection room loge. The watch on his wrist ticked eight o'clock. The studio was dead, lights fading one by one. Tomorrow, action lots of it. But now, tonight, he was alone in this room, looking over the old films of Diana Coyle. In the projection booth behind him, checking the compact spools of film, Jamie Winters, the studio's A-1 cameraman, did the honors of projection.

So here you are, the two of you, late at night. The film flickers, marring her lovely face. It flickers again, and you're irritated. It flickers twice more, a long time, then smooths out. Bad print. Cleve sinks lower in his seat, thinking back three years ago, along about this same hour of night, just about the same day of the month . . . three years ago . . . same hour . . . rain in the dark sky . . . three years ago. . . .

Cleve was at his desk that night. People strode through doors, rain-spangled, never seeing him. He felt like a mummy in a museum where the attendants had long ago tired of noticing him. Just a fixture to buzz doors open for them.

"Good evening, Mr. Guilding."

R. J. Guilding thought it over and vetoed the suggestion with a jerk of one gray-gloved hand. His white head jerked too. "Is it?" he wanted to know. You get that way being a producer.

Buzz. Door open. *Slam.*

"Good evening, Diana!"

"What?" She walked from the rainy night with it shining in little clear gems on her white oval face. He'd like to have kissed them away. She looked lost and alone. "Oh, hello, Cleve. Working late. The darn picture's almost finished. Gosh, I'm tired."

Buzz. Door open. *Slam.*

He looked after her and kept her perfume as long as he could.

"Ah, flatfoot," somebody said. Leaning over the desk, smiling ironically, was a pretty man named Robert Denim. "Open the door for me, country boy. They never should've put you on this job. You're glamor-struck. Poor kid."

Cleve looked at him strangely. "She doesn't belong to you anymore, does she?"

Denim's face was suddenly not pretty. He didn't say anything for a moment, but by the look in his eyes Cleve's doubts were removed. Denim grabbed the door and jerked it viciously.

Cleve purposely left the buzzer untouched. Denim swore and turned around, one gloved hand balled into a fist. Cleve buzzed the buzzer, smiling. It was the kind of smile that drained Denim's hesitation, made him decide to pull the knob again and stride off down away into the halls, into the studio.

A few minutes later Jamie Winters entered, shaking off rain, but holding onto a man-sized peeve. "That Diana Coyle woman; I tell you, Cleve. She stays up late at night and expects me to photograph her like a twelve-year-old kid! What a job I got! Fooey."

Behind Jamie Winters came Georgie Kroll, and Tally Durham hanging onto him so that Diana couldn't get him. But it was too late. By Georgie's face he was already got; and by Tally's she knew it but couldn't believe it.

Slam.

Cleve checked his name chart, found that everybody who was working tonight was already in. He relaxed. This was a dark hive, and Diana was the queen bee with all the other bees humming around her. The studio worked late tonight, just for her, all the lights, sound, color, activity. Cleve smoked a cigarette quietly, leaning back, smiling over his thoughts. *Diana, let's just you and me buy a little home in San Fernando where the flood washes you out every year, and the wild flowers spring up when the flood is gone. Nice paddling in a canoe with you, Diana, even in a flood. We got flowers, hay, sunlight, and peace in the valley, Diana.*

The only sound to Cleve was the rain beating at the windows, an occasional flare of thunder, and his watch ticking like a termite boring a hole in the structure of silence.

Tictictictictic . . .

The scream pulled him out of his chair and half across the reception room, echoed through the building. A script girl burst into view, shambling with dead kind of feet, babbling. Cleve grabbed her and held her still.

"She's dead! She's dead!"

The watch went *tic, tic, tic* all over again.

Lightning blew up around the place, and a cold wind hit Cleve's neck. His stomach turned over and he was afraid to ask the simple question he would eventually have to ask. Instead he stalled the inevitable, locking the bronze front doors and making secure any windows that were open. When he turned, the script girl was leaning against his desk, a tremble in her like something shattered in a finely integrated machine, shaking it to pieces.

"On stage twelve. Just now," she gasped. "Diana Coyle."

Cleve ran through the dim alleys of the studio, the sound of his running lonely in the big empty spaces. Ahead of him brilliant lights poured from opened stage doors; people stood framed in the vast square, shocked, not moving.

He ran onto the set and stopped, his heart pounding, to look down.

She was the most beautiful person who ever died.

Her silver evening gown was a small lake around her. Her fingernails were five scarlet beetles dead and shining on either side of her slumped body.

All the hot lights looked down, trying to keep her warm when she was fast cooling. My blood too, thought Cleve. Keep me warm, lights!

The shock of it held everybody as in a still photo.

Denim, fumbling with a cigarette, spoke first.

"We were in the middle of a scene. She just fell down and that was all."

Tally Durham, about the size of a salt shaker, wandered blindly about the stage telling everybody, "We thought she fainted, that's all! I got the smelling salts!"

Denim sucked, deeply nervous, on his smoke. "The smelling salts didn't work . . ."

For the first time in his life Cleve touched Diana Coyle.

But it was too late now. What good to touch cold clay that didn't laugh back at you using green eyes and curved lips?

He touched her and said, "She's been poisoned."

The word "poison" spread out through the dim sound stage behind the glaring lights. Echoes came back with it.

Georgie Kroll stuttered. "She—she got a drink—from the soft drinks—box—a couple minutes ago. Maybe—"

Cleve found the soft drinks dispenser blindly. He smelled one bottle and tucked it aside carefully, using a handkerchief, into a lunchbox that was studio property. "Nobody touch that."

The floor was rubbery to walk on. "Anybody see anybody else touch that bottle before Diana drank out of it?"

Way up in the glaring electrical heaven, a guy looked down like a short-circuited god and called, "Hey, Cleve, just before the last scene we had light trouble. Somebody conked a main switch. The lights were doused for about a minute and a half. Plenty time for someone to fix that bottle!"

"Thanks." Cleve turned to Jamie Winters, the cameraman. "You got film in your camera? Got a picture of—her—dying?"

"I guess so. Sure!"

"How soon can you have it developed?"

"Two, three hours. Got to call Juke Davis and have him come to the studio, though."

"Phone him, then. Take two watchmen with you to guard that film. Beat it!"

Far away the sirens were singing and Hollywood was going to sleep. Somebody onstage suddenly realized Diana was dead and started sobbing.

I wish I could do that, thought Cleve. *I wish I could cry. What am I supposed to do now, act tough, be a Sherlock? Question everyone, when my heart isn't working?* Cleve heard his voice going on alone.

"We'll be working late tonight, everybody. We'll be working until we get this scene right. And if we don't get it right, I guess we don't go home. Before the homicide squad gets here, everyone to their places. We'll do the scene over. Places, everybody."

They did the scene over.

The homicide squad arrived. There was one detective named Foley and another named Sadlowe. One was small, the other big. One talked a lot, and the other listened. Foley did the talking and it gave Cleve a sick headache.

R. J. Guilding, the director and producer of the film, slumped in his canvas chair, wiping his face and trying to tell Foley that he wanted this whole mess kept out of the papers and quiet.

Foley told him to shut up. Foley glared at Cleve as if he were also a suspect. "What've you found out, son?"

"There was film in the camera. Film of Diana—Miss Coyle's death."

Foley's eyebrows went like that. "Well, hell, let's see it!"

They walked over into the film laboratory to get the film. Cleve was frankly afraid of the place. Always had been. It was a huge dark mortuary building with dead-end passages and labyrinths of black walls to cut the light. You stumbled through pitch dark, touching the walls, careening, turning, cursing, twisting around cutouts; walked south, east, west, south again and suddenly found yourself in a green-freckled space as big as the universe. Nothing to see but green welts and splashes of light, dim snakes of film climbing, winding over spools from floor to high ceiling and back down. The one brilliant light was a printing light that shot from a projector and printed negative to positive as they slid by in parallel slots. The positive then coiled over and down into a long series of developing baths. The place was a whining morgue. Juke Davis moved around in it with ghoullike movements.

"There's no soundtrack. I'll develop it and splice it in later," said Davis. "Here you are, Mr. Foley. Here's your film."

They took the film and retreated back through the labyrinth.

In the projection room Cleve and the detectives Foley and Sadlowe, with Jamie Winters operating the projector in the booth, watched the death scene printed on the screen for them. Stage twelve had been slammed shut, and other officers were back there, talking, grilling everyone in alphabetical order.

On the screen Diana laughed. Robert Denim laughed back. It was very silent. They opened mouths but no sounds came out. People danced behind them. Diana and Robert Denim danced now, gracefully, quietly, leisurely. When they stopped dancing they talked seriously with—Tally Durham and Georgie Kroll.

Foley spoke. "You say that this fellow Kroll loved Diana too?"

Cleve nodded. "Who didn't?"

Foley said, "Yeah. Who didn't. Well—" He stared with suspicion at the screen. "How about this Tally Durham woman. Was she jealous?"

Was there any woman in Hollywood who didn't hate Diana because she was perfect? Cleve spoke of Tally's love for Georgie Kroll.

"It never fails," replied Foley with a shake of his head.

Cleve said, "Tally may have killed Diana. Who knows. Georgie'd have a motive too. Diana treated him like a rag doll. He wanted her and couldn't have her. That happened to a lot of men in Diana's life. If she ever loved anybody, it was Robert

Denim, and that didn't last. Denim is a little too—tough, I guess that's how you'd put it.''

Foley snorted. ''Good going. We got three suspects in one scene. Any one of them could have dosed that pop bottle with nicotine. The lights were out for a minute and a half. In that time any guy who ever bought Black Leaf Forty nicotine sulfate at the corner garden store could have tossed twenty drops of it in her drink and gone back playing innocent when the lights bloomed again. Nuts.''

Sadlowe spoke for the first time that evening. ''There ought to be some way to splice out the innocents from this film.'' A brilliant observation.

Cleve caught his breath. *She* was dying.

She died like she had done everything in her life. You had to admire the way she did it, with the grace, fire, and control of a fine cat-animal. In the middle of the scene she forgot her lines. Her fingers crawled slowly to her throat and she turned. Her face changed. She looked straight out at you from the screen as if she knew this was her biggest and, to a cynic, her best scene.

Then she fell, like a silken canopy from which the supports had been instantly withdrawn.

Denim crouched over her, mouthing the word, ''Diana!''

And Tally Durham screamed a silent scream as the film shivered and fluttered into blackness, numbers, amber colors, and then nothing but glaring light.

Oh, God, press a button somewhere! Run the reel backward and bring her back to life! Press a button as you see in those comic newsreels; in which smashed trains are reintegrated, fallen emperors are enthroned, the sun rises in the west and—Diana Coyle rises from the dead!

From the booth Jamie Winters's voice said, ''That's it. That's all of it. You want to see it again?''

Foley said, ''Yeah. Show it to us half a dozen times.''

''Excuse me,'' gasped Cleve.

''Where you going?''

He went out into the rain. It beat cold on him. Behind him, inside, Diana was dying again and again and again, like a trained puppet. Cleve clenched his jaw and looked straight up at the sky and let the night cry on him, all over him, soaking him through and through; in perfect harmony, the night and he and the crying dark. . . .

* * *

The storm lasted until morning both inside and outside the studio. Foley yelled at everybody. Everybody answered back calmly that they weren't guilty; yes, they had hated Diana, but at the same time loved her, yes, they were jealous of her, but she was a good girl too.

Foley evolved a colossal idea, invited all suspects to the projection room and scared hell out of everyone, proving nothing, by showing them Diana's last scene. R. J. Guilding broke down and sobbed, Georgie squeaked, and Tally screamed. Cleve got sick to his stomach, and the night went on and on.

Georgie said yes, yes, he'd loved Diana; Tally said yes, yes, she'd hated her; Guilding reaffirmed the fact that Diana had stalled production, causing trouble; and Robert Denim admitted to an attempted reconciliation between himself and his former wife. Jamie Winters told how Diana had stayed up late nights, ruining her face for proper photography. And R. J. Guilding snapped, "Diana told me you were photographing her poorly, on purpose!"

Jamie Winters was calm. "That's not true. She was trying to shove the blame for her complexion off on someone else, me."

Foley said, "You were in love with her too?"

Winters replied, "Why do you think I became her photographer?"

So when dawn came Diana was still as dead as the night before. Big stage doors thundered aside and the suspects wearily shambled out to climb into their cars and start home.

Cleve watched them through aching eyes. Silently he walked around the studio, checking everything when it didn't need checking. He smelled the sweet green odor of the cemetery over the wall.

Funny Hollywood. It builds a studio next door to a graveyard. Right over that wall there. Sometimes it seemed everyone in movietown tried to scale that wall. Some poured themselves over in a whiskey tide, some smoked themselves over; all of them looked forward to an office in Hollywood Cemetery—with no phones. Well, Diana didn't have to climb that wall.

Someone had pushed her over. . . .

Cleve held on to the steering wheel, tight, hard, wanting to break it, telling the world to get out of the way, dammit! He was beginning to get mad!

They buried her on a bright California day with a stiff wind blowing and too many red and yellow and blue flowers and the wrong kind of tears.

That was the first day Cleve ever drank enough to get drunk. He would always remember that day.

The studio phoned three days later.

"Say, Morris, what's eating you? Where you been?"

"In my apartment," said Cleve dully.

He kept the radio off, he didn't walk the streets like he used to at night, dreaming. He neglected the newspapers; they had big pictures of her in them. The radio talked about her, so he almost wrecked the thing. When the week was over she was safely in the earth, and the newsapers had tapered off the black ink wreaths, were telling her life story on page two the following Wednesday; page four Thursday; page five Friday; page ten Saturday; and by the following Monday they wrote the concluding chapter and slipped it in among the stock-market reports on page twenty-nine.

You're slipping, Diana! Slipping! You used to make page one!

Cleve went back to work.

By Friday there was nothing left but that new stone in Hollywood Cemetery. Papers rotted in the flooded gutters, washing away the ink of her name; the radio blatted war, and Cleve worked with his eyes looking funny and changed.

He buzzed doors all day, and people went in and out. He watched Tally dance in every morning, smaller and chipper, and happy now that Diana was gone, holding on to Georgie, who was all hers now, except his mind and soul. He watched Robert Denim walk in, and they never spoke to each other. He waved hello to Jamie Winters and was courteous to R. J. Guilding.

But he watched them all, like a dialogue director waiting for one muffed line or missed cue.

And finally the papers announced casually that her death had been attributed to suicide, and it was a closed chapter.

A couple of weeks later Cleve was still sticking to his apartment, reading and thinking, when the phone rang.

"Cleve? This is Jamie Winters. Look, cop-man, come out of it. You're wanted at a party, now, tonight. I got some film clips from Gable's last picture."

There was argument. In the end Cleve gave in and went to the party. They sat in Jamie Winters's parlor facing a small-size screen. Winters showed them scenes from pictures that never reached the theater. Garbo tripping over a light cord and falling on her platform. Spencer Tracy blowing his lines and swearing. William Powell sticking his tongue out at the camera when he forgot his next cue. Cleve laughed for the first time in a million years.

Jamie Winters had an endless collection of film clips of famous stars blowing up and saying censorable things.

And when Diana Coyle showed up, it was like a kick in the stomach. Like being shot with two barrels of a shotgun! Cleve jerked and gasped, and shut his eyes, clenching the chair.

Then, suddenly, he was very cool. He had an idea. Looking at the screen, it came to him, like cold rain on his cheeks.

"Jamie!" he said.

In the sprocketing darkness, Jamie replied, "Yes?"

"I've got to see you in the kitchen, Jamie."

"Why?"

"Never mind why. Let the camera run itself and come on."

In the kitchen Cleve held on to Jamie. "It's about those films you're showing us. The mistakes. The censored clips. Have you any clips from Diana's last picture? Spoiled scenes, blow-ups, I mean?"

"Yeah. At the studio. I collect them. It's a hobby. That stuff usually goes in the trash can. I keep them for laughs."

Cleve sucked in his breath. "Can you get that film for me; all of it; bring it here tomorrow night and go over it with me?"

"Sure, if you want me to. I don't see—"

"Never mind, Jamie. Just do like I say, huh? Bring me all the cutouts, the scenes that were bad. I want to see who spoiled the scenes, who caused the most trouble, and why! Will you do it, Jamie?"

"Sure. Sure I will, Cleve. Take it easy. Here, sit down. Have a drink."

Cleve didn't eat much the next day. The hours went too slowly. At night he ate a little supper and swallowed four aspirins. Then he drove in a mechanical nightmare to Jamie Winters's house.

Jamie was waiting with drinks and film in the camera.

"Thanks, Jamie." Cleve sat down and drank nervously. "All right. Shall we see them?"

"Action!" said Jamie.

Light on the screen. "Take one, scene seven, *The Gilded Virgin*: Diana Coyle, Robert Denim."

Clack!

The scene faded in. There was a terrace by an ocean scene in moonlight. Diana was talking.

"It's a lovely night. So lovely I can't believe in it."

Robert Denim, holding her hands in his, looked at her and said, "I think I can make you believe in it. I'll—damn it!"

"Cut!" cried Guilding's voice offscreen.

The film ran on. Denim's face was ugly, getting dark and lined.

"There you go, hogging the camera again!"

"Me?" Diana wasn't beautiful anymore. Not *this* way. She shook the gilt off her wings in an angry powder. "Me, you two-bit thespian, you loud-mouthed, dirty—"

Flick. Dark. End of film.

Cleve sat there, staring. After a while he said, "They didn't get along, did they?" And then, to himself, almost, "I'm glad."

"Here's another one," said Winters. The camera ticked rapidly.

Another scene. A party scene. Laughter and music; and cutting across it, dark, snapping, bitter and accusative:

"—damn you!"

"—if you fed me the wrong cue on purpose! Of all the cheap, common little—"

Diana and Robert Denim, at it again!

Another scene, and another, and another. Six, seven, eight!

Here was one of Denim saying, "Honest to God, someone ought to shut you up for good, lady!"

"Who?" cried Diana, eyes flashing like little green stones. "You? You snivel-nosed ham!"

And Denim, glaring back, saying quietly, "Yes. Maybe me. Why not? It's an idea."

There were some bristling hot scenes with Tally Durham too. And one in which Diana browbeat little Georgie Kroll until he was nervous and sweating out an apology. All on film; all good evidence. But the ratio was seven of Denim's blow-ups to one of Tally's or Georgie's. On and on and on and on!

"Stop it, stop it!" Cleve got up from his chair. His figure cut the light, threw a shadow on the screen, swaying.

"Thanks for the trouble, Jamie. I'm tired too. Can—can I have these film clips of Denim?"

"Sure."

"I'm going downtown to police headquarters tonight and turn in Robert Denim for the murder of Diana Coyle. Thanks again, Jamie. You been a great help. Night."

Five, ten, fifteen, twenty hours. Count 'em by twos, by fours, by sixes. Rush the hours by. Argue with the cops and go home and flop in bed.

Toddle off to your gas chamber, Robert Denim; that's a good little killer!

And then in the middle of deep slumber, your phone rang.

"Hullo."

And a voice said over the phone in the night, "Cleve?"

"Yeah?"

And the voice said, "This is Juke Davis at the film laboratory. Come quick, Cleve. I been hurt, I been hurt, oh, I been hurt. . . ." A body fell at the other end of the line.

Silence.

He found Juke lying in a chemical bath. Red chemical from his own body where a knife had dug out his dreams and his living and his talking forever and spread it around in a scarlet lake.

A phone receiver hung dangling on one greenish wall. It was dark in the laboratory. Someone had shuffled in through the dim tunnels, come out of the dark, and now, standing there, Cleve heard nothing but the film moving forever on its trellises, like some vine going up through the midnight room trying to find the sun. Numbly, Cleve knelt beside Juke. The man lay half propped against the film machinery where the printing light shot out and imprinted negative to positive. He had crawled there, across the room.

In one clenched fist, Cleve found a frame of film; the faces of Tally, Georgie, Diana, and Robert Denim on it. Juke had found out something, something about this film, something about a killer; and his reward had come swiftly to him through the studio dark.

Cleve used the phone.

"This is Cleve Morris. Is Robert Denim still being held at Central Jail?"

"He's in his cell, and he won't talk. I tell you, Morris, you gave us a bum steer with them film clips. . . ."

"Thanks." Cleve hung up. He looked at Juke lying there by the machinery. "Well, who was it, Juke? It wasn't Denim. That leaves Georgie and Tally? Well?"

Juke said nothing and the machinery sang a low sad song.

One year went by. Another year followed. And then a third.

Robert Denim contracted out to another studio. Tally married Georgie, Guilding died at a New Year's party of overdrinking and a bad heart, time went on, everybody forgot. Well, almost everybody. . . .

Diana, child, is it cold out there tonight—?

Cleve rose in his seat. Three years ago. He blinked his eyes. Same kind of night as this, cold and raining.

The screen flickered.

Cleve paid little attention. It kept on flickering strangely. Cleve stiffened. His heart beat with the sprocketing noise of the machine. He bent forward.

"Jamie, will you run that last one hundred feet over again?"

"Sure thing, Cleve."

Flickers on film. Imperfections. Long blotches, short blobs. Cleve spelled it out. W . . . I . . . N . . .

Cleve opened the door of the projection room so softly Jamie Winters didn't hear him. Winters was glaring out at the film on the screen, and there was a strange, happy look on his face. The look of a saint seeing a new miracle.

"Enjoying yourself, Jamie boy?"

Jamie Winters shook himself and turned and smiled uneasily.

Cleve locked the door. He gave a little soft lecture: "It's been a long time. I haven't slept well many nights. Three years, Jamie. And tonight you had nothing to do so you ran off some film so you could gloat over it. Gloat over Diana and think how clever you were. Maybe it was fun to see me suffer too; you knew how much I liked her. Have you come here often in the past three years to gloat over her, Jamie?" he asked softly.

Winters laughed good-naturedly.

Cleve said, "She didn't love you, did she? You were her photographer. So to even things up, you began photographing her badly. It fits in. Her last two films were poor. She looked tired. It wasn't her fault; you did things with your camera. So Diana threatened to tell on you. You would've been blackballed at every studio. You couldn't have her love, and she threatened your career, so what did you do, Jamie Winters? You killed her."

"This is a poor idea of a joke," said Winters, hardening.

Cleve went on, "Diana looked at the camera when she died. She looked at you. We never thought of that. In a theater you always feel as if she were looking at the audience, not the man behind the camera. She died. You took a picture of her dying. Then, later, you invited me to a party, fed me the bait, with those film clips showing Denim in a suspicious light. I fell for it. You destroyed all the other film that put Denim in a good position. Juke Davis found out what you were doing. He worked with film all the time, he knew you were juggling clips. You wanted to frame Denim because there had to be a fall guy and you'd be clear. Juke questioned you, you stabbed him. You stole and destroyed the few extra clips Juke had discovered. Juke couldn't talk over the phone, but he shoved his hand in the printing light of the developing machine and printed your name W-I-N-T-E-R-S in black splotches as the film moved. He happened to be printing the negative of Diana's last film that night! And you began running it off to me ten minutes ago, thinking it was only a damaged film!"

Jamie Winters moved quickly, like a cat. He ripped open the projector and tore the film out in one vicious animal movement.

Cleve hit him. He pulled way back and blasted loose.

The case was really over now. But he wasn't happy or glad or anything but blind red angry, flooded with hot fury.

All he could think of now while he hit the face of Winters again and again and again, holding him tight with one hand, beating him over and over with the other, all he could think of was—

A stone in the yard of the cemetery just over the wall from the studio; a stone sweating blue rain over her bronzed name. All he could say in a hoarse, choked whisper was:

"Is it cold out there tonight, Diana; is it cold, little girl?"

And Cleve hit him again and again and again!

Dead Men Rise Up Never

When Sherry began to scream I gripped the steering wheel and started sweating. I smelled her sweet and warm in the backseat between the stale smell of Willie and the sharp smell of Mark, and my nostrils took Hamphill into account too. Hamphill smelled soap-clean up in the front seat with me, and he tried to talk to her, calm her. He held her hand.

"Sherry, this is for your own good. Please listen to me,

Sherry. We only got you away from your house in time. Finlay's men, the ones who threatened you, would have kidnapped you today. I swear it. In God's name, Sherry, we're only protecting you."

She didn't believe Hamphill. I saw her dark shining eyes caught, held like crazy, wild things, in the rearview mirror. The car's speed was up to sixty-five. Listen to him, Sherry, I thought, damn you, he loves you, so give him a chance!

"No! I don't believe you," was what she said. "You're gangsters too! I know you!"

She tried to fling herself out of the car. Maybe she didn't know how fast we were traveling. The ground ran past in a windy blur. She struggled. Mark held on to her. There was a shouting, a sudden scream, and silence. . . .

Sherry relaxed too suddenly in the backseat. Willie must have blinked at her dully, not understanding.

"Stop the car." Hamphill groped at my elbow.

"But, boss . . ." I said.

"You heard me, Hank, stop it."

The car sound died away and all you could hear was the ocean moaning along the skirt of the cliff. We were on top of it. Hamphill stared over into the rear seat and Willie's dull voice said, "She's gone to sleep, boss. Guess maybe she's tired."

I didn't turn around. I looked at the gray clouds in the sky and the seagulls looping and crying—at Hamphill's long lean face next to me, bleached to a beaten, shocked white, like a carved wooden mask left to bake and crumble on the sands.

The ocean came in once, twice, three times. Each time Hamphill breathed through his tiny, constricted nostrils. Then, holding her wrists, searching for a pulse he couldn't find, he shut his eyes—tight.

I stared ahead. "There's the cliff house, boss, just ahead. We better get inside it, in case Finlay and his men are following us. I bet they're damn mad at us for this trick. . . ." I trailed off.

Hamphill didn't know I was alive. He resembled something as old suddenly as that ancient wind-shaped, paint-flaked mansion standing on the rim of the stony cliffs.

Loving Sherry had made him young awhile. Now the salt sea wind was at him, rimming his hair above the ears, peeling away his new youth; the tide pounded his guts and sucked away his thinking.

I started the car and drove the last half mile to the cliff house very slowly. I climbed out of the car and slammed the door to waken the boss from his nightmare.

We walked into the house, the four of us carrying her. The front steps groaned when our feet touched them.

Upstairs in a west room with a view we laid Sherry on an old overstuffed sofa. A fine dust puffed from upholstery pores, hovering over her in a powdery sunlit veil. Death had quieted her features and she was beautiful as polished ivory, her hair like the color of waxed chestnuts.

Very slowly Hamphill sank beside her and told her what he thought of her, soft, like a kid talking to a fairy goddess. He didn't sound like Hamphill, the beer baron; or Hamphill, the numbers man; or Hamphill, the racing boss. The wind whined behind his voice, because Sherry was dead and the day was over. . . .

A car passed on the highway and I shivered. Any minute now, maybe, if we hadn't ditched them, some of Finlay's boys might show up—

The room felt crowded. There were only two people who needed to be in it. I pushed Willie and nodded at Mark. We went out and I closed the door and we stood with our hands deep in our pockets, in the hall, thinking many thoughts.

"You didn't have to scare her," I said.

"Me?" asked Mark, jerking a match on the wall and putting the flame unevenly against his cigarette. "She started yelling like a steam whistle."

"You scared her with your talk," I said. "After all, it wasn't a regular kidnapping. We were shielding her from Finlay. You know how soft the boss was on her—special."

"I knew," said Mark, "that we'd collect money on her, then frame Finlay for the deal, have him jailed, leaving us in the clear."

"You got the general idea," I said gently, "only let me bring out the details. The whole thing depended on Sherry's cooperation, once she learned our intentions were for her own good. There wasn't much time to explain today, when we heard Finlay was coming after her, so we grabbed her and ran. The blueprint was for us to hide her, then trap Finlay, let Sherry get a look at him and tell the police it was Finlay kidnapped her. Then they'd salt Finlay away and the whole business would be over."

Mark flicked ashes on the rug. "Only trouble is, Sherry's dead now. Nobody'll believe we didn't kidnap her ourselves. Ain't that swell!'' One of Mark's little pointed, shiny black shoes kicked the wall. ''Well, I don't want nothing else to do with her. She's dead. I hate dead people. Let's load her in a canvas tied with weights and put her out in the bay somewhere deep, then get out of here, get our money and—''

The door opened. Hamphill came out of it, pale.

''Willie, go watch over her while I talk to the boys,'' he said slowly, not thinking of the words. Willie beamed proudly and lumbered in. The three of us went into another room.

Mark has a mouth the shape of his own foot. ''When we gonna get the money and scram, boss?'' He shut the door and leaned on it.

''Money?'' The boss held the word up like something strange found on the beach, turning it over. ''Money.'' He focused dazedly on Mark. ''I didn't want any *money*. I wasn't in this for the *money*—''

Mark shifted his delicate weight. ''But you said—''

''I said. *I* said.'' Hamphill thought back, putting his thin fingers to his brow to force the thinking. ''In order to make you play along, Mark, I said about money, didn't I? It was a lie, Mark, all a lie. Yes. All a lie. I only wanted Sherry. No money. Just her. I was going to pay you out of my own pocket. Right, Hank?'' He stared strangely at me. ''Right, Hank?''

''Right,'' I said.

''Well, of all the—'' Angry color rose in Mark's cheeks. ''This whole damn setup's nothing but nursemaiding a coupla lovebirds!''

''No money!'' shouted Hamphill, straightening up. ''No money! I was only kicking down the Christmas tree to get the star on top. And you—you always said it was wrong for me to love her, said it wouldn't work. But I planned everything. A week here. A trip to Mexico City later, after she got to know me, after fixing Finlay so he wouldn't bother her again! And you, Mark, you sniffing your damn nose at me, goddamn you!''

Mark grinned. ''You should've said about it, boss, how you never intended getting money from kidnapping her, to make me understand. Why, sure, there was no use lying to me. Why, no, boss; no, of course not.''

''Careful,'' I muttered.

''I'm sure sorry,'' said Mark, lidding his small green eyes.

"Sure am. And, by the way, boss, how long we going to be here? I'm just curious, of course."

"I promised Sherry a week's vacation. We stay here that long."

One week. My brows went up. I said nothing.

"One week here, without trying to get the money, sitting, waiting for the cops to find us? Oh, that's swell, boss, I'm right in there with you, I sure am, I'm with you," said Mark. He turned, twisted the doorknob hard one way, stepped out, slammed it.

I put my right hand against Hamphill's heaving chest to stop his move. "No boss," I whispered. "No. He ain't living. He never lived. Why bother killing him? He's dead, I tell you. He was born dead."

The boss would have spoken except that we both heard a voice talking across the hall behind the other door. We opened the door, crossed the hall, and opened the other door slowly, looking in.

Willie sat on the couch-end like a large gray stone idol, his round face half blank, half animated, like a rock with lights playing over it. "You just rest there, Miss Bourne," he said to Sherry earnestly. "You look tired. You just rest. Mr. Hamphill thinks a lot of you. He told me so. He planned this whole setup for weeks, ever since he met you that night in Frisco. He didn't sleep, thinking about you—"

Two days passed. How many seagulls cried and looped over us, I don't remember. Mark counted them with his green eyes, and for every seagull, he threw away a cigarette butt burnt hungrily down to a nub. And when Mark ran out of smokes he counted waves, shells.

I sat playing blackjack. I'd put the cards down slow and pick them up and put them down slow again and shuffle them and cut them and lay them down. Maybe now and then I whistled. I've been around long enough so waiting makes no difference. When you been in the game as long as I have you don't find any difference in anything. Dying is as good as living; waiting is as good as rushing.

Hamphill was either up in *her* room, talking like a man in a confessional, soft and low, gentle and odd, or he was walking the beach, climbing the cliff stones. He'd tell Willie to squat on a rock. Willie'd perch there in the foggy sun with salt rime on his pink ears for five hours, waiting until the boss came back and said to jump down.

I played blackjack.

Mark kicked the table with his foot. "Talk, talk, talk, that's all he does upstairs at night, on and on, dammit! How long do we stick here? How long are we waiting?"

I laid down some cards. "Let the boss take his vacation any way he pleases," I said.

Mark watched me walk out on the porch. He shut the door after me, and though I couldn't be sure, I thought I heard the phone inside being ticked and spun by his fingers. . . .

Late that evening the fog crept in thicker, and I stood upstairs in a north room with Hamphill, waiting.

He looked down out of the window. "Remember the first time we saw her? The way she held herself, the way she took her hair in her hand, the way she laughed? I knew then it would take all the education and smartness and niceness in me to ever get her. Was I a fool, Hank?"

"A fool can't answer that," I said.

He nodded at the sea breaking over rocks, toward a point where fog bands crossed a jut of land that fingered out to sea. "Look beyond that curve, Hank? There's an old California mission out there."

"Under water?"

"About twenty feet under. On a clear day when the sun cuts down, the water's a blue diamond with the mission held inside it."

"Still there, intact?"

"Most of it. They say some of the first padres built it, but the land settled slowly and the little cathedral sank. On clear days you can see it lying there in the water, very quiet. Maybe it's just a ruin, but you imagine you see the whole thing; the stained glass windows, the bronze tower bell, the eucalyptus trees in the wind—"

"Seaweed and the tide, huh?"

"Same thing. Same effect. I wanted Sherry to see it. I wanted to walk along the cliff bottoms, over those big rocks with her, and bake in the sun. Bake all the old poison out of me and all the doubt out of her. The wind does that to you. I thought maybe I could show Sherry the little cathedral and maybe in a day or so she'd breathe easy and sit on a rock with me to see if we could hear the bell in the church tower ringing."

"That's from the bell-buoy at the point," I said.

"No," he said, "that's farther over. This bell rings from in the water, but you have to listen close when the wind dies."

"I hear a siren!" I cried suddenly, whirling. "The police!"

Hamphill took my shoulder. "No, that's only the wind in the holes of the cliff. I've been here before. I know. You get used to it."

I felt my heart pounding. "Boss, what do we do now?"

I shut up. I looked down at the white concrete road shimmering in the night and the fog. I saw the car sweeping down the highway, cutting through the fog with scythes of light.

"Boss," I said. "Take a look out this window."

"You look for me."

"A car. It's Finlay's sedan, I'd know it anywhere!"

Hamphill didn't move. "Finlay. I'm glad he's come. He's the one that caused all this. He's the one I want to see. Finlay." He nodded. "I want to talk to him. Go let him in, quietly."

The car ground to a stop below; its doors burst open. Men piled out, crossed the drive swiftly, crossed the porch; one ran around back. I saw guns with fog wet on them. I saw white faces with fog on them.

The downstairs bell rang.

I went down the stairs alone, empty-handed, clenched my teeth together, and opened the door. "Come on in," I said.

Finlay thrust his bodyguard in ahead of himself. The guard had his gun ready and was popeyed to see me just standing there. "Where's Hamphill?" Finlay demanded. A second gunsel stayed just outside the door.

"He'll be down in a minute."

"It's a good thing you didn't try any rough stuff."

"Oh, hell," I said.

"Where's Sherry?"

"Upstairs."

"I want her down here."

"Particular, aren't you?"

"Shall I hit him?" Finlay's bodyguard asked him.

Finlay looked up the dark stairs at the light in the opening door above. "Never mind."

Hamphill came down very quietly, one step at a time, pausing on each one with pain, as if his body were old, tired, and it was no longer fun to live and walk around. He got about halfway down when he saw Finlay. "What do you want?" he said.

"It's about Sherry," said Finlay.

I tightened up. The boss said, far away, "What about Sherry?"

"I want her back."

Hamphill said, "No."

"Maybe you didn't hear me right. I said I wanted her back, now!"

"No," said Hamphill.

"I don't want no trouble," said Finlay. His eyes moved from my empty hands to Hamphill's empty hands, puzzled at our strange actions.

"You can't have her," said Hamphill slowly. "Nobody can have her. She's gone."

"How'd you find us?" I asked.

"None of your damn business," said Finlay, glaring. To Hamphill: "You're lying!" To me: "Ain't he lying?"

"Talk quiet," I said. "Talk quiet in a house with someone dead in it."

"Dead?"

"Sherry's dead. Upstairs. Keep your voice down. You're too late. You better go back to town. It's all over."

Finlay lowered his gun. "I'm not going anywhere until I see her with my own eyes."

Hamphill said, "No."

"Like hell." Finlay looked at Hamphill's face and saw how much it looked like bone with the skin peeled away, white and hard. "Okay, so she's dead," he said, finally believing. He swallowed. He looked over his shoulder. "So we can still collect money on her, can't we?"

"No," said the boss.

"Nobody knows she's dead except us. We can still get the money. We'll just borrow a bit of her coat, a buckle, a button, a clip of her hair—You can keep the body, Hampy, old boy, with our compliments," Finlay assured him. "We'll just need a few things like her rings or compact to mail to her father for the dough."

A vein in Hamphill's hard-boned brow began to pulse. He leaned forward, stiffening, his eyes shining.

Finlay went on, "You can have the body, we'll leave you here with it, so you guys can take the rap."

"Sounds familiar," I said, remembering our plan to do the same for Finlay. That's life.

"Step aside, Hampy," said Finlay, walking big.

Hamphill fooled everyone the quiet way he stepped aside, turned as if to lead Finlay upstairs, took two steps up, then whirled. Finlay shouted as Hamphill pumped two shots into his big chest.

I shot the gun from one gunsel's hand. The second gunsel, outside, cursed, banged the door open, and sprang inward, his revolver aimed. The second gunsel shot Hamphill in the left arm just as Hamphill clutched Finlay, and they fell downward, collapsing together.

I got the second gunsel easily with one shot. The first one stood holding his awful red hand. Footsteps came in the back door. Willie came lumbering downstairs, bleating. "Boss, you all right?"

"Upstairs!" I said, helping the boss to his feet from Finlay's quiet body. "Willie, take him up!"

The third bodyguard rushed in, maybe expecting to see us all laid out stiff. I made a mess of his hand too.

Willie helped the boss upstairs and came down with some rope he'd found. There were no more footsteps outside. I pulled the door wide, letting the mist in, cooling my face. It smelled so good I just lay against the wall, smelling and liking it. The car was parked, its lights dark, but there was no movement. We'd taken care of everybody.

"Okay, Willie," I said. "Let's tie 'em up."

Hamphill lay like a long gray stick on the couch in the west room, nursing his wound. I closed the door.

"We got a setup, if we want to use it," I said.

He swabbed the wound with a white handkerchief.

I looked at him steadily. "This is the way it'll look to the cops: Finlay and his boys fight over money and shoot each other four ways from Christmas. The police find them here, anytime we want to call and tell them."

Hamphill's eyes fluttered weakly, his voice was small. "Later," he gasped. "Later, Hank. Not now."

"We've got to talk about it now," I said. "It's important."

"I don't want to leave Sherry."

"Look, boss, you're hit bad. You don't feel well."

"Later, Hank," he sighed.

"Yeah," I said feeling cold, but understanding. "Later. Okay."

Downstairs, Mark looked white as new snow. His hands shook as he sucked deeply on a cigarette he'd found on Finlay's body.

"Where were you when the shooting started?" I asked.

"Down at the boathouse on the beach, walking around. I ran up as quick as I could."

"You must be getting old," I said. "What sort of deal did you make on the phone with Finlay?"

Mark jerked, blew out smoke, drew his shaking hand across his unshaven cheek, and looked at his cigarette, then straight at me.

"The fog got me. The waiting got me. My guts got like *that*." He showed a tightened fist to me. "The boss upstairs, talking to her—like water dripping and dripping on my head. So I figured it out neat. You listening?"

"Talk."

"I called Finlay, told him I was double-crossing you guys, that I wanted a cut, that they could have Sherry. I knew Finlay'd come down and we'd get him and his gang and let them take the rap."

"You knew that, did you?"

"You calling me a liar!"

"You were sure quiet about it. We mighta got shot. It mighta worked both ways. We won, you stick with us. If Finlay'd won, you'd be with him, huh? Maybe."

"Hell, no! It was a chance, that's all. Either the cops found us here with Sherry and we got the gas chamber, or we had it out with Finlay. I couldn't tell you or the boss because if he knew he'd have shot me. I got nervous waiting. I wanted a fall guy. Finlay was it. I just didn't think he'd get here when he did; that's why I was down on the beach when things popped. I hoped that Finlay would swipe Sherry, even, and then we'd *have* to get out!"

"Okay," I said, nodding. "But there's still one thing gimmixed up. The boss won't move. After all your trouble fixing a frame, he won't move. So what'll you do now, junior?"

Mark swore. "How long'll we stay here? God, next week, next *month*?"

I pushed him away. "It smells in here. Go open the window."

I was dead tired. I checked the ropes on the three men to be sure they were tied tight, then I stretched out on the couch. Mark went upstairs. I could hear the boss up there, too, talking to somebody now, grunting with pain.

I slept deep, dreaming I walked under green water into that little church off the point, where fish swam with me in a congregation, and the underwater bronze bell rang, and a large squid draped itself like a soiled altar cloth across the pulpit . . .

I woke about four in the morning to the ticking of my watch. I had a feeling something was wrong. It was so wrong that I didn't have time to do anything about it. Someone hit me over the head. I fell, face forward, on the floor. That was all for a while.

I had a terrific headache when I came to. I blinked around in the dark, found my hands tied. It took five minutes to work out of the rope. I switched on a light.

Two of Finlay's men were gone!

I cursed myself out of the ropes tying my feet and raced upstairs.

Hamphill lay exhausted, in deep sleep. He didn't stir, even when I called his name. I shut the door softly and went to Sherry's room.

The couch where Sherry Bourne had lain was empty. Sherry was gone. . . .

The ocean came and dropped itself on the sand and slid out with a foaming sigh as my feet crunched the sand down.

Squinting out, I saw the rowboat—a gray rowboat, barely visible in the moonlight just breaking through the fog.

A large man stood in the boat, with long thick arms and a big head. Willie.

Mark stood on the beach where the waves didn't quite touch his small dark shoes. He turned as I walked up. I looked at Willie in the boat. Mark looked as if he hadn't expected me to show up.

"Where's Willie going?" I said.

Mark looked out at Willie too. "He's got a load."

"A load of what?"

"Canvas with chains around it and bricks inside."

"What's he doing with that at four in the morning?"

"Dumping it. It's Finlay."

"Finlay!"

"I couldn't sleep downstairs with him there. And if you didn't like my plan, I wanted to get him out of the way. One corpse less, if the cops came." He looked at my head. "Somebody hit you?"

"About half an hour ago, and tied me up. While you were down here fussing around, two of the Finlay boys got free and whacked me." I smiled a little, too, to be friendly. "Then they took Sherry and drove off, just a few minutes ago. What do you think of that story?"

"They stole Sherry!" Mark's eyes widened, his jaw dropped.

"You're a damn good actor," I said.

"What do you mean?"

"I mean, why didn't they shoot me and the boss? We shot Finlay, didn't we? So why'd they hit me over the head when a shot in the guts would be better? It doesn't click. It's too damn convenient, you being down here, twice now, when everything begins to pop. Too damn neat you being down here with Finlay's body, giving them a chance to lam."

"I don't get what you're squawking at," snapped Mark. "If you ask me, you should be glad Sherry's gone. Now we won't have to stay here nursemaiding Hamphill!"

"You're just a little *too* glad," I said.

Willie was way out in the night now, looking back, waving at us.

Mark and I watched as Willie lifted the canvas thing and dropped it over the boat side. It made a big splash with ripples.

"Oh, God," I said. I took Mark quietly by his lapels, holding him close so I breathed in his face. "Know what I think?" I breathed. I gripped him. "I think you wanted to get out of here, bad. So you hit me on the head, tied me up, then you took Finlay's men, toted them out to their car, pushed them inside, drove the car down the road, parked it off behind some shrubs, lights out, left them, and came back. A good setup. You tell the boss they slipped their ropes, swiped Sherry and escaped." I looked at Willie in the boat. "All while you were dropping a body in the ocean—only, not Finlay's body!"

"Yes, it is!" He struggled, but I held him.

"You can't prove anything. I don't know anything about Sherry!"

"You should've shot me, Mark, it would have been more convincing." I released him. "You got the cards stacked. I can't prove that was Sherry inside the canvas with the chains and weights. Getting rid of Sherry was the most important thing in your life, wasn't it? No evidence. Gone for good. And that meant we could move on. We'd *have* to move on. The boss'd chase after the escaped Finlay gang to get Sherry back, only it'd be a wild goose chase, because Sherry isn't anywhere but out there, about forty feet under, where that little cathedral is!''

Willie turned the boat around and started rowing clumsily back with slow strokes. I started a cigarette and let the wind whip away the smoke.

''Funny you thought of putting her out there. There's not a better place. If the boss knew, I think he'd like her being there with the bronze bell in the tower and all. It's just your motive for putting her there that spoils it, Mark. You made something dirty out of something that could've been—well—beautiful.''

''You aren't going to tell Hamphill!''

''I don't know. In a way I guess it might be best for us to move on. I don't know.''

Willie beached his rowboat, grinning.

I said, ''Hi, Willie.''

''Hello, Hank. That takes care of Mr. Finlay, don't it?''

''It sure does, Willie. It sure does.''

''He wasn't very heavy,'' said Willie, puzzled.

There was a crunching of feet on the sandy concrete stairway coming down the cliff. I heard Hamphill coming down, sobbing with pain and moaning something that sounded like ''Sherry's gone. Sherry's gone!'' He burst toward us from the base of the steps. ''Sherry's gone!''

''Gone?'' said Mark, playing it. ''Gone!'' said Willie.

I said nothing.

''Finlay's car's gone too. Hank, get our car, we've got to go after them. They can't take Sherry—'' He saw the rowboat. ''What's that for?''

Mark laughed. ''I got Willie to give me a hand with Finlay.''

''Yeah,'' said Willie. ''Plunk—overboard. He wasn't heavy at all. Light as a feather.''

Mark's cheek twitched. ''You're just bragging, Willie. Oh, Hank, you better go get the car ready.''

Maybe I showed something in my eyes. Hamphill glanced first at me, then at Mark, then at Willie, then at the boat.

''Where—where were you, Hank? Did you help load Finlay and drop him?''

''No. I was asleep. Somebody hit me on the head.''

Hamphill shambled forward in the sand.

''What's wrong?'' cried Mark.

''Hold still!'' commanded Hamphill. He plunged his hand into one of Mark's coat pockets, then the other. He drew something out into the moonlight.

Sherry's bracelet and ring.

Hamphill's face was like nothing I'd ever seen before in my life. He stared blindly at the boat and his voice was far away as he said, "So Finlay was light as a feather, was he, Willie?"

"Yes, sir," said Willie.

Hamphill said slowly, "What were you going to do, Mark, use the bracelet and ring on your own time, to get the money?" He jerked a hand at Willie. "Willie, grab him!"

Willie grabbed. Mark yelled. Willie coiled him in like a boa constrictor enfolding a boar.

Hamphill said, "Walk out into the water with him, Willie."

"Yes, boss."

"And come back alone."

"Yes, boss."

"Boss, cut it out. Cut it, boss!" Mark screamed, thrashing wildly.

Willie began walking. The first shell of water poured over his big feet. A second skin of water slid in, foaming soft. Mark shouted and a wave thundered, roared around the shout, folding it as Willie folded Mark. Willie stopped.

"Keep going," said Hamphill.

Willie went in to his knees, then up, inch by inch, over his big stomach, to his chest. Mark's yelling was farther away now because the night wind covered it over.

Hamphill stood watching like a frozen god. A wave broke over Willie into custard foam, leveled out, as Willie plunged ahead with Mark and vanished. Six waves came in, broke.

Then a huge water wall rushed in, casting Willie, alone, at our feet. He stood up, shaking water off his thick arms. "Yes, boss."

"Go up to the car and wait there, Willie," said Hamphill. Willie lumbered off.

Hamphill looked out at the point, listening. "Now what in hell are you up to?" I said.

"None of your damn business."

He began walking toward the water. I put out my hands. He pulled away from me and there was a gun in one hand. "Get going. Go on up to the car with Willie. I got a date for a high mass," he said. "And I don't want to be late. *Now*, Hank."

He walked out into the cold water, straight ahead. I stood

watching him as long as I could see his tall striding figure. Then one big wave came and spread everything into a salt solitude. . . .

I climbed back up to the car, opened the door, and slid in beside Willie.

"Where's the boss?" asked Willie.

"I'll tell you all about it in the morning," I said. I sat there and Willie dripped water.

"Listen," I said and held my breath.

We heard the waves go in and out, in and out, like mighty organ music. "Hear 'em, Willie? That's Sherry taking the soprano and the boss on the baritone. They're in the choir loft, Willie, sending way up high after that *gloria*. That is real singing, Willie—listen to it while you can. You'll never hear anything like it again. . . ."

"I don't hear nothing," said Willie.

"You poor guy," I said, started the car, and drove away. . . .

The Candy Skull

In the morning light, shadows of the children ran and ran across the pink and blue tiles of the plaza, while on the bronze bench Old Tomás sat, very withered, very indignant, waving his scarred hands at them. One small Mexican boy held a cape and wooden sword; another enacted the part of the enraged bull.

"No, no!" cried Old Tomás. "No, this way, and this!" He rose suddenly and stood to show the boys how to make a veronica, *so!* And another, *so!* "You see! With the body *this* way, see?"

The small boys ran, dodged, squealed.

Later they came and said, "Show us your scars, old one."

And Old Tomás pulled out his handwoven shirt to bare his right hip, once more to show them where the bull had gored thirty years ago. The boys touched the scar. "How long since you fought the bulls, old one?"

"Before your mothers were born," he replied.

A young Spanish woman crossed the plaza tiles. She wore a tailored gray gabardine suit; her hair was black and shining. Her head was high. She did not look at Tomás as she passed and went up the steps into the tourist hotel.

Tomás watched her all of the way. He saw how her ankles took the clear morning light. He saw how her dark shining hair was. His eyes followed. His tongue moved on his lip, ever so little.

On the second-floor balcony of the hotel a moment later a young pink, blond man suddenly appeared. Old Tomás narrowed his vision, his eyes tight, his mouth pressed shut. The young pink man on the balcony looking down. The clean, loud, tourist American who had driven into town last week. Old Tomás looked up at the clean man on the balcony. And when the clean tourist American turned and went back into his room, Tomás spat upon the pink and blue tiles and would no longer play with the children at their game.

Roby Cibber awakened this morning with a feeling as if something had happened. He couldn't tell exactly what or how or why, but something out of the ordinary had occurred during the night. He sat up and hung his legs over the edge of the bed and looked down at his feet for a long time. Then he remembered where he was.

He was in Guanajuato, Mexico, he was a writer, and tonight was the Day of the Dead ceremony. He was in a little room on the second floor of a hotel, a room with wide windows and a balcony that overlooked the plaza where the children ran and yelled each morning. He heard them shouting now. And this was Mexico's Death Day. There was a smell of death all through Mexico you never got away from, no matter how far you went. No matter what you said or did, not even if you laughed or drank, did you ever get away from death in Mexico. No car went fast enough, no drink was strong enough.

He looked over at the lamp table in the dim light and he did not recoil. With only a dull movement of his heart in his chest, he saw the white object that lay upon the table.

A small white sugar-candy skull.

It was the the kind of skull they eat on *el Día de Muerte*—the Day of Death. It was made of white sugar and it would crumple if you held it tightly. It had sockets and teeth and it glinted like a hard-packed snowball.

It had his name on it.

Roby.

Scrawled across the top in a thin pink candy rope—his name.

Roby.

The skull hadn't been there when he'd gone to sleep last night.

It was there now.

The room was cold. He got up and threw back the vast wooden doors over the windows that shut out the night air.

He caught a glimpse of himself, blond and pink faced, in the wall mirror as he stepped out on the balcony to take the sun and breathe the good air. He did not look back at the skull on the table. He didn't want to look at it. He looked instead, from the balcony, upon the small green plaza below with the rococo bronze bandstand and the trees clipped into round green drums and the tiles laid blue and pink on the walk where people strolled arm in arm on Thursdays and Sundays with the music hammering and crashing out into the silent Mexican sky.

There was no music now. Children ran on the tiles. Old Tomás sat on a bronze bench, instructing them on something or other.

Roby Cibber went back into his room. He touched his face. He needed a shave. It was good, feeling the warm, early-morning sunlight. It was nice living and moving about. His stomach was sickish—too much tequila last night with Celia Diaz. His throat was sore—too much singing.

Someone rapped on the door. He started, laughed at himself, opened the door.

"Buenos días, señor."

The little cleaning woman stood in the hall. Would it be possible that he was ready for breakfast? The ham and eggs were awaiting him and she would clean his room and set it right for him if he so wished—was this possible?

This was possible. He then turned and caused her to follow him in to the table, where he pointed at the small sugar-candy skull. He spoke to her in Spanish. Did she know where this came from? Had she seen anyone enter his rooms during the night?

She looked at the skull and laughed. Death is a good thing in Mexico; it is a thing to talk of at dinner, at breakfast, with or without a drink, with or without a smile. No, señor, she gave him to understand, she had seen no one enter or leave his room. Was not the sugar skull fine? Such good lettering of the señor's name!

Yes, he had to admit, the lettering was fine.

He went down to breakfast unshaved.

*   *   *

As always, there was ham and eggs. The Mexican people, once they have happened on a good food, he thought, flay the thing to distraction. Ham and eggs every morning now for two weeks. Since arriving in Guanajuato, bearing his typewriter, it had been the same thing each morning at nine. He stared at his plate, gently grieved.

Celia Diaz came across the dining room, smiling. She wore a tailored gray gabardine suit, and her hair was black and shining.

He rose to let her into her place, and they said their good-mornings. "It's a nice morning," she said. "A very nice morning."

"Yes," he said.

She had dark hair, a great lot of it, and dark eyes, large and inquiring and gentle, and full lips, and she did not look as a woman looks getting up in the morning. She was an anachronism. She looked as if it were eight o'clock, the core of the evening, everything at its highest point, everything fresh and delightful. He looked at her. He didn't look away.

"You were tired," she said quietly.

"I *am*," he said. "I came to Mexico a tired man, I live in Mexico a tired man, and I shall leave Mexico a tired man. It is a continuous state, having nothing to do with wine, women, or guitars. Nor is it the altitude, which frequently causes me to have hot and cold flashes in the middle of the afternoon. No, it is none of these."

"Perhaps I know what it is," she said, not flickering her steady gaze that was always on him.

"You couldn't possibly know," he said.

"But I *do*."

"No, no. You'd never guess." He shook his head.

"I know Americans—they are always afraid of the same thing in Mexico. They always look over their shoulders in fear, they do not sleep, they digest poorly. They laugh and say it is the change in climate. It is not," she said. "I know what it is."

He put down his fork. "What, then, is it?"

"Death," she said.

The sunlight fell through the wide French window and touched upon half her face and illumined all the silverware and blazed upon the painted wooden bowls hung from the walls.

She placed a small candy skull on the table.

"I stopped at your room just now," she said. "The cleaning woman was there. I saw this on your table."

He looked at the skull.

"You're afraid," she said.

The lettering was very exquisite, very fine.

"Yes," he said at last, settling back in his chair. "I'm afraid."

They had coffee to finish up the breakfast. Then they went out into the green *zócalo*. They passed Old Tomás, who sat on the bronze bench. "Señorita, señor," he said.

"Tomás," they said, walking on, glancing at him briefly. The children came to play with Old Tomás after they had walked by, with capes and wooden swords.

Celia and Roby sat on a bronze bench and had cigarettes, one after the other.

"Who would want to hurt you?" she asked.

"I don't know." He flung down a used match. "Dammit, I don't know anyone in Mexico!"

"Why did you come to Mexico?"

"To write. And there was that friend of mine, Douglas McClure."

"Yes, I knew him. He was here in Guanajuato last year. He left suddenly one night. I never saw him again. I was surprised. He never wrote me."

"Or me. His last letter was from here, last September. Then he went up in thin air. Never heard from him again. I know what you're thinking—I'm one of those half-cocked adventurers looking for trouble. Frankly, I'm selfish as hell. I came down to collect material for my novel. On the side, I'm looking for McClure. He wrote about you, Celia, in three of his letters. That's why I thought you might be able to help me."

"I am not much good." She lifted her hands. "One week he was here, the next gone. He was very nice. We talked much and had many dinners together. When he vanished, I said to myself, ah, these Americans. I did not worry. Did you look for him in Acapulco?" She smiled shyly.

"Acapulco! That's all I hear. Everyone tells me, 'Go to Acapulco!' That's where all the people go who vanish. I went. I didn't see any beachcomber that looked like Douglas McClure. Anyway, he was in this town last of all. His letters about you were very flattering, Celia. I thought, well, maybe this Celia Diaz has a Spanish sweetheart who got jealous of Douglas and killed him."

"That is all very flattering and romantic, but hardly true," she said. "I am the modern Mexican woman. I am disliked by my people, I walk alone, I do not follow the customs. But I am no one's woman yet. There was no jealous sweetheart to hurt your friend. Tell me of this sugar skull you found in your room."

"I'm warm," he said. "I must be close to Douglas. Some nights I almost feel how close he is to me. I expect to run into him at the Thursday night band concert, or in a bar. Whoever left this sugar skull in my room was pretty silly. If they think they can scare me off, they're wrong. I'm scared, but I won't go away. The sugar skull is a mistake. It only confirms my suspicions. They should have let matters stand, not bothered me. Maybe I am close to Douglas, but maybe I would have missed the next clue, missed Douglas, and gone back to the United States next week."

"Maybe you *can't* miss the next clue," Celia replied, logically. "Maybe they knew your next move was so obvious you couldn't miss your friend. Therefore they warned you before you made the move. Not a very pleasant warning. What *is* your next move?"

"I don't know."

"But they know. It's not something you'd have to do today, but something you'd have to do before you finally left town next week. What would that be, Señor Roby? What would you do in the next week, what would you see that you have not already seen?"

He had the answer.

She saw that he had the answer and she put out her hand swiftly to gentle him. He drew deeply on his cigarette and flickered his eyes and his breath came in and out of him in deep moves of his lungs.

"Tell me," she said, after a time. "What is the one place where you have not been that you will go before you leave town next week?"

He took a deep breath, let it hiss out slowly.

"The catacombs," he said.

The graveyard was at the top of the hill. It looked over all of the town. The town was hills—hills that issued down in trickles and then creeks and then rivers of cobblestone into the town, to flood the town with rough and beautiful stone that had been polished into smooth flatness over the centuries. It was a pointed irony that the very best view of the town could be had from the cemetery hill, where high, thick walls surrounded a collection of tombstones like wedding cakes, frosted with white angels and iced with ribbons and scrolls, one against another, toppling shining cold. It was like a cake confectioner's yard. Some tombs were as big as beds. From here on freezing evenings you could look down at the candlelit valley, hear dogs bark sharp as tuning forks banged on a flat stone, see all the funeral processions coming up the hill in the dark, coffins balanced on shoulders.

Roby Cibber stood halfway up the hill, looking at the cemetery wall.

"Don't go up today," said Celia. "Can't you wait until tomorrow?"

His voice was flat. "No. Now that I've thought of it, it's the one place. It was in my mind all the time, but I wouldn't go look. I wouldn't let myself believe until today. I had to look everyplace else first. The last place I wanted to look was in the catacombs. I've heard of that horrible place and those mummies standing wired against the walls."

He walked up the hill slowly and looked at a little soft-drink stand. He laughed wearily. "It's warm. Celia, have an Orange Crush with me. We need something."

"You look sick."

"I'm going to be a whole lot sicker. I'm going to be sick all the rest of my life, after today."

They stood in the sunlight, drinking down the bottled drinks, making foolish sucking noises on the bottle necks with their lips, not thinking anything.

He finished his bottle and looked at the little girl who tended the stand. She held a little candy corpse in her hand. She was eating it.

He didn't move. He watched her eat it.

Then he turned sighing, and walked up the hill, not talking, with Celia's shadow moving long and easy beside his own shadow, up and up to where the wrought-iron gates swung, squealing, opening on ancient hinges to the graveyard.

By the church, by the plaza, under the dark green trees, the people sat waiting. They waited for something to happen. When it happened they would get up and run around and be part of it. The sun was lowering over the many hills, showing in dull flashes the tin sidings of the silver mines high up. The people waited in the square until finally it was very dark.

Roby Cibber came down the street slowly. He stopped and looked in the many windows. He went in one place and had a beer. Celia was with him, would not leave him. He didn't think of her, though. It wasn't important.

Douglas McClure was up on top of that hill, right now. In the catacombs.

You walked up the hill and paid the graveyard attendant a peso and he flung back a steel door and you went down a spiral stone stair into the earth, into the catacombs. You entered a long dim hall with one hundred twenty-five mummies facing each other, standing against the walls, their mouths open, their beards intact. Looking as if they had leaped up at your entrance, screaming silently.

You walked along the line of standing dead. You looked into the bony, tight-skinned faces.

Until you came to the body of Douglas McClure.

Roby Cibber walked up the slanting street until it gave into the plaza before the church. Somewhere he lost Celia.

A brass band with five busy members marched briskly up one alley, flinging off a tune with the vicious, unpredictable centrifuge of a musical wheel. The men in handwoven pants beat drums, spat into trumpets, or chewed lovingly their long black clarinets. Roby heard them dully, with no appreciation, as they moved by him.

What will you do now?

I don't know. I'm sick. I'm afraid. Tonight, I need people all around me, on all sides, to protect me. I need noise. I'm going to stay here, in the middle of the fiesta, until Celia comes. I won't go up any dark alleys. I won't be alone one moment. I'll stand here in the plaza where *he* can't get me!

Who?

The person who killed Douglas McClure.

The band marched up on the bandstand, played *Yankee Doodle*. It came out of the horns with a strange loss, changed by the breath that blew it and the minds that thought it before the blowing. It was not quite *Yankee Doodle*; it was something frightening.

I'm going to be killed, thought Roby Cibber.

Don't talk like an ass. Go to the police.

What good would that do? Maybe they already know about McClure's body being in the catacombs but kept it quiet so as not to get in trouble with the American government. Those things happen.

A bull was carried into the square, a papier-mâché bull carried on the shoulders of Old Tomás, grunting, charging about. The bull rested on a reed frame, or what appeared to be reeds.

How did Douglas McClure die?

He had a strange hole between his eyes.

A bullet hole?

No. A *strange* kind of hole. I don't know.

The people jumped up from the benches. Something exploded. Old Tomás, lighting fuses on the bamboos and reeds under his papier-mâché bull, ran about the plaza, chasing people before him.

The bull erupted. Involuntarily Roby cried out. The bull gave off great balls of flame. From tubes under the bull shot out, one after another, brilliant, round, blazing fireballs that hit, streamed, gushed into the crowd! The crowd buckled, fell back, closed in. Old Tomás shuffled forward, the bull on his shoulders, laughing. The bull's eyes glowed, flashed, banged out loud traces of yellow-and-orange fire. There were hidden Roman candles, dozens of them, in and under the bull. All these stabbed the air, spurting, beating the children mercilessly with swift fire. The children waved red kerchiefs. The bull charged. Everyone screamed and laughed.

Under the green unmoving trees people stumbled and fell over benches to get out of the way of the fire-throwing bull. A little boy caught a fireball in his shirtfront, leaped into a trough, splashing. Now the bull was all fire, all aglow, all illumination. People held onto each other, panting, holding their sides, gasping for breath from the game.

Roby Cibber let himself be taken into the crowd. He began to run, first slowly, his face ashen, then more swiftly. He felt the need to be at their very center, to whirl, to fall, to laugh, to clutch at them, to use them as shields for himself against whoever might be watching and waiting for him. And he wanted to forget. He ran and laughed. At first it was not a very good laugh. Then it was hysterically exhausted, but he kept leaping hedges as the bull charged first at him, then at someone else. The bull whirled in all directions, booming out firecrackers. An immense cloud of smoke filled the air. Somebody set off a dozen rockets that pierced the sky and blew out into a grand high architecture of red across the stars.

The bull charged again. The crowd parted away from Roby Cibber. He turned, crying out in confused delight. For a moment there was no fear but the simple fear of the firecracker bull and old shambling Tomás. A fireball caught him on the ear. He cried out. There were explosions. He felt something hit him in the arm. He dogged. He laughed. He stumbled over somebody.

Celia was there.

He saw her in the crowd at the edge of the square, standing, watching his wild gyrations.

He freed himself by pushing and shoving and shouting all through the rolling mob until he made a path through to her.

He almost fell as he reached her.

She looked at him with a look of ancient, tired horror.

She was looking at the blood pouring from his arm, warm and constant.

"You've been shot," she said.

The band blared away in a mechanical tumult.

He fell down upon his knees and held onto Celia, and her arms came down to hold him and try to lift him up. . . .

Doctors are no use in Mexico. If you are hysterical, they are so calm and quiet in their inefficiency that you want to scream. Maybe you do, a little. The doctor bandages your wound quietly. It is the fiesta, señor. No more, no more. Some happy man fired a gun. Simply an accident. You will not prosecute, señor? Who is there to prosecute. No one. And this—this wound of the señor's—perhaps only a Roman candle made it, eh? No? Well, it *is* deeper. Yes, I will admit, a bullet. But only from a happy soul. Forget it, señor, forget it!

Roby Cibber came from the doctor's office, Celia with him.

"Did you see who fired the shot, Celia?"

"I saw nothing. Nobody saw. There was so much running and noise. But you are lucky, only a flesh wound."

"That doctor! Sitting there, philosophizing on death! You're not safe anywhere in Mexico, alone or in a crowd."

"Perhaps it would be better if you went back to the United States."

"No. I'll stay. I've got to get Douglas out of the catacombs and shipped home where he belongs. Then there'll be the investigation. In the morning, though—I'm bushed." He looked at her coldly. She was alien. Everything was frightening and alien. He wasn't even certain of her now. Maybe she—

"You're tired," she said. "You'd better get to bed."

He returned to his hotel.

The funeral awaited him.

It was on a little shingle, lying on his bed, the funeral.

He closed the door after switching on the light and he lay against the door looking at the funeral.

It was a tiny funeral. There was a tiny priest with a tiny nut for a head, holding a tiny black book and raising a tiny hand in a holy gesture. There were little altar boys bearing small banners. There was a small coffin and a small sugar-candy corpse in it. And there was an altar with a picture of the corpse on it.

The picture was of Roby Cibber.

He looked around. Someone had gone through his luggage, found an old photo of his, clipped it small and pasted it on the little altar.

There was no note with the funeral. The funeral was enough. These little shingles with tiny figures were sold in the market for *el Día de Muerte*. But this one was just a little out of place on his bed in the waiting, silent room, and he was cold, very cold, and he began to shiver.

There was a tapping on the door behind him. He started. Then, coldly, he opened the door.

"*Señor!*" A hiss. Old Tomás stood in the dim hall. There was the smell of sweat and wine. "It is important that I see you."

"I'm tired."

Tomás looked in at the bed, at the little funeral.

"It is about *that*, señor." Tomás pointed at the funeral. "A little while ago I came through the hall. I saw someone go in your room with that small funeral. I thought you would want to know this."

Roby blinked several times. "Did you see his face?"

"It was no man, señor. It was a woman."

"A woman?"

"Señorita Celia. I saw her."

"You'd better go downstairs. I'm cold and you're drunk."

"She did not see me. She held the funeral in her hands and went in and came out a few minutes later. You are not well, señor?"

Roby held on to the door, shutting his eyes. "I am not well."

"Señor, I have watched the señorita each day, with you. This is not a thing for Mexican women to do. It is not our custom for a woman to be on the streets with a man, or to see a man alone, or to walk alone. And yesterday, Señora Licone, who makes sugar skulls, said to me, 'Ah, that Celia woman, she is insane. She came to me and asked me to make a sugar skull and put the name of the *americano* on top of it: Roby.' I thought nothing of this thing, señor, until tonight, when I saw her take the funeral in, and then, when you were hurt at the fiesta. I thought all of these things over and came to you.''

Roby sat down heavily, careful of the bandage along the right side of his chest. "Can you take me to Señora Licone tonight?"

"*Sí, señor.*"

"I must talk to her about the sugar skull."

"*Sí.*" Old Tomás wet his lips. His dark face grew darker, his dark eyes glowed. "I thought all of this strange, señor, for in the past, there was another *americano*—"

"Another!"

"Sit down, señor. You look very pale. Yes, another *americano*, at this hotel, a year ago. He and the señorita were together much. I saw them go in and out of the hotel together—"

Roby talked quietly to the floor. "Celia, Celia—"

"And then one day that other *americano*, he vanished!"

"Yes, I know."

"And this Celia, she showed surprise at his being gone. A clever woman. She removed his luggage herself, of this we may be certain."

"Why didn't you go to the police?" Roby studied the man.

"For what, señor? An *americano* goes away, perhaps to the United States. Is that murder? Is that bad, señor? No, it is only this week, and the things I have seen that make me think. The woman Celia with you, your injury tonight, the sugar skull, the little funeral. Then I think back. I remember this other *americano*. Then I come to you. Will you see Señora Licone now, señor?"

"I'll see her. Where do we go?"

"A little way."

They went down the street of the coffin makers. Even this late at night there was a tapping and sawing of wood. Through the open door you saw the coffin makers joking at their work.

Celia, thought Roby Cibber, sweet, gentle-eyed Celia. What happened? Did you love Douglas McClure and did he do something to you that was not of your Mexican logic and custom? And then did you kill him, in some sudden passion, as most killings occur in Mexico? Oh, death is quick down here. It's not the slow brooding poison and the plan. It is the instant act for which, a moment later, you are sorry. A blow, a knife, a gun—quick, and over. Did Douglas say or do something, try to hold or kiss you? Did your family dislike him? Was your reputation hurt by being seen with him? A simple thing to us Americans, but not to you— was that it, Celia? And so you killed him, in one passionate instant, took his luggage from his room. It looked simply as if he'd gone away. Then you let an unidentifiable naked body be found, to be put in the catacombs. Maybe so you could go down and laugh at him once in a while, I don't know. And then I came, and you tried to warn me away, but I'm not going.

"This way, señor."

They turned down a dark alley. The stars were clear and cold. A dog barked across the stone valley. A guitar picked out a fine, clear, crystal chord. A voice sang somewhere, sadly.

"How much farther, Tomás?"

"A little way, señor."

They went up a hill in the moonlight. . . . There was no way to get McClure's body out of the catacombs, was there, Celia? thought Roby. It was found and put down there, but you couldn't bribe anyone to get it out; it would have given you away. Maybe you didn't *want* to get it out. Maybe you've been playing with me. Maybe you *wanted* me to find Douglas there.

The moon was a white pallid eye staring over the sky and the empty land. Their shadows hung under them; they breathed hard with climbing.

They turned in at a familiar-looking building. There were banners on the outside fence, played by the wind.

"This is the bullring, Tomás?"

"Yes, the bullring."

"Does Señora Licone live here?"

"She has no home. She lives beneath the bullring and there she makes her sugar skulls and the little shingle funerals. *Here*."

They walked out into the clear, moon-filled silent space of the bullring. The sand was a white dimpled sea and the *barreras*— the stands—went around in moon-drenched circles, empty and quiet.

"How do you feel, senõr?"

"Not so good. That was a climb."

"Look over there," said Tomás.

They looked. Tomás walked to a black bundle that lay on the sand. "Why, señor, someone has left a bullfighter's equipment here."

There was a scarlet cape. There was a little *birreta* and there were some tiny black ballet slippers and a sword that shone in the light.

"Someone forgot them," said Roby uneasily.

Tomás bent to touch the articles. "It is a shame these were forgotten. These are good things." He picked up the *birreta* and handled it carefully. "Have you seen the bullfight, señor?"

"A few times. I didn't like it."

"Señor, you *americanos*." Tomás fitted the *birreta* to his head. In the moonlight his body straightened. He held his hands down. "How do I look, señor?"

"Fine, fine. Now if you'll take me to Señora Licone—"

"Do I not look fine?"

"Fine indeed, but—"

"Did you know that once, many years ago, señor, I was the best bullfighter in all of Mexico?"

"Undoubtedly, but—"

"Please, señor, to listen." Tomás was very tall suddenly, with the moon over him casting his shadow long on the sand. Suddenly he was not hunched, the muscles were released, the dark chin was up, the old eyes flashed with new fire. "Once I fought three bulls here—in one day!" he cried. "Oh, there were people in all the *barreras* to the sky. When I was done they cut off the ears of the bulls and gave them to me. The people threw down hats and gloves and purses at me. It was like a rain." He said it proudly.

Roby looked at him and said not a word. They both stood looking at one another coldly.

Tomás bent and took up the sword and the cape. "I handled the veronicas so, and so—" He whirled to show how it was done. "Beautifully." He bent and put on the little ballet slippers in place of the *huaraches* he had kicked off. "Now, señor—" He walked toward Roby.

"Señora Licone?"

"Yes, yes, the maker of candy skulls." Tomás pointed. "There she is now, you see?"

Roby turned. Simultaneously Tomás struck him a blow on the back of the neck. "Señor!"

Roby cried out. He leaped back and almost fell. He clapped his hand to his neck and discovered it was pierced by three tiny needles to which were attached little fluttering ribbons, red, white, and green. He pulled them out and cast them down. "Tomás!"

"Señor!" cried Tomás. "The banderillas. The pikes for the neck of the bull. Have you seen the bullfight, señor, in which the **bandilleros** stick the banderillas into the neck of the bull? This I have just done!"

"Tomás, Tomás!" shouted the American, backing up.

Tomás struck at him with the sword. The sword went through Roby's leg, in and out. He collapsed and fell bleeding.

"Tomás!"

Tomás bent over him in the moonlight.

"Do you know what happened tonight, señor?"

"Tomás," gasped the sprawled man.

"I tried to kill you in the fiesta. It was easy, with my gun hidden under the framework of the charging bull. But you escaped, señor!"

"Take me to the candy woman, Tomás!" Roby could not breathe. His mouth opened and shut violently. He was sick.

"There is no candy woman. Do you know what will happen tomorrow morning, señor?" He shouted. "Tomorrow the woman Celia will ask for you. And you will be gone from the hotel. Your luggage gone. *You*, gone!"

Roby tried to get up.

"Get up," said Tomás. "I am ready for you."

Roby gained his feet. Pain was firing his wounded leg. He stood, swaying. "Tomás, you're crazy. Put down the sword, you fool."

"No."

"Why should you want to kill me?"

"Because."

Tomás adjusted the *birreta* on his head. It would have been ridiculous, save for the pain and the blood and the stark moonlight and the clear sky. "I'll shout," said Roby. "People will hear."

"You would not do that, and spoil the game, señor. Then

I would have to kill you quickly. The sword between the eyes.''

Roby shivered. He saw Douglas McClure in the catacombs again. Now the strange hole in the skull was understood. The hole of a bullfighter's sword. This was how McClure had died.

''We shall have a little game, señor. I am the greatest toreador in the world. You, señor, will be the bull. You will charge me, I will lead you on. You will charge again. I will nick your arms, your legs, your chest. The moon will watch. And the stars will fill the *barreras*.''

''What have I done, Tomás?''

''Each day I have watched you go in and come out of the hotel. I have seen Celia with you. She is of us; she is not of you.'' Tomás stood there, tall and proud. ''In the sunlight you walked and laughed and did not speak to me. Each day, each day I saw you touch her and laugh with her, and I hated you, señor, yes, even as I hated the other one. The one last year who went in and out of the hotel—the young *yanqui*, the ridiculous tourist. And Celia had only eyes for him, as now it is only you she sees. She has no eyes for Tomás. Tomás who was once the toast of all Mexico, from Oaxaca to Guadalajara and Monterrey! No, Tomás is old now, no longer can he dance in the ring. No bull would look at him, much less a woman. Tomás is not fit for swine. People spit on him. Tomás was gored by a bull many years ago—''

He made a jerking motion of his hand. The smooth flat of his belly was revealed under the shirt, the scarred, flat, brown belly with the gore mark deep-puckering it.

''See, señor? See? My mark of honor! My profession! But what are scars to young women? You walked and laughed with her. I watched. I watched her with the other. And when I could no longer see them together, I guided him here one night, I the toreador, and he the silly animal, and I killed him. Now you have come, and you too shall die!''

''Tomás, I hold nothing against you, old man—''

''I am not old!'' raged Tomás, running lightly forward, making a vicious sweep with the sword. ''She thinks me old, yes. That Celia one! Each day she passes me on my bench and does not look at me, and each day of each year I have gazed at her beauty as she walked. And I said to myself, these *yanquis* shall not have her. As many as come to walk with her will I kill. One and then two and then three, and perhaps a dozen before I am caught. *They* shall not have her. *I* will have her." He cut the air with the sword. "Now, move, *yanqui*! Do not stand; move, run, charge me! Give me a fight!"

"My leg, I can't move."

"I will *make* you move!" And Tomás beat him across the face with the sword until the anger made Roby leap forward on his agonized leg. Tomás dodged. "Good!" he cried, swirling the cape. "Another!" Roby stumbled forward. "And another! Good, good!"

Roby stood panting. Tomás looked at the moon. "It is late. It is time for the finish. You will run and I will put the sword in your brain." He held the cape, so, fluttering in the cold wind. The moonlight lay over all.

Roby's leg was pulsed like a massive heart. He could not see well. The earth tilted and the stars tilted. "Tomás," he said, gently.

"Come," said Tomás, waving the cape, the sword out, cold, shining in the wind.

"All right," said Roby.

"Now," said Tomás.

"Now!" Roby leaped.

The sword glittered.

Roby fell, rolled sidewise, kept rolling. He struck the legs of the toreador. He grabbed. Tomás shrieked. Tomás fell. They were together on the white sand, wild, and in the cape, with the sword held now by one, now by another.

Then one of them got clear, stood up, the sword in his hand. The sword sank down through, pinning the other to the white moonlit sand. "This is for *me*," said the one with the sword wildly, swaying. He pulled the sword out and put it in the squirming body again. "And this is for Celia!" Out and in again.

"And *this* is for Douglas McClure!"

When Celia met Roby he was coming down the street, limping, in the early morning, limping, fresh from the doctor's office, carrying something small and white and sugary in his hand. It was very early. The sun was just rising among the blue hills and the church bells were sounding as she saw him from a distance. Roby stopped, stood, took a deep breath of the incredibly sweet charcoal air. Then he lifted the little white sugar skull with the name Roby on it, and he broke it into several fragments and finished eating it even as she walked up and said good morning. Chewing and swallowing, he smiled and answered her.